LORD JAMES HARRINGTON AND THE SPRING MYSTERY

James and his wife Beth are hosting the annual spring fair when wealthy recluse Delphine Brooks-Hunter is murdered. While James is summoned to the reading of her will and is tasked with solving an intriguing riddle, Beth tackles her own mystery after discovering a homeless man suffering from amnesia. As they delve deeper, a number of questions emerge. What links Delphine to the fairground folk? Who would harm such a refined lady? Are rumours of wartime espionage true? As they unravel the truth, they uncover more than they bargained for . . .

LYNN FLORKIEWICZ

LORD JAMES HARRINGTON AND THE SPRING MYSTERY

Complete and Unabridged

LINFORD
Leicester

First published in Great Britain

First Linford Edition
published 2018

A catalogue record for this book is available
from the British Library.

ISBN 978–1–4448–3763–6

Published by
F. A. Thorpe (Publishing)
Anstey, Leicestershire

Set by Words & Graphics Ltd.
Anstey, Leicestershire
Printed and bound in Great Britain by
T. J. International Ltd., Padstow, Cornwall

This book is printed on acid-free paper

1

The staff at Harrington's Country Hotel and residents of the nearby village of Cavendish, fussed around the manor's extensive grounds with the utmost efficiency. The spring fair wouldn't open for another three or four hours, but the early and fastidious preparations had always been an intricate part of its continued success.

At the house itself, waiters and waitresses wearing white cotton aprons in the style of Parisian waiters, carefully arranged tables in the luxurious dining-room and set up additional seating alfresco on the stunning, newly-built terrace.

Lord James Harrington pushed up the sleeves of his pale lemon pullover and surveyed the scene from the far end of the terrace. It certainly was a hive of activity. Paul, the *maître d'hôtel*, gently chivvied his workers along, highlighting areas that required extra attention, all the while taking his instructions from James' wife,

Beth. Without doubt, she had an eagle eye for colour and design and James watched on fondly as she took the lead. She called across to him, her accent still faintly American, thanks to her upbringing in Boston.

'Sweetie, how's it looking?'

He leant against the door frame and slipped his hands into the pockets of his linen trousers. There was something extremely endearing about her childlike excitement. In all the years they'd been hosting the May Day fair, her enthusiasm had never dipped: he knew these English traditions were a delight to her even after all of these years.

'Absolutely marvellous, darling,' he replied and met the gazes of several of their helpers. 'You're all doing a splendid job and I must say, Beth, you've chosen a particularly lovely colour-scheme.'

A smile lit up her impish face as she carried on with her impeccable organisation. The colours were typically seasonal; pure white linen tablecloths with daffodil yellow napkins, and fresh golden tulips delicately arranged into posies on each table.

The alfresco fresco area, built with Sussex sandstone, had turned out exactly as they had asked. It seemed only yesterday that he'd spotted the design in a hotel brochure featuring accommodation beside the Bay of Naples. Of course, the Italian climate suited an outside dining area; but, he'd suggested to Beth, why not here? The British summers were, by and large, dry and warm and, with the long summer evenings ahead, it seemed a shame to cocoon oneself inside, especially with the outstanding views of the South Downs and the distant sparkling blue of the sea in the distance.

Unfortunately, the whole project had nearly been cancelled, what with that unpleasant business before Christmas. The suspicious death of a local farmer, Alec Grimes, along with the attempted murder of his son, had put everything on hold.

Prior to discovering his criminal activities, they'd asked the builder and architect Ian Connell to work on the design and he had drawn up a set of detailed plans. James knew he'd make a good job of it because he'd carried out work for a number of villagers. What a pity the young man had got himself involved with that evil vixen, Diana, who'd shared his office. Now, Ian was under lock and key and probably ruing the day he ever met her. After some consideration, James decided that as he had already paid for the plans, they might as well go ahead with the work.

After a few telephone calls, he had called in some favours from the builders who'd constructed James' own home a couple of miles away. The owner of the firm had recently died, but his two sons had carried on the business and were happy to oblige.

They'd completed the terrace during the winter months and installed a number of wide glass doors that ran the length of the dining-room. James' chest had swelled on seeing those doors open for the first time. It had been such an inspirational idea and, even now, that wonder stayed with him as he watched Paul push the doors fully open to connect the dining-room with the garden beyond. The sunshine poured in and he could hear Pat Boone's 'April Love' drifting from the wireless.

The grounds were undergoing the final preparations for the May Day fair. In the distance, men were fixing the last bolts and screws to the rides of the fairground. The rides extended along one side of the field and included a wonderful merry-go-round with vibrant painted horses, an exhilarating swing ride, a strong man gauge and robust bumper cars, always a popular choice with everyone. The children had their own miniature versions of the same rides. Dotted here and there were a number of smaller side-stalls for those wishing to win a coconut or play hoopla. He heaved a satisfied sigh. The glorious weather added to his benign mood and he looked forward to what promised to be another enjoyable May Day celebration.

At the far end of the field, a number of vehicles trundled in and parked in an orderly line. They comprised ice-cream vans, candy floss and toffee apple vendors, hot dog stands and lemonade bars. For once, Beth had decided she'd take a complete rest from contributing to the Women's Institute catering and, at first, James had felt a little disappointed as he loved her lemon drizzle cakes and home-made elderberry wine. But he completely understood why. The Women's Institute reigned supreme in Cavendish and their marquee tent was already crowded with women of all ages scurrying in and out with home-made jams, scones, cakes and pastries, eager and ready for the fair's annual competitions. They were unlikely to miss a lemon drizzle cake.

'Oi, oi.'

A feeling of comfort always flowed through him when he heard the familiar cockney tones of his good friend, Bert Briggs. He turned to greet him.

'Ah Bert. You're looking very chipper today.'

'I love it, mate, love it. You can't beat the May Day shindig, can you? Looks like you're gonna 'ave a full 'ouse today. Weather's done you proud, too.'

'Yes,' said James, scanning the cloudless sky, 'couldn't have asked for a better day.

I hear you're helping Donovan out with the drinks?'

Donovan Delaney, the local publican, was a stalwart of all village festivities and ensured he had all the local beers on tap for his thirsty customers.

'Yeah, we've set the beer tent up between the WI and the platform for the Morris Men. Have you got an order for what's 'appening? I don't wanna miss anything.'

James pulled out a slip of paper from his shirt pocket.

'Yes, here we are. We officially open at midday and kick off with the school band. Then we have the egg and spoon races, donkey derby and suchlike throughout the day. Oh, and before anything, the children are doing a dance to introduce the May Queen. Peter Mitchell's lent us his open-top lorry to bring her in. I believe the villagers have made a good job of transforming the vehicle into something fit for a princess.'

James turned the paper to continue reading. 'The Morris Men are performing some traditional May Day dances. In the WI tent, we have the judging for best cakes, scones, chutney and all that with the best home-brewed wine in the beer tent. Plant and vegetable judging is taking place at around three, I think.'

'And what's going on 'ere?' Bert said waving a hand at the classy dining area around him.

'Ah, well, Didier has prepared a special May Day menu for those who prefer to sit down and eat properly.'

'You mean the posh geezers who want to view things from a distance.'

James grinned. He could always count on Bert to keep his feet on the ground. He'd been a friend to James since a chance meeting in childhood at the Natural History Museum in London, where their respective schools had chosen to arrange an outing on the same day. For some inexplicable reason, he and Bert had hit it off immediately and they'd remained firm friends since that day.

Bert, a true Cockney, came from an impoverished background and could have easily taken the wrong path in life. There was no doubt that, at times, he veered a little too close to the wrong side of the law for James' liking, but he understood his reasons for doing so. As a child it had meant the difference between eating and starving. James preferred not to dwell on it and asked few questions, if any, about his friend's activities.

'My posh geezers, as you describe them, are simply our guests at Harrington's. We have a few regulars in but some have arrived specifically for the May Day fair. I have to admit that many of them will feel happier eating here than munching on a toffee apple.'

Bert slapped him on the back. 'Right, well I'd best go and 'elp Donovan set his beer barrels up. He's got a new ale on tap. By the way, did you go and see your film?'

James' eyes lit up. 'Oh yes, *The 39 Steps*. Jolly good. Kenneth More plays the lead particularly well. You ought to go and see it.'

'I've 'eard there's gonna be a good film out later in the year with Peter Sellers called *I'm All Right Jack*.' Bert tapped his nose. 'I've got a mate in the business. He's a cameraman and he's been working on it.'

'Bert, is there anyone you don't know?'

'I'll let you know if I find out,' he winked as he made to leave.

At the sound of brisk footsteps, James turned to see the rotund frame of his head chef, Didier, striding efficiently toward him.

'Ah, Didier, how are things going?'

Didier, a short man with an almost perfectly round face, stood smartly in his chef's whites and beamed with pride. 'Today, Lord 'arrington,' he announced with a subtle French accent, 'I 'ave the wonderful spring menu. The lamb is divine and you will salivate at the very thought of eating this dish.'

Before Didier could launch into the details of his menu, Anne Merryweather, the vicar's wife, called from the doorway that led to the reception area.

'James. So sorry, there's a telephone call for you in reception. An elderly lady who insists on speaking with you personally.'

James noted Didier's disappointment as he acknowledged Anne's message. He grasped the chef's elbow. 'Don't worry,

Didier. I will not only return to hear of this wonderful menu, but I will be partaking of it later today.'

He made his way through the dining-room and into the reception area of the hotel. The doors to the main entrance were open wide, allowing a warm breeze to float in and affording a framed vista of the extensive drive to the front of the building. He accepted the receiver from Anne, who returned to a polished walnut table just inside the entrance and continued working on the flower display that provided a beautiful centrepiece.

'Hello, Lord Harrington here.'

An efficient, elderly voice greeted him. 'This is Delphine.'

James searched his memory. Delphine? He didn't know a Delphine and yet the name sounded familiar.

'Delphine Brooks-Hunter,' she continued, answering his hesitation. 'I live in the old Coach House.'

'Good Lord, of course! I'm so sorry, Miss Brooks-Hunter.'

'That's quite all right, my dear, I wouldn't expect you to be waiting for my call. I hardly go out, let alone contact you from one year's end to another.'

James assured her that he remembered her very well, but couldn't help admitting his surprise at hearing from her. Delphine Brooks-Hunter, he recalled, was around seventy years of age and rarely ventured further than her beautifully fragrant garden and the village shop.

'Well, Miss Brooks-Hunter — '

'Call me Delphine, dear. Brooks-Hunter sounds so terribly formal, don't you think?'

James grinned. 'It's a little shorter, too. Now, Delphine, what can I do for you?'

'I'd like to come to the May Day fair. Can I do that?'

James' eyes widened and he almost stumbled over his words. 'Yes, of course you can. It'll be wonderful to see you. Any particular reason why?'

'Mmm?'

'Why you want to come this specific year?'

'Yes, dear, I want to enjoy myself.'

James couldn't help but smile. 'Well,

enjoy yourself you shall. Do I take it that you require some transport? I know you're not far as the crow flies, but it's quite a way to walk or drive.'

'You assume correctly, Lord Harrington.'

'Please, call me James.'

'James, yes, I've seen you swanning around in that lovely car of yours.'

'Ah, the Jaguar. Yes, luxuriously comfortable and a stylish ride.'

'No, dear, not the Jaguar. I said I wanted to enjoy myself. I rather fancy having a go in that little sports car you have.'

'What, the Austin Healey? Are you serious?'

The Austin was his pride and joy; a sleek, 1957 two-seater sports car that had rolled off the production line just the previous year.

Delphine replied that she'd never been more serious in her life. James continued grinning. What a wonderfully spirited woman. Age was obviously not something that slowed her down. He checked his watch.

'Well, Delphine, I can be with you in

around ten minutes. Will you be ready?'

'I already am.'

He placed the handset on the cradle and rubbed his hands together. How wonderful. Anne returned to the reception desk with a vase of handpicked tulips.

'Not bad news I hope?' she asked, setting the vase down. 'She sounded quite anxious to speak with you.'

James assured her that it was anything but bad news and repeated the conversation. Anne listened eagerly as she discarded some discoloured leaves from the display and gave James a bright and cheery smile.

'She sounds quite a character — let's give her a day to remember.'

James knew he could rely on Anne to help make Delphine welcome. 'Yes, let's, although I rather think she plans to do that anyway.'

He reached down to a ledge behind the reception desk and retrieved his car keys, along with his straw Panama.

'Anne, could you let Beth know where I am? I shouldn't be too long.'

Didier stood in the doorway — his eyes hopeful of some attention. It wasn't lost on James.

'Ah Didier, I have to go and rescue an elderly villager from her confines. But, when I return, you will have my full attention, *oui*?'

Didier bowed his head and managed to radiate some positivity above the grimace. Again, it wasn't lost on James. Didier Le Noir was a magician in the kitchen, but also rather needy with it — like a small boy who craved constant attention and praise. He made a mental note to lavish time and energy on his chef once he'd settled Delphine at the fair. He turned on his heels and made to go, but then he turned again and called out to him.

'I say, Didier?'

Didier's eyebrows rose in question.

'Could you make sure we have a table for three? We'll have someone joining us for lunch and I want to make a fuss of her. Can't do that without some tasty morsels, can I?'

James then strode out of Harrington's toward the Austin, knowing that his small but subtle compliment had gone some way to brighten Didier's day. Settling into his car, his thoughts turned to Delphine; he was curious as to why such a reclusive old lady was so keen to attend their May Day celebrations.

2

Beth meandered from stall to stall, checking over the finer details before the May Day Fair officially opened. She chatted enthusiastically with the villagers who, as they did every year, gave up their time and effort to help make the day a success for themselves and their visitors. Any proceeds at the end of the day were to be shared between the church, a building that always needed attention, and the events committee. With the number of festivals and traditions celebrated in Cavendish the funds were always in need of boosting and May Day helped to refill the pot.

She looked on as the local Cubs and Scouts, led by schoolteacher, Mr Critchton raced from pillar to post erecting signs, setting out chairs and generally being a support wherever required. They were distinctive in their shorts, green jumpers and yellow scarves. Many of them had a number of badges sewn onto their sleeves to denote their Scouting achievements.

The vicar, and the Harringtons' good friend, Stephen Merryweather, sat cross-legged on the grass alongside his two boys, Luke and Mark, discussing the best strategy for winning a coconut.

'D-don't go for power, get your aim right.'

'Like when we play cricket,' said Mark, leaping up and pretending to bowl.

'I rather th-think underarm would be better.'

'Like marbles,' said Luke delving into his pocket and bringing out a blue and yellow marble. A small catapult fell to the ground. He held it up triumphantly. 'Can't I use this to knock the coconut off?'

Beth smiled as Stephen attempted to explain why that wouldn't be acceptable. Beyond them, she glimpsed the local butcher, Graham Porter, and Cavendish's doctor, Philip Jackson, heaving the traditional hog roast into place, while Bert figured out a safe way to light the fire below it. Bob Tanner's folk band, The Taverners, practised a final jig and the Morris Men stretched their limbs and went over to examine the ales set up at the beer tent.

Anne, wearing a beautiful canary yellow summer dress and a pale lemon cardigan, caught up with Beth. 'There you are — I've been looking all over for you.'

Beth greeted her warmly. 'Oh Anne, isn't this going to be the most perfect day? We couldn't have asked for better weather. Stephen must have ordered it specially.'

Anne gave her a knowing look and stood back. 'You look really pretty, Beth. Are they new?'

Beth surveyed her white Capri pants topped with a striking blue and white gingham blouse. 'Yes, they are!' She clapped her hands in excitement. 'I couldn't resist the Capri pants, they're so flattering and they go so well with plimsolls. I wanted to be smart but, you know, I didn't want to be too dressy, especially wandering around fields.'

'Oooh, yes, and you can't beat flat shoes if you're on your feet all day.'

'You're quite right. Did you want me for something?'

'Yes, I have a message from James.' Anne went through the details of his telephone call with Miss Brooks-Hunter. Beth couldn't contain her delight.

'How wonderful,' she said. 'I haven't seen her in months. She's a real gem of a lady, Anne, and amazingly frank and funny. I always think it's a shame she doesn't socialise more — everyone who meets her adores her.'

'She doesn't come to church,' replied Anne. 'Is she not well enough?'

'Oh, she's well enough, she just chooses not to.' Anne couldn't help but show her surprise. Normally, ladies of Delphine's vintage were the stalwarts of the Sunday service. Clearly, she commented, this lady went against tradition.

'She is definitely her own woman.' Beth searched the crowds. 'I need Bert to help me retrieve the village stocks from the old stables.'

'Stocks!' said Anne in horror.

'We always get the stocks out,' she said as they strolled over to Bert, whom she'd spotted in the distance. 'We've three of them. We don't actually lock anyone in, of course; it's just for fun, and whoever volunteers to sit in them gets a free ice-cream. You buy three wet sponges and do your level best to drench the victim. It's a hoot.' She waved her arms to catch his attention. 'Bert?'

Bert, who had now moved on from helping Donovan and Graham to assisting the Cubs as they secured the maypole in position, returned the wave.

'Watcha. How's my favourite titled lady?'

'I'm very well, thank you. When you've finished there, could you possibly help me get the stocks out?'

' 'Course I can. Can't let you do that on yer own — not wiv' those lovely clean togs on. I'll get Pete Mitchell to 'elp. Where are they — normal place?'

'Yes, in the old stables, where you put them last year.'

Bert summoned a couple more Scouts to finish the maypole and sought out

Peter who managed an orchard on the outskirts of the village. Together with Beth and Anne, they made their way along the side of the hotel and toward the stable entrance.

To Beth's continual dismay, the stables had sunk into disrepair some years ago. James' father was not a horseman and had sold the animals at auction many years ago. When they'd opted to allow the house to be used as a hospital during the war, the stable block was not maintained and didn't receive the attention it deserved so the place had slowly fallen into ruin. James assured her it was saveable and certainly the main structure appeared strong. To Beth, though, it was fit for the bulldozer. As if reading her thoughts, Pete posed a question.

'Are you going to do up the stables, your Ladyship?'

'It's on James' to do list,' she replied. 'The men who laid the terrace are giving us a quotation. The hotel's getting such a wonderful reputation because of its setting and its outdoor pursuits, so it seems the obvious course of action to buy some horses, especially as we're right on the South Downs. It's perfect countryside for riding.'

'Can't get a better view, that's for sure.'

Beth agreed. The country house was nestled in a huge meadow at the foot of the South Downs, in the heart of Sussex. Surrounding them were farms and woodland and, to the south, distant sea views of the coast. To the north was the quaint village of Cavendish, over which the Harrington family had presided for the last two centuries. Yes, it would certainly be nice to have horses back in the fields.

'Mummy! Mummy!'

Anne turned to see Luke waving frantically.

'Mummy, me and Mark are learning how to Morris dance. Come and watch!'

Beth insisted Anne should go and see this momentous occasion. 'After all, there's nothing to see in here except some old timber and cobwebs. I'll be back in a while; tell the boys I want to see their performance.'

Anne assured her she would and

followed her excited son back to the fair.

Beth, Bert and Pete continued toward the barn-building. The doors had long since disappeared and the wooden structure was dry and brittle. Beth linked arms with her cockney friend.

'Do you think we can save it?'

'I reckon so. This is the side that gets all the weather, so it'll need quite a bit o' work. But the rest of it's sheltered by the trees at the back. It's not as bad as you think.'

They stepped inside.

'Looks all right in here,' Pete said as he studied a rusty old tractor. 'You ought to restore that. They're right handy little motors.'

Beth grimaced at the rust heap on four wheels stored there since before the war. 'Do you think it'll work?' she asked.

Bert grinned. 'Pete's a dab hand with mechanics, as is your 'usband — I'm sure it'll scrub up nice.' He scanned the stables. 'How many 'orses did they keep 'ere?'

Beth pondered the question as she mentally counted the number of dilapidated stable blocks. 'I guess around twenty in its heyday. They only had a handful when I moved here.' She turned to the men. 'Wouldn't it be grand to have twenty chestnut geldings here for our guests?'

Pete and Bert both mumbled that they much preferred motorised transport and if they had to see a horse, they'd rather be betting on it.

'Sorry, Beth,' said Bert, 'but whenever I've ridden a donkey on the beach, I always end up with a sore bum. It'll be even worse on an 'orse.'

Beth observed Bert fondly. She loved his accent and his down to earth language.

They spent the next few minutes picking through bits of junk dumped during the renovation of Harrington's. Items of scored and faded furniture had taken the place of livestock, along with rolls of unused wallpaper, broken tiles, lengths of timber and a hideous stuffed, moth-eaten fox in a glass case. High in the rafters, Beth could see old birds' nests and thick cobwebs. She shuddered — she hated cobwebs and decided not to venture too far into the rubble.

'Is this what we're looking for?' Pete pointed across to one of the stalls.

'Yeah, that's them there,' said Bert. 'There's only two, though — 'aven't you got another one?'

'Yes, there it is over there,' Beth said, nodding to the opposite stall. Bert nudged Pete.

'Right, come on then. Let's get our 'ands dirty.'

As the men shifted the stocks, Beth wandered further into the barn, trying to envisage how it would look with a little tender, loving care. Bert was right, the inside was surprisingly unscathed. The individual stables would come up a treat with a coat of fresh varnish or paint. She'd always adored the stables she'd seen in a magazine about horse riding in Kentucky. The ranches there were a sight to behold with their buildings painted in rich rustic red, behind pristine white fences. How lovely that would look here.

A familiar rush of adrenalin hit and she knew, straightaway, how the finished stables would look and feel. But one thing did concern her and that was the cost. Renovating the stables was one thing, but keeping horses — well, that would need careful budgeting. She'd need to have a serious chat with James before they committed themselves to anything. He was the money man and would know whether the project was viable.

A groan interrupted her thoughts. She turned. Bert and Pete were outside with the first set of stocks. There it was again — coming from the far stall. Her gaze settled on a shovel leaning against the wall. She gingerly lifted it up, careful not to make any noise, and trod gently toward the corner. A field mouse scurried over a mound of straw and disappeared out of sight.

She peered; the mound of straw moved and two feet, in desert boots, extended out. Beth brought the shovel up above her head and took a deep breath.

'Who's there?'

The person under the straw yawned. Beth relaxed a little and nudged the sole of one boot with her foot.

'You — what're you doing here?'

A man cleared the straw from his body and squinted. Beth studied him. He didn't appear to be terribly menacing. If anything, there was something tremendously calming about him. He rubbed the sleep from his clear blue eyes and brushed a wave of thick, blond hair away from his forehead. Beth caught her breath — my, but he was handsome.

'I'm so sorry,' he said wearily. 'Is this your place?'

Beth quickly replaced the shovel and helped clear the straw from his legs. He wore a pair of tatty jeans and a checked shirt with the sleeves rolled up. Beth guessed him to be in his early twenties. 'Well, yes, it is our place,' she replied, 'but we don't tend to sleep here.'

Their eyes met and they laughed. Any tension that she had felt disappeared.

'No, I don't suppose you do.' The young man gave her a genuine smile. His voice was deep and he was well-spoken; Beth imagined him to be privately educated. She narrowed her eyes.

'How long have you been sleeping here?'

'Just a couple of days.' He closed his eyes and brushed the straw from the back of his head. He gave a helpless shrug. 'It seemed pretty derelict, so I thought I'd get away with it.'

Beth's jaw dropped. 'You've been sleeping like this for a few days? Where's home?'

The man ignored the question and gathered together what few belongings he had — a threadbare woollen jumper and a small leather wallet. His eyes were hopeful.

'I don't suppose I could have a wash?'

'Not until you answer my question.'

'Oi!' shouted Bert. 'What's all this then?'

The young man stood up and swayed, prompting Bert and Pete to rush alongside and support him.

'Sit him down,' Beth said. 'Over there, on that old chair.'

Pete, being younger and fitter, took the young man's weight and delivered him to the said chair. Beth turned to Bert.

'Bert, be an angel and ask one of the waiters to bring some tea, would you?

Strong, with sugar, and get them to make up a cheese sandwich.' Beth checked her watch. 'We really must get the remainder of the fair set up. Pete, I can manage here — can you get the stocks over to the green? James has gone to pick someone up, but I'm sure someone will help. They're the only things not in place.'

Pete told her not to worry and dashed across to a horse-stall to pick up the next set of stocks. Beth, meanwhile, put her hands on her hips and studied the stranger. He really did appear terribly dazed — almost vulnerable. She wondered when he had last eaten — he was probably faint with hunger. She pulled an old milking stool across and sat down next to him.

'Where's home and what's your name?'

He appeared bemused. 'I've come from London,' he replied, 'but that's not home. Truth is, I can't remember. I don't know who I am or where home is.'

'But that's impossible! You must have some idea.'

'Everyone at the Mission calls me Jim.'

Beth knew James teased her about this,

but she always felt people resembled their names; but this young man didn't look like a Jim to her. She imagined a Jim to be dark and swarthy. And a Jim, in her eyes, would never be a young man.

'You don't look like a Jim to me. You look like you should be called Rupert or Oliver.'

The man laughed and Beth was immediately drawn to his winning smile. Dimpled on each cheek. She felt herself blush and quickly rebuked herself for such a reaction.

'It's short for Gentleman Jim,' he said. 'Most of the men at the Mission are from pretty rough areas and some are mixed up with drink or drugs. But me, I don't know. I think I had a fall or something and I can't remember anything.'

'What Mission?'

'St Mary's in Bethnal Green.'

'And how long have you been at St Mary's?'

Beth took a sharp breath when she learnt he'd been there for several years. He couldn't be more than twenty two or twenty three, so that would mean he had been fifteen or sixteen when he arrived. Surely that couldn't be right!

Behind her, she heard Bert whistling a tune from *South Pacific* as he approached with a tray full of goodies. Strong tea, as requested, a bottle of ginger beer, cheese and ham sandwiches and a slice of apple pie.

'Silver service at the OK Corral,' he chortled. 'Get yer gnashers round that lot.'

Beth had never seen anyone so grateful.

Gentleman Jim took the tray from Bert and placed it on his knees, looking as if he didn't know where to start.

'Is this all for me? Are we sharing?'

Beth assured him that it was all his. She suggested he ignore any manners or etiquette and tuck in. He did so with gusto. Beth stood up and drew Bert to one side. She explained what she knew to date and Bert gave it some thought. He quickly observed the young man.

'Bethnal Green's my stamping ground. I'll see what I can find out about 'im. You gonna let him stay 'ere?'

'I think I should discuss it with James

first,' replied Beth. She scanned the crowds in the distance. 'Is Philip about? It'd be good for a doctor to cast an eye over him — see what he thinks, especially with the man's memory loss.'

'I'll go and get him now,' said Bert. 'Pete's putting the stocks out. Anne and Elsie are organising everyone.'

Beth sent up silent thanks as Bert rushed off to track down Philip. Anne had become a particularly close friend and Elsie Taylor, who owned the local café-come-restaurant, was a godsend and one of the most organised people she knew — there would be no last-minute disasters with those two at the helm.

Gentleman Jim devoured the sandwich, swigged all of the ginger beer and finished off the tea and apple pie. Beth watched on. He couldn't have eaten in days. Colour began to return to his face.

Her shoulders fell in relief at the sound of James' voice.

'Hello all, I hear we have an intruder.'

The young man quickly put the tray on the stable floor and stood up, doing his best to swallow his food as he mumbled an apology. Beth gestured for him to sit back down as she repeated his story.

James turned to the stranger. 'You really can't remember anything?'

'No, I'm afraid not,' replied the young man. 'I'm a bit of a lost sheep.'

James frowned. 'Well, what's brought you here?'

The man explained that he'd decided to have a trip to Brighton. He raked his fingers through his hair. 'I managed to get a ride down on a coach that was taking some children to the seaside, but I'm hitching back. I saw this place in the distance and it looked familiar.' He shrugged. 'So, here I am.'

'Yes, here you jolly well are. But what do you mean, it looked familiar?'

Gentleman Jim shook his head. 'I don't know what I mean.' He tilted his head toward Harrington's. 'The house there, I know it, I'm sure I do. It's the first time I've seen something that may have some meaning for me.'

James raised an eyebrow at Beth. He asked Jim to excuse them and steered her toward the stable entrance.

'What d'you think?' he asked quietly.

'He seems an awfully nice young man; not your normal tramp or layabout.'

'Yes — going by his accent, I would say he's from a rather well-to-do family.' James studied the manor house ahead of him. 'I wonder why this place is so familiar to him. Do you recognise him at all?'

Beth assured him that she didn't. 'Could he have been sent here as an evacuee during the war? Perhaps his Dad was here. But if he can't remember who he is, how is he going to know?' She faced James. 'But, more importantly, what are we going to do with him?'

'Well, the chap needs a bath and a set of clothes for a start,' replied James. 'I'll get Mrs Tubbins onto it.' He knew their head cleaner would be cut out for such a job.

'Sweetie, there's a single room free at Harrington's — why not let him stay for one night? I can't imagine he would be an embarrassment. And, he's about the same build as Oliver and Harry, so I'll pop home and get some fresh clothes for him.

We may as well make him welcome.'

'I say, steady on, Beth — we don't want him moving in.'

Beth gave him a tender kiss. 'I'll go and get him fixed up for the next couple of days. Has Miss Brooks-Hunter arrived?'

James said that she had and was, at this minute, being served a glass of Pimms on the terrace. 'Charlie Hawkins is going to escort her around the fair, and Didier is serving the three of us lunch at one o'clock. I thought, with Charlie coming every year, he could fill her in on the general running of things and the history behind May Day and all that.'

'He's good company,' replied Beth. 'She'll enjoy that.'

Charlie Hawkins was a widower in his mid-thirties who was also the village librarian. He'd lost his wife to an illness several years previously and was now bringing up his two young children on his own. James was very fond of the man and afforded him a great deal of respect.

Gentleman Jim shuffled toward them carrying his tray of empty plates and cups. 'That was delightful. Thank you so much for your kindness.'

James took the tray from him. 'Our hospitality doesn't stop here,' he said. 'Beth's going to arrange a bed for the night for you, before we set you on your way. We'll have a chat later — see if we can't fathom out why this place is so familiar to you.'

'I'd love it if you can,' replied the young man. 'I even knew where the stables were.'

James watched the young man as he followed Beth to the house. How strange that he knew the house and the stables. They were not exactly in plain sight, so one would have to know they were there. Who on earth was he and how had such a well-mannered young man ended up living rough? And how did anyone lose every ounce of memory? James sensed an interesting mystery to solve.

Perhaps he'd have the young man stay for a few days to see if he could unravel it.

3

In the distance, and timed to perfection, the church bells pealed the arrival of the May Day Queen.

Through a tunnel of flower garlands held high by youngsters, six-year old Natasha Jackson, Philip's daughter, made her entrance to herald the start of the Spring Fair. Peter's flatbed lorry had been transformed into a pink and mauve carriage with strands of ribbon that fluttered in the breeze. A simple wooden chair which had been painted gold and decorated with a huge yellow bow was fixed to the back. Natasha wore a pink lace and cotton dress, silk ballet shoes and had a silver-coloured tiara. She waved a wand with a star fixed on the end and occasionally her eyes sought out her parents, to make sure they were nearby.

The arrival of the May Day Queen brought the whole place alive and signalled the start of the festivities.

Children giggled and screamed as they played ring-a-ring-a roses in time with the music of the carousel. Across the field, Bob Tanner's folk band belted out a lively jig, while the Morris Men 'Stripped the Willow' with great enthusiasm, bells jangling on the leather straps around their calves.

The enticing aroma of fried onions, hot-dogs, toffee apples and hog roast mingled together and drifted across the field prompting many people to start queuing for food.

The spring sun enticed villagers from their winter confines to enjoy the fresh air, the tasty food, the fairground rides and the various competitions.

The arrival of the early warm weather had triggered the first airing of spring fashions. The ladies, in particular, had been quick to discard dark, winter colours for bright flowery designs. An assortment of outfits in varying shades of yellows, blues and greens resulted in a vibrant spectacle. Although the older gentlemen remained more formal, the younger men had opted for linen trousers and short-sleeved shirts. Some, thanks to the influence of American singer Elvis Presley, had opted for jeans and slicked-back hair.

Boys and girls raced from one exciting ride to another; dads competed on the strong man machine, while mums scrutinised entrants to see if they stood any chance of winning the many baking and chutney-making competitions. It came as no surprise to James that both Elsie and Mrs Keates came away with the first prizes of the day — best scone and best Victoria sponge, respectively.

Both excelled in the kitchen and he particularly admired Elsie for investing her talents and skills into setting up her café on the road to Charnley. Unusually for a woman, she'd rejected the traditional path of marriage and children, preferring instead to launch herself as a lone business woman by turning a small, run-down building into a thriving and popular dining venue.

Mrs Keates had come to his attention during his investigation into the death of Alec Grimes and she had quickly become part of the Cavendish social scene. James felt sure that if Elsie and Mrs Keates ever decided to enter into a business partnership, they'd be a formidable force in the catering world.

Graham Porter, the amiable butcher with huge meaty hands, narrowly missed out on the strongman competition to a tall, muscular man whom James had never set eyes on before. He appeared to be known to the fairground family so was probably used to handling heavy machinery and equipment. James loathed judging people solely on appearance, but he really didn't like the man's countenance — furtive, with shifty eyes.

'N-not a nice fellow, I-I can tell you.'

James recognised the endearing stammer of Stephen, the local vicar, and quickly sought an answer.

'Do you know who he is?'

'I understand he r-runs the Waltzer. G-goes by the name of Derek Jacobs.'

'And you've taken a dislike to him?'

'Mmm, all God's children and all that, but he r-really has a very rude and aggressive manner. D'you hire him every year?'

'No,' replied James. 'This is the first time. I normally book Lambs — a family enterprise from Eastbourne — but they were already booked, so this Jacobs lot were second choice. They seem a little rough around the edges, but I s'pose most fairground people are.'

Dr Philip Jackson ambled toward them, a bottle of beer in his hand. 'Lovely day, James. Everyone seems to be enjoying themselves and Natasha is in her element as May Queen.'

'Yes, she's as pretty as a picture,' replied James. 'By the way, did you manage to check over our mystery man?'

'Yes. Not much to report, really. He certainly seems to have some sort of memory loss — amnesia, of course, but not sure what type. He can't seem to pinpoint anything very much apart from the Mission in Bethnal Green. Bert said he and Beth are going to try to find out a bit more. Interesting case; never come across one before. If he's around for a while, I'll study him for a few days. It'll be like being back at university.'

James gave a wry smile. 'Mmm, Beth has taken rather a shine to him, so the one night I promised him will no doubt turn into several. He's a good-looking chap, so I'm sure the ladies will be after him once they know he's here.' He tilted his head and grinned. 'Take the pressure off you.'

Philip had the grace to look bashful. It was no secret that the handsome wavy-haired doctor was a hit among the ladies of Cavendish. It didn't sit well with him at all and he often bemoaned the trivial nature of illnesses female residents asked him to attend to. Luckily he and his wife, Helen, adored each other, so any lady trying to pursue the said doctor was always rebuffed and sorely disappointed.

He doffed an imaginary hat and went to join Helen, who waved a hello at them. James returned the greeting then reached inside his trouser pocket for his cigarettes.

'Have you met the mystery man yet?' he asked Stephen.

'N-no. Beth updated Anne who then updated me. I've been promised a full report later.'

'We could do that over lunch. Where are you eating?'

'N-no say in the matter, I'm afraid,'

replied Stephen. 'We tend to f-find that we eat on the go at these events. Luke and Mark graze their way around the field like two sheep.'

James laughed, recollecting the very same thing with their twins when they were young. 'You can't keep the youngsters away from toffee apples and hot dogs, can you?' He slapped Stephen on the back. 'Well, enjoy. Beth and I are about to indulge Delphine Brooks-Hunter with Didier's finest.'

A flash of envy crossed Stephen's face. 'P-perhaps I could tell Anne I'm not feeling well and join you.'

James grinned as he said his goodbyes. 'We're eating outside, Stephen. She'd rumble you straightaway. I'll book us all in for afternoon tea. I'm sure your boys will be ready to sit down by then. If they're not, we'll get someone to look after them.'

Leaving Stephen happy in anticipation of a civilised break later in the day, James made his way through the crowds to the calm of the terrace.

'Hello, Lord Harrington,' said Adam. 'I

put this table by for you — hope that's all right?'

The young and loyal Adam had, according to the *maître d'*, asked to wait on James, Beth and Delphine. Only eighteen, he'd developed quite a crush on Beth and always gave impeccable service as a result — although James hoped he served all diners with a similar dedication.

'Thank you, Adam. Is my wife in the area, or am I going to have to hunt her down?'

'In the area, your Lordship. There she is, with your other guest.'

James squinted as he searched the crowds and finally spotted Beth and Delphine strolling arm in arm toward him. Delphine, he decided, was pure elegance and never allowed age to dictate the clothes she wore. Most women in their seventies had relinquished fashion for comfort, but Delphine had refused to do so. Today, she wore a tailored skirt with a cowl neck sweater and cream court shoes. With Beth in her Capri pants and shirt, they cut a stylish pair.

45

As he waited, he studied the new patio from a diner's perspective and decided he was delighted with the whole thing; a stunning addition that replicated his vision in every detail. The terrace ran the length of the house and was decked with terracotta pots brimming with buttercup-yellow daffodils and purple crocuses. Twenty round tables were spaced appropriately and bedecked with pristine tablecloths and fine crystal glasses. Navy blue cushions lay on every chair and canary yellow parasols were opened, providing shade for the diners.

'So sorry we're late, sweetie,' said Beth, pecking him on the cheek.

James assisted both ladies to their chairs. 'I don't think you are, darling. I was just admiring the terrace. Are you enjoying yourselves?'

Delphine closed her eyes and smiled. 'It's been a perfect start to a perfect day,' she said. 'Your librarian chappie, Charlie, is a delight and your wife is the most charming hostess. Now I'm looking forward to sampling the menu and making more excursions around the stalls. I'm determined to see everything.'

Beth added: 'Charlie covered the far end, but we've only touched on the flowers and vegetables so far.'

As Adam distributed the menus, James settled back in his chair. 'You haven't sampled Didier's culinary skills, have you? I think you're in for a treat.'

After some deliberation, they ordered drinks, which were promptly delivered. Delphine sipped delicately from her sherry glass, while James and Beth enjoyed flutes of sparkling Cinzano and studied the dishes on offer. Delphine examined the menu.

'My, my, quality takes precedence here,' she said. 'I can see why so many people speak of Harrington's in such positive terms.'

'Our treat, Delphine,' replied James. 'Please do choose whatever takes your fancy.'

Adam waited patiently at a distance and, after a subtle nod from James, came forward to take the order.

'Unanimous decision, Adam. We'll go for Didier's spring special — prawns wrapped in smoked salmon with hollandaise sauce. We'll follow that with the crown roast of lamb with buttered baby potatoes and carrot royale.'

'Good choice, your Lordship,' replied Adam. He gathered the menus in and bowed to the women. 'Lady Harrington, Miss Brooks-Hunter.'

'What a well-mannered young man,' said Delphine. 'So few appear to be these days,' she added with sudden melancholy.

Her mood wasn't lost on James. 'Oh, I don't know. I think it may be a matter of age thing. We all get to that stage where we think times have changed for the worse, don't you think?'

Delphine sat up brightly and agreed. They turned their chairs to obtain the best view of the activities in the arena. Their guest frowned quizzically at a section of the crowd.

'Who on earth is that?' she said, staring into the distance.

James manoeuvred himself to see. 'Who, the chap dressed like a tree?'

'Yes — did he think it was fancy dress?'

Beth laughed. 'No, Delphine, he's the Green Man. You know, the ancient pagan figure. We always have the Green Man at the May Day fair. It's tradition. He's part of the Morris-dancing team; in fact, I think beneath all that undergrowth, you'll find Jack Hedges from the greengrocers.'

'Of course,' said Delphine. 'I should have known. It's so long since I've been to a May Day fair.' She patted Beth's hand and spoke to James. 'I remember coming here with my sister Juliet and we'd watch the maypole dance. On this very green and here we are all these years later doing the same thing.

James' ears pricked. 'You have a sister?'

'Yes dear, she's lived in Cornwall for some time.'

Beth tilted her head. 'I didn't realise you lived here as a youngster.'

'I didn't, dear, but May Day was a popular one and we used to visit quite frequently. My sister lives up on the moors in Cornwall. Quite remote it is, wouldn't suit me. She moved there years ago.'

Delphine drifted back to what appeared to James to be a sad and reflective state of reminiscence. He made an effort to lighten the mood, and she quickly returned from her daydream and insisted on knowing more about the May Day festivities and, in particular, the Green Man. She placed a hand on James' arm.

'I know that you're quite an expert on local folklore.'

'Not sure that I'm an expert,' he replied. 'More of an amateur enthusiast. My friend, Bert, probably knows more than I do.'

She dismissed his claim of ignorance as poppycock. 'And Bert's not here, dear, so I'll need to hear it from you.'

'Right-ho,' said James as he took a sip of Cinzano. 'Well, quite simply, the Green Man is the god of vegetation. He sort of symbolises the natural world — the earth, particularly the forest. I mean, most of England was forest once upon a time, so it could be a pretty scary place to pop into.'

A shadow was cast over James; he looked up. 'Bert! I thought you had taken up residence in the home-brew section.'

'Bit early in the day to murder John Barleycorn, Jimmy boy.'

Delphine jumped at the comment and asked what on earth he meant. Beth answered. 'John Barleycorn is a folklore term, Delphine.'

'That's right, missus,' joined in Bert. 'To make beer, you 'ave to murder the barley. The proper term is to hammer it. There's a folk song about it; centuries old it is. And the Scottish poet Robbie Burns wrote his version of it:

"There was three kings went into the east,

Three kings both great and 'igh,

And they 'ave sworn a solemn oath,

John Barleycorn should die'.'

The elderly spinster patted the vacant chair next to her and invited Bert to join them. 'How wonderful.' She winked at James. 'Two folklore enthusiasts. I hear you're the real expert on the Green Man.'

Bert sat down as James formally introduced the two. He asked Adam to bring some beer to the table.

'Sounds like Jimmy was doing a fine job without me,' replied Bert. 'I'll correct 'im if he goes wrong.'

James cleared his throat and thanked Bert in the most sarcastic way possible before returning his attention to Delphine.

'Anyway, as I was saying,' he said. 'In those days, people had to go into the forest to hunt and gather and whatnot. Well, during the winter, it was always pretty sparse and bare. When the spring arrived, everything began growing again and the locals at the time all thought there were some spiritual goings-on needed to make that happen, hence the Green Man.' James glanced at Bert. 'Is that right?'

Bert confirmed that it was as he began rolling up a cigarette. 'That's right. He's the god of the forest, and seen as a sort of huge tree or bush with a face.'

'Must be terribly hot inside a costume in this weather,' Delphine chuckled. 'Let's hope there are no nettles among the foliage.'

Their salmon appetiser arrived. Delphine studied the plate with interest. 'What an excellent idea. Now, I've eaten prawns and salmon for many years, you know, but never together.'

'Yes, our Didier is remarkably good at making something special from quite simple ingredients,' replied James. 'Decidedly delicious.'

'Your young waiter is also decidedly delicious,' replied Delphine. 'What a shame I'm a little too old for him.'

Beth giggled and playfully scolded Delphine for being so naughty.

'When you get to my age, dear, you can say whatever you want. No one really has the heart to scold. It's great fun.' She turned to Bert. 'So, tell me, Mr Briggs. Are there any juicy stories about the Green Man?'

'D'you know what, missus,' replied Bert. 'There is, although it's not juicy, more sinister. Some Wicca traditions think 'e's more of a Horned God.'

Delphine and Beth frowned. James clicked his fingers in triumph. 'Cernunnos! Yes, I remember learning this. He's the horned god that you find in Celtic mythology and totally different to our friendly trunk over there. Cernunnos is portrayed as a man with a shaggy beard and wild, unruly hair. I don't think there's anything evil about him, though — just a little more menacing than anything else.'

'Talk o' the devil,' Bert picked up his

beer. 'I've got some jobs to do.' He made a quick and polite excuse to leave as another guest approached.

'Afternoon all.'

'George!' James stood and shook hands with his old pal, Detective Chief Inspector George Lane. George was another friend from younger days and a fellow cricket team member. Bert, as a result of his occasional dodgy deals, tended to find an excuse to leave if George pitched up although nothing untoward had ever happened between them. James hoped it would stay that way. He pushed out a chair for him. 'I thought you were on duty.'

George remained standing. 'Just left off; thought I'd pop in for the fishing competition. Nice to have someone with their own stretch of river.'

Delphine clapped her hands. 'How wonderful. Is the river brimming with fish?'

Beth enthused that it was, most definitely, brimming with all sorts. 'We have bream, perch, tench and, of course, trout.'

'How wonderful. Are you averse to an old lady trying her hand?'

George couldn't help but express his surprise and was also a little confused as to who this lady was. James immediately introduced them to each other. Then it was Delphine's turn to express surprise.

'A Detective Chief Inspector! How fortunate that you've arrived today.'

'Why's that, Miss Brooks-Hunter?' asked George.

James looked on with some concern as she dismissed her comment with a wave of her napkin.

'Oh, no reason, dear. Just me being mischievous. Won't you join us?'

George checked his watch and excused himself, but expressed his willingness to lend her his fishing rod, an offer she happily accepted.

The rest of the dinner was spent happily enjoying the fresh and succulent meal placed in front of them. James couldn't remember tasting such juicy and tender lamb and called for Didier who rushed to his table as if he feared the worst.

'Is the lamb not to your liking, Lord 'arrington?'

'On the contrary, Didier. I've never tasted lamb like it.'

'Beautiful,' Beth added.

Delphine quietly applauded him with a twinkle in her eye. Didier bowed, his face flushed a little. 'It is most kind of you, most kind. If you excuse, I must continue in the kitchen.'

He briskly marched back to his domain, his head a little higher than when he'd arrived. Beth gave James a fond smile. 'You made his day.'

'Yes, poor chap looked so downhearted this morning when I had to shoot off. I thought a few added compliments wouldn't go amiss.'

Delphine patted her lips dry and folded her napkin.

'Perhaps, James, you would escort me around the rest of the fair,' she suggested. 'I'm sure Beth is eager to spend some time with her friends and play the hostess.'

'Absolutely, old thing.' He swung round and called to Adam. 'I'll settle up with you later today, Adam. Put the bill by the cash register.' He wagged his finger at the young waiter and pushed a generous tip into his pocket. 'I know Didier insists I have meals on a complimentary basis, but that will never do. This is a business, after all.'

Adam bowed sheepishly and began clearing the table. James finished the last of his drink and caught Beth's attention. 'Are you coming with us?'

Beth explained that she'd like to catch up with some of the villagers and ensure that everything was running as it should be.

'The sign of a true hostess,' said Delphine. 'We'll bump into you on the way round, dear.'

'I'm sure we shall,' replied Beth. She tugged James' arm as he helped Delphine out of her chair. 'Did you mention something about afternoon tea?'

James had momentarily forgotten all about that and quickly announced that they were going to rendezvous back on the terrace at around four o'clock with Stephen and Anne.

'You've yet to meet the new vicar, isn't

that right, Delphine?' he added.

'I've seen them in the village,' she replied. 'They appear to be a lovely family; and how refreshing to see a vicar with blood in his veins. Not like that old crock we had before. He was like someone from a Dickens novel.'

James and Beth grinned at each other as they left the terrace. Beth turned right for the coconut shy where their sons, Oliver and Harry, were holding court. On holiday from their studies at Oxford, they frequently came home to help with the village festivities. Harry was always keen to lend a hand and had signalled his intention to join the 'Harrington's' business after completing his studies.

James and Delphine began their tour to the left, where a lucky dip was taking place. Delphine held onto his arm.

'So exciting, isn't it? I do hope nothing will happen today. I'm having such a good time.'

She didn't allow James to ask what could possibly happen to dampen the proceedings, but her tone made him somewhat wary. His intuition was tested further when they reached the fairground Waltzer, where Derek Jacobs acknowledged him and appeared to scowl at Delphine. James frowned. What on earth was all that about?

Over the next hour, they happily played a number of amusing fairground games and Delphine was delighted to win a goldfish, which she promptly gave to the nearest child.

Further along the route was the gingerbread man, a stalwart at the Spring Fair. James bought a couple of biscuits from him.

'Have to have some gingerbread, Delphine. It's lucky.'

Delphine gave a sideways look. 'Lucky?'

'Yes, centuries ago there were always gingerbread stalls at village fairs and they're considered as lucky. No one really knows why, but I believe there's a religious element to it. The Philippines believe that ginger has the power of driving out evil spirits.'

'I've heard of that, dear. And you know that the Polynesians built roofs over their altars with ginger leaves?' She took a bite.

'Let's hope we have some luck today.'

James went on to buy some home-made scones for her from the WI tent and a jar of Lilac and Rose Crumb's fresh lemon curd. The sisters, or the Snoop Sisters as he preferred to call them, eagerly sought out information about James' lady-friend but found out very little because no one knew her that well. He knew it was wrong to gloat but, for once, he had the upper hand with the Crumbs — where Delphine was concerned, anyway.

Delphine held onto his arm firmly and, as they reached the merry-go-round, she fondly reminisced about her love of the prancing horses.

'So colourful, and so magical, too,' she said. 'Don't you adore the music of the merry-go-round?'

The organ and the accompanying bells, drums and flutes were playing a robust version of 'It's a Long Way to Tipperary' and James had to admit it that a fairground organ always sent a wave of nostalgia through him. Reg Jacobs, brother of the loathsome Derek, walked toward him, wiping his hands on an oily rag.

'Everyfing all right, guv'nor?'

'Absolutely splendid, thanks. Business booming?'

Reg glared at Delphine. 'Could say that.' His eyes narrowed at the elderly lady. 'Enjoying yerself?'

Delphine allowed Reg a brief acknowledgement and pulled James away.

'Now, where do I go for a spot of fishing?' she asked.

Delphine's assertive tug took James by surprise and he bade a quick goodbye to Reg. What a strange encounter that had been.

He led her into the wooded copse to meet up with George at the river. All the while he wondered about the somewhat frosty atmosphere between the Jacobs family and the old lady. Had she done something to upset them? It wouldn't be too much of a surprise, given their general demeanour.

But Delphine never really went anywhere, so where would she have met them? Perhaps it would be best to ask.

Reg and Derek Jacobs might just as well have put a curse on her with the looks they gave her. He wondered if it would be too forward to ask, especially as he didn't know her that well. He chewed his lip and made a mental note to try and turn the conversation toward the fairground people during afternoon tea. It would be interesting to see how she reacted.

4

With Delphine safely ensconced with George,
James strode back to the fair and sought
out Bert, who was standing alongside pub
landlord, Donovan Delaney. Dublin-born
Delaney had only moved to Cavendish a
few years previously. He'd married a Sussex
girl, Kate, and they now had two small
children. With his Irish charm and banter,
he had quickly settled into the community
and had an uncanny knack for knowing
exactly what his customers wanted. For
the Spring Fair, he'd done some extensive
research and kegs inside the beer tent
were evidence of that, bearing names such
as Sussex Gold, May Day Celebration
and Victoria Spring Ruby Mild.

The usual suspects had gathered by
the barrels — Graham Porter and Pete
Mitchell and, in the far corner, Mr
Chrichton, the primary school teacher,
who appeared to have a lady-friend in
tow. Chrichton waved hello across the

crowd and James reciprocated as he wandered over to Bert.

On seeing James approach, Donovan quickly grabbed a pint jug and began pouring.

'You'll be wanting something to quench your thirst, James.'

James licked his lips and enquired as to the name of the ale he would soon have his hands on.

'This, your very fine Lordship, is South Downs Harvest, brewed by Harveys.' Donovan held the glass up. 'A light ale, with a rich dark colour, and the taste of single malts, made with water from the local spring.'

James took the glass from him and supped the top half inch. He closed his eyes as the refreshing ale swirled around his mouth and eased its way down.

'I say, Donovan! What a splendid little number that is. Almost like a mild. I think even the ladies will enjoy this one.' He examined the contents of Bert's glass. 'What are you drinking?'

'Home-made lemonade!' Bert's eyes went heavenward. 'I got caught with the

Merryweather kids and they insisted I 'ad a drink with 'em.' He peered into his glass. 'Actually, it's not too bad.'

Donovan continued taking orders for ale as James steered Bert out of the tent and into the fresh air. Bob Tanner and his band were thumping out 'Midnight Special' and the young children raced around the green in front of them playing tag and generally having a marvellous time.

James' son, Harry, was assisting the old blacksmith, Mr Friar, with donkey rides. Helen Jackson and the formidable Dorothy Forbes, from the Cavendish players, delicately licked their vanilla ice-creams whilst discussing how best to win the turquoise vase from the hoopla stall.

'Another success, Jimmy boy.'

'Yes, it's all going rather splendidly, isn't it?'

'Your old bird enjoying 'erself, is she?'

James winced. 'Ye . . . s.'

His friend picked up on his hesitation. 'What's up?'

James rubbed the back of his neck. 'What do you know about the fair people, Bert?'

Bert pulled a face. 'Not a lot. I've seen 'em around on a few bank 'olidays and summer fêtes, but they tend to be the second or third choice for the likes o' this type of do. I think they're what you might call rough around the edges.'

'Surely all fair people are like that?'

'Not necessarily. Your lot from Lambs' are nothing like this. What's to do, then?'

'Oh, I don't know,' replied James. 'It's the little things she's said and the rather evil eyes she's received from the Jacobs. There's just something that doesn't add up. It's as if they've had some sort of run-in. But not just a one-off tiff, more as if they have a history.'

Bert sipped his lemonade. 'P'haps they 'ave. I mean, we don't know much about the old bird, do we? She's an 'ermit, ain't she?'

James agreed that, although a charming and spirited lady, Delphine remained rather a mystery and he was sure there were many layers beneath the surface. He wished he knew what the problem was with the Jacobs though. The Reverend interrupted his thoughts.

'A-absolutely perfect day. Anne and the children are having a w-wonderful time. No Beth?'

'She's around, somewhere — probably with Elsie tasting all the food in the WI tent.'

'Or in-interrogating the mystery man from the stables.'

'Tch, Lord, yes,' said James. 'I'd forgotten about him. Strange business that. You know he's got amnesia, don't you?'

Stephen explained that Anne had been apprising him with continual updates.

'Well, one parting shot across the bow was that he's sure he knows this place. Not Cavendish — I mean the house, Harrington's.'

'Could he have been evacuated d-during the war?' asked Stephen.

'Mmm, we thought about that, although the house wasn't used for evacuees. I don't recognise him at all, neither does Beth. I got Harry and Oliver to pop in, too, as they're about the same age, but they're similarly clueless.'

'P-perhaps George can make some enquiries?'

Bert pulled a face. 'I wouldn't fink so. He's not missing, is he? Unless he's got a record, in which case they may have his fingerprints on file somewhere. Just lost his memory. Jackson's the man to speak to. Might be able to give 'im some treatment.'

James explained that Dr Jackson was already on the case. He took out his cigarettes and offered the contents. Stephen declined, but Bert took advantage. After lighting up, he jutted his chin at Bert.

'You know that Beth is going to recruit you to visit the Bethnal Green Mission?'

'Yeah, yeah,' replied Bert. 'I sor' of offered, to be honest. We'll take a run up later in the week, see what we can find out.' He tutted. 'Another mystery to solve, Sherlock.'

Stephen grimaced and commented that he hoped it wouldn't be anything like the Alec Grimes affair the previous Hallowe'en. James assured him that the village was not exciting enough to have so much intrigue going on. But Stephen's eyes quickly lit up.

'T-talking about intrigue. I h-heard

rumour that Miss Brooks-Hunter had been a spy during the war.'

'A spy!' said James. 'But that can't be possible. She doesn't strike me as being the spying type.'

Bert agreed. 'But even if she was, she's about seventy. The war only ended thirteen years ago. She's a bit old to have been mixed up in that sort o' thing.'

'I-I wonder if they meant the Great War?'

'And where, Stephen, are you obtaining this alleged information?' asked James.

Stephen's face took on an embarrassed expression. 'You're quite right, shouldn't listen to gossip. I th-think Anne overheard something in the WI tent.'

A collective groan rang out as James asserted that the rumour probably came from Rose and Lilac Crumb, the Snoop Sisters. He'd never come across such a pair of tell-tales in all his life and had decided, long ago, they must lead incredibly mundane lives to feel the need to make up so many stories. He advised Stephen to take any rumours coming out of the WI tent with a pinch of salt.

'You never know quite where they've come from,' he added, 'especially if the Crumbs are in the vicinity.'

On seeing a fellow horse-racing enthusiast, Bert excused himself and passed his half-glass of lemonade to Stephen.

'W-where is Miss Brooks-Hunter?' he asked. 'Are we all still having tea together?'

James checked his watch. 'Yes, absolutely. She's down at the river with George, doing a spot of fishing.'

Stephen's eyes widened in surprise. 'G — goodness. You don't expect someone like D — Delphine to go fishing.'

'Yes, she's a game old dear, that's for sure.' James squinted in the sunshine and shielded his eyes. 'I say, there's George over there buying an ice-cream. No Delphine with him, though.' He made to go. 'Excuse me, old chap. I promised to look after her, so I'd best make sure that all is well.'

With a block of vanilla ice-cream in one hand and a beer in the other, George explained that Delphine had decided to visit the fortune-teller and had since returned to the river.

'She said she wanted some peace and quiet,' he continued, 'so I've left her sitting by the river. I promise she'll be with you for tea on the terrace.'

Mrs Jepson, the Harringtons' cleaner, made a beeline for James to tell him how lovely the day was. She'd volunteered to be the fortune-teller for the afternoon and had embraced her role by dressing in a long, olive-green tiered gypsy skirt with a headscarf and rather large dangly earrings.

'I say, Mrs J, you do look the part,' said James. 'Are you having fun with it?'

'Well, I don't know about fun,' she replied in her Sussex lilt. 'I mean, I don't really know what I'm doing. Still, I tell everyone they're going to have a nice time and that those they love will always love 'em. Don't want to spoil anyone's day, do I?' She fanned herself with her hand. 'Somethin' odd happened, though, when that elderly lady came in. The one you brought over, Mr Lane.'

'Go on,' said George, curiously.

The two men gave her their full attention.

'Well, I was just going through me normal routine, you know, you're going to enjoy the day and all of that. Well, she shook her head and said no.'

'No?'

'That's right. I said, whatever do you mean? And she said, that's not right, dear. Something bad *will* happen to me today, you wait and see.'

'Good Lord.' James looked at George. 'What d'you think she meant by that?'

George finished his ice-cream and shrugged. 'No idea. What's gonna happen here? Everyone's enjoying the sunshine. Probably the wittering of an old woman.'

James let the comment go, but he really didn't feel that Delphine Brooks-Hunter ever wittered. Indeed, she seemed the least likely out of all the elderly residents he knew to have that in her character. He made his excuses and decided to stroll toward the river, just to check that she was all right.

He picked his way across the main arena, where Dorothy Forbes had begun to judge the dog show and, as was her way, being very officious with it. Further along, Donovan and Kate Delaney were taking a soaking in the stocks by their children, who were beside themselves with laughter. Mr Chrichton and his lady-friend sat on a park bench nearby, their faces almost hidden by a mountain of candy floss.

The arena heaved with visitors and villagers alike, all chatting and laughing, while an announcement came through the public address system advised that the judging for flowers and vegetables was under way. The queue for the donkey ride, which stretched for twenty yards, proved how popular it was. It was the first time they'd booked them and it probably wouldn't be the last.

He passed Mrs J's fortune-telling tent and followed the trodden undergrowth that led to the river. Most of the fisher-men had taken up positions upstream where the best fishing was. *And so they should*, James thought, as he'd put up a £5 prize for the winner, plus a free fishing licence for the year. George, however, wasn't bothered about winning; he simply enjoyed the pleasure of the sport and liked to choose a secluded area where the occasional otter swam and turquoise kingfishers shared the spoils.

The wooded area beside the river had blossomed in the spring warmth and an assortment of beautiful woodland flowers stretched into the distance: daffodils, wood anemone and purple bluebells carpeted the ground ahead of him and caught the dappled sunlight. Their fragrance, although mild, was evident and James breathed in the fresh scents of flowers and ferns with utter delight. Thrushes, finches and blackbirds sang high above him. A more peaceful and contented scene he could not envisage.

In the distance, he glimpsed George's chair. At no time in their friendship had James ever known his friend to use a proper, low-slung fishing chair. Instead, he carted around a deckchair with a cushion and blanket to ensure maximum comfort. It appeared to be empty and James guessed that Delphine was standing in the shallows, trying her hand at fly-fishing. As he approached the clearing, he saw it was empty.

He frowned.

Then his stomach churned.

Oblivious to the branches scratching at his clothes, he ran toward the clearing to find Delphine on the ground, curled up into a ball.

'Oh my Lord!' he cried, rushing to her side. 'Delphine? Delphine, can you hear me?' He felt for a pulse and let out a huge sigh of relief. 'Delphine, can you hear me?'

He yanked the travel blanket off the deckchair, wrapped it around her and placed the cushion under her head. Searching for signs of life along the riverbank he decided the best option was to simply shout.

'I SAY, CAN ANYONE HEAR ME? IT'S JAMES HARRINGTON, WE NEED HELP!'

'Over here,' a distant voice called. 'What's up?'

'WE NEED A DOCTOR. CAN YOU TRACK DOWN PHILIP JACKSON?'

'Will do!'

James cradled Delphine in his arms and discreetly checked for signs of foul play. After what Mrs J had said and Delphine's odd comments to him earlier, he seriously wondered if something untoward had happened. It hadn't, for one minute, dawned on him that this would result in her being harmed. As far as he could make out there was no blood or any sign of a struggle. Perhaps she'd fainted. A hint of a moan passed her lips. James leant in.

'Delphine, it's James. You're quite safe, someone's gone to get the doctor. We'll soon have you out of here.'

Delphine's response was barely audible. 'It was him, you know.'

James' ears pricked. 'Him? Who? Did someone attack you?'

'The tree.'

He frowned. The tree — what on earth was she talking about? She had to be suffering from concussion.

'The leaves.'

James stroked her cheek and assured her that he knew what she was talking about, even though he hadn't a clue. As she drifted in and out of consciousness, her face contorted in frustration.

'The tree . . . That man . . . God . . . '

He heard footsteps approaching and turned to see Philip and Beth running toward him.

'Gre . . . ' Delphine whispered as she finally lost consciousness.

Philip knelt down beside her and took her pulse while Beth clung to James.

'What happened?'

James recounted the events that had led to him finding her, although he held back on his reasons for wondering about her safety. He repeated her peculiar phrases about a tree then gave Beth a questioning look.

'Perhaps she had a little too much to drink with lunch?' suggested James. 'What do you think?'

Beth pooh-poohed the idea, explaining that she'd hardly drunk anything. Philip urgently delved into his bag for smelling salts.

'Is she on any sort of medication, do you know?'

'Haven't the foggiest, I'm afraid,' replied James. 'This is the first time I've really spent any time with her.'

'You know,' Beth added, 'we don't

know much about her at all, except that she's an absolute dear, with an amazing zest for life.'

Philip checked her pulse and looked at them with a stony expression. 'Well, I'm afraid that her amazing zest has given up. I'm sorry, James, Beth, but she's dead.'

5

Beth reached for a hanky and dabbed her eyes.

'Are you quite sure, Philip? Her pulse was very weak.' James said with his arm around his wife. 'I'm sorry — I shouldn't be questioning your expertise.'

Philip pushed himself up. 'That's all right. It's a shock when something like this happens, I know. I'll organise an ambulance to collect her. Shame — she seemed like a lovely lady. A real character.' He put a hand on James' shoulder. 'I'll get things sorted.'

James struggled with the notion of leaving Delphine, but Philip insisted there was no point in staying.

Beth blew her nose. 'If people ask, should we say she's been taken ill? We don't want to dampen spirits. Do you think that's underhand, sweetie?'

James was quick to reassure her. 'No, it isn't but I don't think many people knew who she was. I think it would be best to tell those people who did meet her. Come and join us when you can, Philip.'

Leaving Philip to tie things up, they took a slow walk back through the wooded glade. James fondled Beth's fingers.

'Her death was too sudden, don't you think, Beth?'

Beth tilted her head. 'She was in her seventies, and we don't know what ailments she had. Perhaps she had a weak heart. This was an exciting day for her and it may have been too much.'

James disagreed and began going through the odd phrases she'd spoken before her passing, then he gazed skyward for inspiration. 'She was trying to tell me something. She'd been dropping hints all day about something awful happening. And the way the Jacobs people treated her was really quite contemptible. And — '

Beth tugged his arm. 'James, will you listen to yourself? You hardly know this woman. Perhaps she was delusional, and who's to say what history there is between her and the Jacobs family? I can't for one minute understand why, but let's be realistic. We don't know these people.'

James' heart was heavy as they continued on. 'I suppose you're right. She really was a wonderfully spirited lady, wasn't she?'

Beth agreed, expressing her regret at not having known her for longer.

A twig snapped behind them. They turned to see the grocer, Jack Hedges, stumbling toward them. Beth frowned at James. 'Is he drunk?'

Jack, a rather large, overweight man, waved and tottered along the trodden pathway to join them. He still had his Morris outfit on with the bells around his long socks jangling; his face was painted bright green from his stint as the Green Man. He got to within five yards and fell against a large oak tree. James rushed forward.

'I say, are you all right, Mr Hedges?'

Jack's energy seemed to dip and he slid down the tree trunk to the ground and rubbed the back of his head. 'Someone nicked my outfit.'

Beth studied the back of his head.

'You've got blood in your hair. Did you knock yourself out?'

Jack closed his eyes. 'No, but someone tried to knock me out. I think they did for a couple of minutes — when I came to, my outfit was gone.'

'But you're wearing your outfit,' Beth said. She touched his jacket and felt a residue between her fingers. 'And you managed to get that sticky stuff all over you — that's a devil to clean off.'

'Wha' sticky stuff?' he asked.

James peered over Beth's shoulder. 'Oh, it's from one of the shrubs. Don't worry about that, it'll come out in the wash. You say your outfit was gone?'

'That's right. Not this one; I 'ad the Green Man one on over the top.'

James baulked. 'Of course, that's what she meant!' He turned to Beth. 'The man . . . the face . . . the leaves.'

'James, what on earth are you talking about?'

'Delphine. She said it was him, the tree that attacked her. That's what she meant. The Green Man — the Horned God, or whatever you want to call it. She didn't faint, she was attacked!'

Beth pursed her lips. 'Oh no! You're not getting involved in another mystery or, more to the point, creating another mystery! Not after the last one.'

Neither of them could forget the Alec Grimes affair when Beth's life was put at stake. James hesitantly laughed her statement off and assured her that he had no intention of getting involved. He grabbed Jack's hands and helped him to his feet.

'I'm pretty certain a crime has been committed,' he said. 'I'll report it to George. The only reason I got involved in the Grimes case was because no one believed me. This is cut and dried assault on an elderly lady ... and our chap Hedges, here. I'll simply ask around and listen to a few snippets of gossip.'

Beth glared at him. 'I can't believe you're even considering it. Why involve yourself? Tell George everything and let the professionals do their job. You really are the limit, James, and you should know better.'

'I say, steady on,' said James. 'I'm only trying to help.'

'I know, darling, but this is serious! If that woman was attacked you cannot treat this as a game. It's not an episode of Paul Temple.'

James gritted his teeth in frustration. He knew she was right, of course, but it didn't stop him from wanting to find out about things. 'Sweetheart,' he said, squeezing Beth's hand, 'I'm well aware that it's not a game and I'm certainly not going to treat it as such. I'm angry and upset that someone has assaulted a dear old lady and I simply want to get to the bottom of it.'

Beth closed her eyes. 'I know you do. I do too if I'm being frank, but all I'm saying is — be careful. Don't get too involved.'

'I promise I won't. Any information I glean today, I'll pass on to George.' He kissed the back of her hand. 'Anyway, you've adopted your handsome young man as a mystery, so the least you can do is let me have mine.'

'But yours are always so dangerous. If I see you getting too entangled, I will ban you.'

'Ban me from what?'

Beth frowned, struggling to think of something. 'Oh, I don't know. Playing cricket for Cavendish.'

They stared at each other and burst out laughing.

'James,' she continued, 'I'm just saying, *please* be careful.'

James bowed. 'And I will, Lady Harrington. You have my word.'

With Jack Hedges staggering between them, they returned to the fair, where James made the grocer comfortable at a table at the end of the terrace. A waitress delivered a pot of tea and large brandy while James stood on tiptoe to pick out George in the crowd.

★ ★ ★

The ambulance came and went from the front of the house and no one appeared to notice the activity or that Miss Brooks-Hunter had left.

Keen to keep to a normal schedule, James instructed that afternoon tea should take place on schedule at 4pm, where a number of people had joined him and Beth on the terrace. After they'd delivered the news of Delphine's death, the atmosphere was subdued and even the pots of stimulating Assam and freshly-baked cakes and scones failed to lift the mood. Seated around the circular table with them were Stephen, Anne, Bert and Philip Jackson, who confirmed to them that he'd found some bruising around Delphine's throat.

'Oh dear,' said Beth. 'How dreadful. I can't believe anyone would want to harm such a wonderful woman. What is the world coming to?'

Philip watched his daughter enjoying a donkey ride. His wife, Helen, walked alongside holding her hand. 'I've no idea but I hope that whoever is responsible is found soon. I can't imagine why anyone would want to hurt an elderly lady.'

Adam quietly walked around the table ensuring that all guests had full cups, plenty of cake and dollops of Cornish clotted cream for their scones although appetites had subsided considerably. He then remained some distance away, ready to be summoned if needed.

Anne turned to James. 'You think something untoward has happened, don't you? Do tell.'

Stephen emitted a loud 'tch'. 'Really, Anne, d-do remember that a lady has died.'

Anne quickly apologised and assured everyone that she was as devastated as everyone else over the death of Miss Brooks-Hunter. 'I'm not being insensitive, really I'm not. She seemed such a kindly soul, but do you really think there's something going on?'

Although he wasn't hungry, James prepared a scone more out of habit than necessity. 'Well, George is asking a few questions as we speak. Delphine certainly hinted that something untoward would happen today, and what's-his-name . . . Jack Hedges, he didn't get that bump on his head by accident.'

'That's a fact, darling,' replied Beth. 'He had his costume stolen, too.'

'Yes,' Philip said, 'I've sent him down to the hospital for a couple of stitches and to get him checked out for concussion. He'll be fine and his wound will heal quickly.'

Bert rubbed the stubble on his chin. 'George said they'd found the Green Man outfit behind some bushes by the river.' He turned to James. 'Who else was down there?'

James explained that George always occupied a less popular section of the riverbank so no-one would have seen anything. 'I think Dorothy Forbes' husband, Ted, and Alan Newton, the kennel owner, were nearby. Indeed, I believe it was Alan who went and found you, Philip.'

Philip said it was. 'You'll probably have to draw up a list of all the fishermen for George. He'll need to question them.'

'W-what a to-do,' said Stephen. 'And on such a lovely day.'

A sombre murmur went around the table and James did his best to steer people away from dwelling on Delphine's untimely death. And, as the tunes from the merry-go-round drifted across the field, the mood slowly lifted and, before too long, the conversation turned toward the activities of the day.

Alongside the main arena, several elated women proudly showed off their winning rosettes from the baking competitions; Dorothy was generous in her praise where the dog show was concerned, and the members of the Cavendish and Charnley allotment societies had, between them, scooped a number of prizes for their displays of fruit, vegetables and plants. All in all, with the exception of Delphine's passing, it had been another glorious success.

'One th-thing, I will say,' said Stephen. 'Excuse me for commenting, but I-I didn't take to the people running the fairground.'

A joint nod prompted James to agree.

'Yes, I shan't hire them again. We've always had Lambs', but I was too late booking. I shall telephone them first thing tomorrow and book them for next year before anyone else does. You know, it's very strange that Delphine rang this morning, wanting to attend this particular year — the year that the Jacobs family were here.'

Beth frowned. 'What's so strange about that?'

He went on to explain the approach and attitude shown to her by all of the fair people, in particular by the two brothers, Reg and Derek Jacobs. 'I mean, if looks could kill, she would have collapsed the moment she'd arrived.'

Bert stubbed his cigarette out. 'Well, one thing's for sure, Jimmy boy. She prob'ly knew who attacked her.'

'H-how on earth do you know th-that?' asked Stephen.

'Well, it stands to reason, don't it?' replied Bert. 'You don't nick someone's costume just for the fun of it. It's a disguise.'

James contemplated. 'Mmm, I think you have something there.' His audience waited for him to continue. 'I mean, she said 'it's him' as if she recognised him.'

'W-we'll never know now,' said Stephen.

Anne nudged him. 'Don't be silly. James is going to investigate, aren't you?'

'You two are as bad as each other,' Beth said with a hint of frustration. She jabbed a finger at James. 'You're going to leave this to the professionals. The last time you played amateur sleuth we were almost killed, so put any notion of investigation into the dustbin.'

James crossed his legs and watched as Anne replenished everyone's cups. It was true, of course. All that business last year with Grimes had almost torn him apart, especially when he realised how much danger Beth was in. Thank the Lord for friends. Bert did his fair share where the rescue was concerned; George quickly followed with a large contingent of constabulary, and Stephen, just with his presence, put a sense of calm in place for him.

But he was itching to find out more. It was another one of those jigsaws where he'd found the corner pieces. He couldn't let someone else complete the outer rim. Perhaps he should speak with George and see if he could be of assistance.

'Right, your Ladyship,' said Bert, 'when are we goin' to Bethnal Green?'

Anne handed round a plate of lemon sponge cake. 'Oh yes, I'd forgotten all about the mystery man. What an eventful day! Have you learnt any more about him?'

Beth explained that she hadn't really

anything new to report. 'Harrington's is certainly familiar to him,' she added, 'but he doesn't know why. He's not sure what age he is or how he ended up in the East End.'

Bert took a swig of tea. 'Well, before we make the journey up to the smoke, why don't you get a photo of 'im and show it around? Someone might remember some-thin'.'

Stephen quickly pushed his Kodak Brownie across the table to him. 'There's a c-couple of snaps left to take on the film, so you'd do me a huge favour if you used them. W-we've still got some pictures from Christmas on there, so please do take it.'

Beth slid her chair back. 'Let's go do it now. The sooner we get those pictures, the sooner we can make a start.'

James brushed some crumbs from his trousers. 'I say, why don't you get Mr Chrichton to develop the film for you? He's got a darkroom up at the school and it'll save waiting for the chemist to do it. Also, darling, why don't you take your young man out for a spin in the Jag? Take him around the village and the area. You never know, it may jolt a few more memories for him.'

'That's a great idea. Come along, Bert.'

Bert snatched the last piece of lemon sponge and followed Beth into the manor house. At that moment, George Lane arrived at their table and made himself comfortable on a vacated chair.

'Ah, George,' said James. 'Everything sorted?'

'Yes, we've done as much as we can do here. Miss Brooks-Hunter's body is on its way to the morgue, the Green Man costume is in the back of my car, and Philip here is writing up his findings for an official report. I'll get our own doctor to do a proper examination. Philip thinks there's some odd bruising around the neck. Do you know if there's any family?'

'She mentioned a sister in Cornwall, but that's about it,' replied James. 'I don't believe she ever married, although I seem to remember a gentleman on the scene when I was a youngster. But you don't take much notice of older people at that age, do you?'

Anne suggested there was sure to be plenty of information in her house, and George, to her surprise, agreed. His manner encouraged her to add that perhaps James could go across and search through her belongings. George reverted to his gruff demeanour.

'Mrs Merryweather, this is a police enquiry. I'm not about to ask Lord Harrington to rummage through the victim's belongings.'

Anne sank back in her chair. James watched, bemused, and noted Stephen's exasperation toward Anne. She really did love a puzzle and clearly wanted to contribute. He switched his attention back to George.

'Is there anything you do want me to do?'

'It's in hand. Keep your nose out.' George shielded his eyes as he scanned the main arena ahead of him. 'Winding down?'

James checked his watch. It was almost five. 'Yes. A few people have drifted off home now. I'd best start chivvying the stallholders to pack up if they haven't already started. Anne, would you mind asking the WI lot to start reducing their cake prices. They may have already done so. We don't want them going to waste.'

Anne, always eager to help, said she'd go straightaway. 'I think I'll get a few cakes for us. Do you want any?'

James felt in his pockets for some change. 'Yes. If Elsie or Mrs Keates have some of their wares, do get a few and we'll take them to the old folks' home. George, you'll take some, won't you?'

George sarcastically remarked what a stupid question that was and handed over some of his own change. 'I'll wait for you to get back, then I'd better make a start on Miss Brooks-Hunter.'

Philip rose from his seat. 'Yes, I'd best round up Helen and Natasha and make a start on this report.'

Stephen and Anne left with the doctor. James waited for Adam to clear the table before speaking.

'I say, George, do you think this was a premeditated attack?'

George pulled his pipe out of his pocket. 'I think so, yes. The police doc's going to take a look at her later. Not sure if anyone meant to kill her, but . . . '

'So we're looking at murder?'

'Or manslaughter. The fact that Mr Hedges was knocked out suggests there was some planning. But either way, it's not good. An elderly lady who was no bother to anyone. What's the world coming to, James?'

James left his friend with his thoughts and wandered toward the stalls. It certainly seemed a rum do that such a dear old lady should be attacked. There must have been some sort of motive for it. People don't go around killing old ladies and knocking out Morris dancers. Mind you, he didn't think people knocked vicars over the head, but that's what happened to Stephen last year. He'd heard the phrase twice now; first Beth, now George and they were right to question — what *was* the world coming to?

He reached the ice-cream van and came across Chris and Joan Trent, two rough vagabond individuals who were part of the Jacobs crowd. Chris, a cousin from what he could gather, ran the ice-cream van, while Joan served hot dogs from a van alongside him.

'Ah, hello,' he said, 'I thought I'd pop round and just tell you to start packing up. I think most things have come to a natural end now. Business been good?'

'Brilliant,' Chris said, handing him a vanilla cornet. 'Couldn't 'ave asked for better weather for ice-creams.'

'And plenty of kids for the hot dogs,' Joan said adding that children loved frankfurters.

James agreed that people did tend to bring their appetites with them. He alerted them that the food in the WI tent would be sold off cheap if they wanted to get some cakes and jam, for which they thanked him. They appeared to be a pleasant couple — not like the Jacobs brothers. That reminded him.

'I say, have you been with Reg and Derek for long?'

'About ten years on and off,' replied Chris. 'We're family and all, but we're independent as businesses go. Occasionally they ask us to help out at things like this if they know we're needed.'

'Good show. Well, thanks for coming and all that.' He continued on and arrived at the swings, where Jackie Connor was already dismantling the equipment.

'I say, do you need any help? I can grab a few sturdy chaps for you.'

'Nah, s'alrigh', replied Jackie happily. 'I'm used to doin' all this on me tod.'

James told her about the cake sale and she assured him that she'd be getting plenty from the WI to feed the family.

'Jolly good. D'you have a big family?'

'Ten of us, all connected to the Jacobs lot and we all stick together.' She threw a set of chains into a wheeled container.

At that moment, Reg Jacobs arrived. James put on a welcoming expression, but there was something about him that James didn't warm to. Indeed, both Reg and Derek Jacobs gave the impression of being absolute bounders — swarthy and rough in lifestyle and manner. Jackie told him to clear his stuff away. Reg grunted a response and loped back to where he'd come from. James winced.

'Is he all right?'

'Yeah, 'e's a righ' charmer,' she replied. 'A smile'd crack 'is face. Worse today.'

'Oh? Any reason?'

She massaged the base of her spine. 'Nah, nuffin' you've done. Just someone rubbed him up the wrong way.'

James said he was sorry to hear that, but silently wondered why any of the villagers would do such a thing. But, having interacted with the brothers, he could understand how it might happen. One word out of place could be an annoyance for any member of the Jacobs family.

'Well, I hope it didn't spoil his day too much,' he added. 'Did you want me to have a word?'

'Nah. You can't put the 'istory of one family righ' in a day.'

James couldn't help but look both quizzical and confused. She told him not to fret.

'It'll come ou' in the wash.' She turned her back on him and continued working.

James made his way to the beer tent. Had that comment been something to do with Delphine? Did the old lady have family links with the Jacobs? Surely not! If she had rubbed Reg up the wrong way, did he retaliate? He watched Reg from a distance as he bullied his young charges into dismantling the carousel. He certainly didn't treat his associates with any respect. Did that treatment go as far as murder?

6

A few days later, with the events of the May Day fair well and truly behind them, James and Beth relaxed on the patio of their own home on the edge of Cavendish, a red-brick chalet-style house built in the 1930s. James' father had insisted on moving to a more manageable property due to rising costs, as the upkeep of the old manor house had been simply overwhelming for a family of five. James admitted he felt more at home here than he ever did at Harrington's, especially while bringing up his own children; it seemed far more homely than the great stately pile nearby. And, turning Harrington's into a country hotel had been an inspired decision.

On the dark green cast iron table between them sat two bone china cups filled with tea and two plates bearing toasted teacakes oozing with butter. Beth, her eyes closed, faced toward the sun, while James scanned the pages of *The Times*.

'I see England are playing football against Portugal this week; up at the Empire Stadium' he said, more to himself than anything. 'I wonder if Bert's going?'

'Perhaps,' replied Beth. 'Will you go?'

'I'll see if there's time. We have the folk day on the last Saturday in May, so we've to get that organised. We must remember to incorporate Oak Apple Day, too, but I think the Scouts and the Guides are organising that.'

England had two bank holidays in May and Oak Apple Day was part of the later celebrations that commemorated the restoration of the English monarchy in 1660. The day was set aside for dancing and singing and was a nice addition to the folk day. During the celebrations, villagers wore sprigs of oak leaves and, if you were seen without decoration, you would have to accept the punishment meted out by the children in the village, namely receiving a pinch on the bottom or being stung by nettles. The children, of course, relished this opportunity to play mischief with their elders. James folded his paper and placed it on the table.

'I haven't seen England play for a couple of years. I wonder if our mystery man would like to go.'

'We can't keep calling him our mystery man,' said Beth. 'Shouldn't we give him a name?'

'I thought he had a name!'

'But he doesn't look like a Jim,' said Beth, reaching for her plate.

James took a bite from his teacake. 'Mmm, I must admit that I agree with you. It doesn't suit his character, does it? You've spoken to him a few times — how does he strike you?'

'Well-mannered, thoughtful, kind, considerate. And handsome. He has lovely thick blond hair and the most gorgeous blue eyes.'

James gave her an old-fashioned look. 'Yes, he certainly is a handsome fellow, isn't he? What sort of blue are his eyes?'

Beth described them as the flash of blue that you see in the wings of a kingfisher. James grinned. 'You've certainly observed him at close quarters, haven't you?'

She playfully slapped him. 'You are simply teasing me, James. He's half my age and you're naughty to suggest such a thing. He answers to Gentleman Jim and we shouldn't saddle him with another name. The poor dear is confused already, what with no memory.'

'Why don't you shorten it to GJ? That'll rid us of the name Jim. He looks more like a GJ than a Jim. What do you think?'

Beth bobbed her head thoughtfully and met James' eyes. 'Yes, I like it. Let's ask him if we can call him GJ.'

The sound of the doorbell interrupted their musing. James went through to the hall and opened the front door to the postman who handed over several letters. Alongside him was Charlie Hawkins who presented him with a book.

'You said you wanted some information on amnesia,' he said, smiling brightly. 'Well, in our medical section I found this, which might enlighten you.'

'Splendid! Thank you, Charlie.'

James watched their postman cycle down the drive then invited Charlie in for tea and cake. Charlie held his hand up and expressed his regrets.

'I've left Professor Wilkins in charge of the library while I popped out. Got to get back.'

Professor Wilkins, the historian and curator of the museum, more or less lived in the library when he wasn't giving lectures or travelling to historic sites. With the discovery of some Roman remains last year, his days were now filled with itemising and archiving the artefacts. James bade Charlie farewell and returned to Beth.

'Charlie just dropped off a book about amnesia — and the post has just been delivered.' He leafed through the letters and examined the postmarks. 'I think this is from Fiona. I wonder if she's coming up.'

Fiona, James' sister, normally visited at that time of year. He passed it to Beth and frowned at the next envelope. It was typewritten and posted locally. He gently opened the envelope and pulled out a letter.

'Oh. It's from Bateson, the solicitor.'

'Really? I wonder what he wants.'

James scanned the contents and quickly twisted to face Beth. 'Good Lord, listen to this. 'Dear Lord Harrington. We are writing in respect of the late Miss Delphine Brooks-Hunter who died on 5th May 1958. As her solicitors, we are instructed to adhere to her wishes and invite you to the reading of her last will and testament on Friday, 16th May at 10 a.m. This meeting will take place at our address in Cavendish. Please confirm that you are able to attend at this time as Miss Brooks-Hunter was insistent you be there. Yours sincerely,' etc.'

He rested the letter on his lap. 'Why on earth would she want me there? I hardly knew her.'

Beth agreed that it all seemed very strange. 'I guess all will be revealed on the day,' she replied. 'I can't imagine many people will be there. Her sister, I suppose.' She waved the letter in her hand. 'By the way, this is Fiona and she's planning to come up a little later than usual — around July time. That'll be fine, won't it?'

'Absolutely. I'll telephone her later to confirm.'

He studied the next envelope; another local postmark with the address written in a frail hand. Instinctively, he thought of Delphine, and then quickly dismissed the idea. But, on unfolding the letter, her address was clear at the top of the page. He read the contents quietly and, at the end, simply stared into space. Beth, having refilled both teacups, noticed his stunned expression.

'What is it? You look as if you've seen a ghost.'

James offered the letter to her and she proceeded to read.

''Dear Lord Harrington. I asked Mr Bateson to post this letter when he contacts you. By the time you read this, I shall be . . . dead,' Beth's jaw dropped, and she was speechless for a while before resuming. '' . . . unless my killer makes a mess of the whole affair, in which case, you may come and interrogate me (over tea) and listen to the ramblings of an old lady. I will have called to attend your charming fair and have enjoyed every moment of the day with you and your family. I know that my demise will surely occur at this event, as this is where my attacker will be . . . '' Beth paused again to look at James in amazement.

''But', she went on, ''I feel I must apologise for making your wonderful venue the scene of my final appearance. I do hope it doesn't spoil the day too much. You will receive a letter from my solicitor and I implore that you attend this appointment for two reasons. One, I want you to observe the people who attend the reading and, two, I want you to remain behind to speak with Mr Bateson. He needs to discuss a very special request that I have for you. I do hope that you will carry out my final wishes. If our trendy vicar is to be believed, I shall be listening from the other side! Good luck, Delphine Brooks-Hunter.''

Beth sat in a daze for some time. James got up, put his hands in his pockets and strolled to the edge of the terrace. Even the stunning group of roe deer in the far field could not command his attention.

Beth eventually joined him. 'I think you

need to tell George about this.'

'Yes, I think you're right. Although she must know that the police would be investigating her death. What does she want me to do?'

Beth gave him a helpless shrug. 'One thing's for sure. You're not going to find out until next Friday.'

7

Mr Bateson brushed a speck of dust from his black pinstriped suit and gently eased down into the chair behind his magnificent oak desk. There were few papers on show but those placed there were neatly stacked. The wall-to-wall carpeting hushed any noise, inside or out. James likened the atmosphere to sitting on a church pew waiting for the service to begin. Only the ticking of the mantel clock disturbed the quiet.

Above Bateson's head was an exquisite painting, which had probably been created by the solicitor himself. James had often observed him by the river with his water-colours and easel. He resembled a rambling artist more than he did a respected solicitor; a slender man with wild, chestnut hair, better suited to wearing an artist's smock than a legal gown.

Those summoned to his office sat in a half-circle around the desk. James chose to position himself at the end and struggled to hide his surprise at the sight of the individuals who had gathered. Indeed, he'd quickly invented a tickly cough in order to excuse himself so that he could fetch a glass of water before returning, feeling more composed.

For next to him, sat the decidedly unsavoury bunch from the fairground, including Derek and Reg Jacobs. They reminded him of the gangsters from the East End that Bert occasionally spoke of. Next to them was Jackie Connor looking somewhat pale and drawn. Chris and Joan Trent stared into space, appearing to avoid eye contact with everyone. Joan, in particular, fiddled nervously with her handkerchief.

The man seated at the far end was a stranger to James and to say he was built like a prize fighter would be no exaggeration. He had a squashed nose, cauliflower ears, and eyes that were too small for his face. A rugby player perhaps. James struck the thought from his head. Schools included rugby in their physical education but, from where he was sitting, he wondered if the man had even bothered attending an educational facility. The more likely cause for his appearance would be boxing.

But where was Delphine's sister? Perhaps she was not well enough to attend. He acknowledged everyone graciously, but all he received in return were looks of suspicion and hostility. Crossing his legs, he silently wished that Bateson would get on with it.

A few seconds later, Bateson lifted his gaze from the papers in front of him and scanned the room. Satisfied that everyone was accounted for, he cleared his throat.

'Thank you for attending,' he began. 'As you know, Miss Delphine Brooks-Hunter of the Coach House, Cavendish, died unexpectedly on the fifth of May and her instructions were to gather the people she had listed in this room for an announcement in respect of her last will and testament.'

Reg Jacobs grunted and stabbed a finger at James. 'What's 'e doin' 'ere?'

James shifted uneasily in his chair as Bateson continued.

'Lord Harrington is on the list, Mr Jacobs. It is of no concern to you as to why. If Miss Brooks-Hunter wished him to be here, then here he shall be.'

He picked up a solitary piece of paper, scanned it quickly and replaced it on the table. He rested his elbows on the desk and clasped his hands.

'It would appear that Miss Brooks-Hunter foresaw her demise and, as a result, the police are investigating what they think is a suspicious death.'

James observed the reaction in the room and frowned at the lack of surprise. They scrutinised one another warily as if each was wondering who of the others was guilty. He found his mouth lacked saliva. Was one of these people responsible for her death?

'Because of this,' Bateson continued, 'Miss Brooks-Hunter instructed that no funds be made available at present, except for her funeral. She has written separately to the Reverend Stephen Merryweather with her instructions and wishes. Should the police establish that Miss Brooks-Hunter was murdered, no funds and/or inheritance, be it money or possessions, will be released to the family.'

The Jacobs and Trents turned red with rage. Jackie Connor raised a fist at Bateson.

'Whatcha talkin' abaht? You cahn't. It's as much ours as 'ers. Bleedin' stuck-up cow. She's dead an' we're due a share.'

'Instead,' Bateson firmly interjected, 'they will go to local charities and institutions. We will reconvene here once the police have completed their investigations. I will be in touch.' Quick to ward off any arguments from his audience, he quickly turned to James. 'Lord Harrington, I wonder if I could have a word with you — alone.'

Derek Jacobs glared at the two of them. Bateson, aware of the impression this gave, promptly added that it was concerning the folk day.

James did his best to act the part. 'Yes, of course. I was hoping to catch up with you about that. Is now a good time?'

James felt Reg Jacobs breathe on his neck. 'Whatchu doin' 'ere?'

He turned to face him. 'To be honest,

Mr Jacobs, I have no idea. I was on the list, as Mr Bateson said. I hardly knew Miss Brooks-Hunter, but there you are. Perhaps she has something to bequeath to the village — given that I sort of look after that aspect of things.'

Jacobs glared, grunted and finally trudged out after the rest of the group. Bateson called for tea, closed the door and signalled for James to return to his chair.

'What did you make of it all, Lord Harrington?'

James crossed his legs and straightened a seam in his trousers. 'Well, they're certainly a motley crew. What I don't understand is who these people are to Delphine? Are you able to enlighten me?'

'Mmm, I can understand why you'd question that. You probably won't believe me when I say they're family.'

'What! Immediate family?'

Bateson winced and made a 'yes and no' gesture with his hands. 'There are two sides to the Brooks-Hunter family; two very different sides. Delphine descends from the mother's side and the Jacobs from the father. Delphine's parents, you see, were not married.'

James pulled a face. 'Oh, I see. Well, that puts a different slant on things. Not good these days, let alone back then.'

'Exactly. The families of the two young lovers were from completely different backgrounds and, against their wishes, the couple had three children before they were torn apart — two girls and a boy.'

'Delphine and her sister?'

'And a brother. The families eventually either split the couple up or they themselves came to their senses. Delphine and her sister remained with the mother's side of the family, while the brother was farmed off to the father's side.'

'Delphine's family were wealthy and well-educated,' stated James.

'Exactly. The Jacobs family were decidedly dodgy, even back then, so they're as different as chalk and cheese.'

'My word, it's like Romeo and Juliet. Delphine, presumably, never married? No children?'

'Correct. Her sister, to my knowledge, remained a spinster, although I've never met her so I may be wrong. Delphine never mentioned any children. So, the only family she has are the people you saw here today. For reasons that I cannot establish, they had some sort of hold over her.'

'Otherwise she'd have left everything to the sister,' James surmised.

Tea arrived and Bateson played host as he allowed everything outlined so far to sink in. James remarked that it must have been a hell of a predicament for such a gentle lady.

'D'you think she'll leave all her money to them if everything is proven to be above board?' he asked. 'I suppose you must know, because you had the will drawn up.'

Bateson shrugged.

'Miss Brooks-Hunter insisted a solicitor from London should draw up the will. Once it was written, she entrusted it to me. I'm afraid I won't have access to its contents until I have the results of the police investigation.'

'How mysterious. And where do I come into it? Delphine's letter stated that she wished for me to stay on. I presume it's not just for social chit-chat.'

'You presume correctly,' said Bateson. He slid open the drawer in front of him and drew out some papers. 'Miss Brooks-Hunter is unlikely to leave much to her blood relatives. As little as she can get away with — that's the impression she gave me in our talks together. The majority, I'm sure, will go to her sister. She is aware that the Jacobs and Trents will try to get their hands on her belongings. I have forewarned the police, who assure me they will be keeping an eye on her home, the Coach House.' Bateson opened an envelope and brought out a key, which he handed to James. 'In the meantime, she has a front door key for you, and this.' He slid a piece of paper across to him.

James took the items and noticed Bateson's bemused expression. 'I don't quite know what you're going to make of it, but the key to her fortune, excuse the pun, is in this letter and the riddle contained therein.'

'Riddle?'

'Yes. She tied all of her fortune up but has never said how or where. This,' Bateson tapped the paper, 'apparently explains everything.'

James gently unfolded the paper and read the contents aloud:

'Fortune comes to those who search,
Beneath the Rose of rich red earth,
A window through which Man can gaze,
Encapsulate and clear the haze.'

He frowned at Bateson. 'What on earth is that supposed to mean?'

Bateson was equally perplexed and read the rhyme for himself. 'Well, I really don't know. Not my thing, I'm afraid.'

James slumped back. 'No, it's not my sort of thing either. I struggle with the crossword. All right, answer me this. Why me?'

'Aah, that I *can* answer,' replied Bateson. 'Delphine summoned me at the end of last year. She'd heard about your involvement in the Alec Grimes affair and the lengths you went to to get to the bottom of things. You're also an upright and honest citizen, Lord of the Manor, and so on. Who better to solve the riddle?'

James clenched his jaw. Why couldn't she have just sent a telegram giving him the answer? He hated riddles. He had never been any good at conundrums and now, here he was, sitting on what could be a fortune and it all rested on deciphering the words from this piece of paper. He would have to enlist some help, otherwise who knew how long it would take to decipher.

'Where's the sister?' he asked.

'In Cornwall. She's elderly, like Delphine, but we're still trying to contact her.'

'Does she have somewhere to stay?'

'I've no idea.'

'Well, we'll put a room by at Harrington's for her. Perhaps you'd let her know if you're able to speak with her?'

'Of course.'

'Anything else I need to know?'

Bateson assured him that he felt that was enough to be going on with and James commented that it was indeed. He safely secured the riddle and the key in his inside pocket. A thought flashed through him and he swung round.

'I say, Bateson. I recognised most of the people here today, but who was that great lumberjack of a man opposite?'

'Another of the Jacobs gang. Ray 'Bruiser' Jacobs.'

'Bruiser!'

Bateson collected his papers together and looked at James wryly. 'Mmm, used to be a bare-knuckle fighter.'

'Thought as much.' James hoped to goodness he didn't have to come up against him in the physical sense. He bade Bateson cheerio and trotted down the steps and out onto the High Street. Across the green, he saw Stephen clipping the box hedge surrounding the vicarage garden and made his way over to him.

'Hello Stephen. I understand that you're organising Delphine's funeral.'

Stephen straightened up and placed his shears on top of the hedge. 'Y-yes, believe so, although the police won't release the body just yet so I'm not sure when it's going to be. How did you g-get on at Batesons?'

'There are two words that I would say

to that. Interesting and intriguing. Both are not for discussion here. D'you fancy lunch at Elsie's today? I have a proposition to put to you and Anne.'

'Oh?'

'Yes, in fact, I think I'm going to need a bit of help with what I've been asked to do. I may see if Bert's available, too. Can you make one o'clock — you and Anne? I'll pick you up about a quarter to.'

Stephen assured him that would be fine and went straight indoors to tell Anne. James returned to his beloved Austin Healey and fired up the engine. It was the perfect day for a spin and he decided to put the car through her paces by taking the long way home. The roof was down, the wind whipped around him as he raced through the country lanes.

Fragments of the riddle teased him and snippets of his conversations with Delphine at the fair popped in and out of his head. The task was daunting. Although he hardly knew Delphine, he was fonder of her than he wanted to admit and didn't want to let her down. He hoped he could live up to her expectations.

He eventually arrived home and bounded up the front steps to update Beth on the morning's activities.

* * *

Elsie escorted James, Beth and the Merryweathers to their table. James had called ahead and she'd kindly reserved his favourite table by the bay window which gave a view of the road and the trees beyond.

'You know,' Elsie said in her Sussex lilt, 'I always wonder why you come here when you've got your lovely big country hotel up the road.'

James winked at her. 'Elsie, it doesn't pay to get complacent. When I see the excellent home cooking and the delicious cups of tea that are placed before us, I see you as a competitor.'

Elsie's face flushed to the roots of her blonde hair. He knew she was flattered that her clientele included Lord and Lady Harrington but he couldn't deny it: she was a natural cook and whatever she served, be it simply poached egg on toast or a more elaborate dish, the cooking came from the heart. He truly adored the atmosphere of the café as well as the food.

'Is Bert not coming?' Anne asked.

'Unfortunately, the 2.15 at Brighton racecourse has proved more popular than lunch at Elsie's. Sorry, Else, but it's his loss. I say, what's your special for the day?'

Elsie's eyes danced and Beth encouraged her to spill the beans. 'I guess you have something you're proud of, by the expression on your face.'

'I have, your Ladyship.' She allowed her beaming smile to surface. 'Well, I hope you don't mind, your Lordship but, when we was helping you out at the Christmas dinner for the old people, you mentioned your grandmother's Welsh Rarebit.'

'That's right, I gave you her secret recipe.' He wagged a finger at her. 'My guess is that it's not a secret anymore.'

Elsie did a quick scan round her café to ensure no one else was listening. 'I won't tell anyone the recipe and I've already given it a special name.' She directed their attention to the chalkboard.

TODAY'S SPECIAL: Grandma Harrington's Welsh Rarebit.

'H-how wonderful,' Stephen exclaimed. 'O-one of my favourite snacks.'

It didn't take long for them all to agree that they needed to taste Grandma Harrington's cheese on toast, so they swiftly placed an order as one of Elsie's young waitresses served tea. Anne arranged the cups.

'Is there a secret ingredient to Grandma's cheese on toast?' she asked.

'I believe that my grandmother always put a little extra mustard and Worcestershire sauce into the mix,' replied James. 'Gave it a bit of a kick.'

With tea distributed, James quickly set about explaining the morning's events to everyone — from his surprise about Delphine's relatives, to the mysterious riddle presented at the end. Anne couldn't conceal her delight.

'And you want us to help you?'

'Yes. If I'm being frank, I *need* you to help me. I haven't got a clue what the riddle means, so I am calling for your brain cells to awaken and I ask for a sense of detection should we visit her home.'

'How wonderful!' replied Anne. 'I've always wanted to see inside that Coach House.'

'A-Anne,' began Stephen, 'I do wish you weren't so en-enthused about this, after what happened last time.'

'Sorry Stephen, but you have to admit, it is captivating.'

'Yes, that about sums it up,' said James. He turned his attention to Beth. 'And you've no need to worry about me sticking my nose in where it's not wanted. George is investigating the crime — not me. I'm simply investigating the riddle and getting to the bottom of Delphine's fortune. *And*, I've been requested to do so officially by her via Bateson.'

Beth held her hands up. 'You've convinced me, Sherlock. Just make sure you don't step on George's toes.'

Grandma Harrington's Welsh Rarebit arrived and the conversation died as everyone tucked in to melted Sussex cheddar and Gruyere, infused with English mustard, Worcestershire sauce and a dash of

Tabasco drizzled over home-made bread toasted to perfection.

'S-so, are we to see this riddle?' asked Stephen.

James scanned the room like an undercover spy. Feeling in his inside pocket, he brought out a sheet of paper.

'The original and the house key are locked in the safe,' he explained. Unfolding the paper, he quietly recited the contents.

'Fortune comes to those who search,
Beneath the Rose of rich red earth,
A window through which Man can gaze,
Encapsulate and clear the haze.'

Anne, Beth and Stephen looked at one another blankly.

James's head fell. 'Oh Lord, it doesn't make any sense to you, either, does it?'

'Well, I-I shouldn't think she meant for it to be deciphered in five minutes,' said Stephen.

'Sweetie,' said Beth, 'what we need to do is keep working on it; go round to the house and rummage around a little. She must have given you the key as part of the riddle.'

Anne agreed and suggested there must be something in the house that would provide a clue to deciphering the rhyme. Stephen took a pen from his pocket.

'I–is it all right if I copy it? I can always ponder over it before sleeping.'

'Absolutely,' replied James. 'But, for heaven's sake keep it safe — or, at least don't let any rumour of you having it get back to the Jacobs lot. Especially Bruiser.'

'He sounds a delight,' Beth said with sarcasm. 'It makes you wonder how two people from such different backgrounds became lovers.'

'It certainly does,' replied Anne. 'I mean, young ladies were always chaperoned back then. Ladies of a certain standing in society simply never mixed with the lower classes. It just didn't happen.'

'Maybe one of the Jacobs was in service and they fell in love,' said Beth.

'Or,' Anne said, wide-eyed, 'perhaps Delphine was a descendant of Bohemian people? Perhaps she mixed with artists and musicians?'

She and Beth giggled with each other

but, James conceded they might not be wrong. Delphine hadn't been any run-of-the-mill elderly lady sitting in a chair knitting. No, he felt she had had a colourful history, one that toyed with danger. It wouldn't have surprised him at all if she had mixed with the Bohemian set.

After some small talk about the folk day, James paid the bill and suggested a slow drive home. They shrugged on their jackets and wandered outside where Anne linked arms with Beth.

'By the way, did our mystery man recognise anything on your village tour?'

'Not a thing,' replied Beth. 'But Bert's got a photograph now, so we're going up to London to see what we can find. We're going up on Sunday morning. We thought if we get there early, we could take a trip to Petticoat Lane, too.'

'Oh gosh, can I come?' asked Anne. 'I've never been there. I hear it's supposed to be fantastic.'

Beth assured her she was most welcome. Petticoat Lane market was a hive of activity on a Sunday morning with long rows of market stalls selling all manner of things: bric-a-brac, clothes, animals, food and yards of material, sold by men and women from various backgrounds and cultures. Many of Bert's dealings appeared to be carried out on a Sunday morning around this area.

'W-what about my sermon?' asked Stephen, a little aggrieved.

'Oh Stephen, I'll only miss the morning service,' replied Anne. 'This is going to be fun.'

James grinned at Stephen's crestfallen face and slapped him on the back. 'Don't worry, old fruit, I'll give you some moral support. Perhaps you could do a little chat about our young man? See if he's known to anyone.'

Stephen brightened. 'W-what a good idea.'

James unlocked the car, a little happier now that he'd shared the burden of solving the riddle.

8

James observed Bert as he surveyed his breakfast plate; sitting on it were two bacon rinds, the corner of a crust and the end of a sausage. The two of them had savoured the delights of the traditional English: crispy-fried bacon, Portobello mushrooms, beans, tomatoes, sausages, toast and two poached eggs.

Beth had invited Bert to breakfast in order to discuss their trip to Bethnal Green, but James also requested his friend's assistance in his own mystery, although Bert had yet to learn of the riddle. James, of course, had no qualms about asking his old friend for some help. The bond between them went back many years and James could recall its commencement as if it was yesterday.

He relished Bert's honesty and lack of pretence. He was a true cockney and he felt privileged to know him and to have him as his friend. Unfortunately, with his other good friend being a Detective Chief Inspector, he feared that one day his friendship would be compromised. Bert was forever doing deals close to the edge of the law and James was sure that eventually he'd slip up. Today, however, would not be that day.

Bert dug his fork into the last piece of sausage. 'So, Jimmy boy. We're digging into another mystery, but this one's all legal and above board.'

James assured Bert they had the full permission of the late Miss Brooks-Hunter and the police. After the affair with Alec Grimes several months ago and the unfortunate attack on Stephen, acting within the law certainly gave them a sense of security.

'And wha' exactly are we looking for?' asked Bert while chomping his food.

'Anything to help us solve a riddle.'

Bert's chewing slowed considerably as he took the news in. Then he looked at Beth to confirm what he'd just heard.

'That's what he said, Bert.' She poured more tea. 'It's actually quite fascinating and exciting, too. There's a fortune to be found and we, or rather James, has been entrusted with finding it.'

James reached inside his back pocket and brought out the slip of paper with the rhyme on. He placed it on the table for Bert to read. After some time, Bert simply frowned.

'What's tha' supposed to mean?'

'We've no idea whatsoever. We're hoping that visiting the house may give us a clue.' James finished his tea. 'Are you coming, Beth?'

Beth checked the clock and dabbed her lips with a napkin. 'I'm collecting our young man and meeting Charlie Hawkins to discuss the folk day. I figure something may jog his memory if we keep visiting places.'

'You're probably right,' replied James. 'If he remembers Harrington's then there must be something else he'll recollect. And we'd best have a chat about the folk day when I get back. I've not even thought about guests or anything. Do we have people for dinner tonight, or are we on our own?'

Beth told him they were on their own

and, out of courtesy, extended an invitation to Bert, which he declined. 'You two do enough entertaining, so 'ave some time to yourself.'

And, with breakfast finished, James and Bert went on their way.

★ ★ ★

The Coach House was a long and narrow two-bedroom property. During the nineteenth century it had served as a stopping point for coaches and consisted of a stable, a blacksmith's forge and a cottage. In early 1930, the whole building had been knocked into one, creating a unique dwelling.

It had front and rear gardens and a large bay window where the stable doors once opened into a cobbled courtyard. The courtyard made up part of the front garden.

The property was on the edge of a small wood, which backed onto the far end of the grounds of Harrington's Country Hotel. Bert nudged James and gazed at the garden.

'Roses. They're in the riddle, aren't they?'

An enormous variety of England's favourite flower grew en masse all around the house. The riddle, James recalled, mentioned a rose, but where on earth would he start! One couldn't go around digging up every rose bush in sight. And, anyway, surely that was taking it too literally. Delphine might as well have sent a map telling them the treasure was under the third rose from the apple tree. Bert groaned as George Lane emerged from the front entrance and greeted them with his usual gruff demeanour. James gave a cheery wave.

'Ah George, what are you doing here?'

'Just going through some of her things,' he replied. 'Build up more of a picture if I can.'

'Well, I'm sure that Bateson put you in the picture about my reasons for coming?'

George assured him that he did, but eyed Bert suspiciously. 'Couldn't you have found someone else to help?'

James couldn't help but laugh at Bert's innocent protestations and accusation of slander.

'You've never 'ad reason to nab me, George, so button yer lip and leave me be.'

George grunted and returned to the house while shouting back: 'We've finished everywhere but the kitchen but if you find anything you think we may need to know about, tell me.'

James and Bert followed in behind.

The interior of the Coach House was as immaculate as the exterior. Unlike many of her generation, Delphine seemed to have had no sentiment where ornaments were concerned. She preferred the occasional photograph of distant climes and had managed to create a modern, yet cosy feel to the place.

Each room was decorated in the same or similar colour scheme — natural colours, where the fabrics and carpets could be changed in an instant. James made a mental note to bring Beth along next time. No doubt she would take some ideas away with her and incorporate them into whatever needed decorating next.

Two shallow steps took them into the lounge, where a polished coffee table played host to a number of fashionable women's magazines and a record sleeve of Gershwin's *Rhapsody in Blue* — the record itself remained on the turntable. A number of humorous caricatures hung on the walls and a well-worn copy of *Carry On Jeeves* by Wodehouse. There was no question in James' mind, the woman had outstanding taste in everything — what a lady!

As if reading his mind, Bert put in, 'I only met 'er once, but I think I would've liked this old gal.'

George peered round the door. 'There's not much beyond this. All the rooms are lovely, but nothing much in them. Her drawing room's got a few papers that may help.' He scratched his head. 'By the way, what exactly is it you've got to do?'

James went through a bite-sized version of events and showed him the riddle set by Delphine. His friend grimaced. 'Rather you than me.'

'Oh, I don't know. I thought that at first, but I suppose it's similar to detective work. Just need to find the clues.'

George grunted, shrugged and indicated where the drawing room was.

'Some of the papers may shed some light on things for you.'

Unlike the lounge, the drawing room was wallpapered in a chintz design of summer flowers, many of them roses. Two rather traditional oil paintings hung on opposite walls and large, Georgian-style glass doors opened to a small, well-kept cottage garden at the rear. Three wing-backed chairs were arranged round a rectangular table and in the comer, stood a large mahogany writing desk with drawers on both sides and a bottle-green leather top.

Bert aimed straight for the desk while James, from a distance, studied the paintings. He didn't know much about art, but wondered if these were valuable in any way. At the same time, these were landscapes with not a rose in sight. He quietly reminded himself not to take the riddle so literally.

'Oi! Oi!' Bert said, waving James over. 'Looks like an address book.'

He passed it to James, who flicked through the pages. Most of the names and addresses were crossed out with a brief explanation why — the main reason being death. Indeed, throughout the whole book he could find only four current addresses: his own, Delphine's sister, the abominable Reg Jacobs, and one that was unfamiliar to him. He fondled his ear lobe.

'Bert, have you ever heard of a chap by the name of Kushal Patel?'

Bert didn't need to consider, giving James a quick shake of the head. 'Nah. I think I'd remember a name like that. What is it, Indian?'

'Yes, I believe so. He's listed as living in Richmond, near Kew. Nice part of the world. Moved about, too. Kensington, Oxford, Harrow and now Richmond.'

'Not short of a few bob, then.'

James agreed. Richmond was a beautiful, leafy suburb of London, close to Kew Gardens, Wimbledon and Hampton Court. If Mr Patel lived by the river, he was certainly a wealthy and respected man. James drummed his fingers on the book.

'I wonder if he's a doctor or something? You don't live there without a worthy profession to your name, especially from that part of the world. Those of a foreign persuasion tend to work doubly hard to achieve that status. There's a phone number listed. D'you think I should call?'

Bert picked up the Bakelite telephone receiver on the desk and held it out. 'No time like the present.'

James took the receiver and made himself comfortable behind the desk. He dialled for the operator. Within a few seconds, a voice answered.

'Ah, hello. I'm calling from Cavendish . . . ' He quickly checked the number on the phone. '694. I wonder if you could direct me to a number? I have it listed as 3612 and the chap lives in Richmond. Can you do that for me?'

The operator assured him that she could. James watched Bert rummage through drawers and bookcases as he listened to various clicks coming down the line.

'Putting you through now, sir.'

James sat up. 'Hello?'

A well-spoken man, with a soft Indian accent, answered. 'Hello?'

'Ah, hello, is this Richmond 3612?'

'It is.'

'Jolly good. I wonder if I might speak with a gentleman by the name of Mr Kushal Patel?'

'This is Kushal Patel. Who is this?'

James noted a slight wariness in Mr Patel's tone but put it to the back of his mind. It was imperative he gained some sort of rapport with the man.

'Ah, good, my name is Harrington. Lord Harrington — '

'Oh, my goodness!' said Mr Patel. 'Good morning, Lord Harrington. I am sorry if you think me rude.'

'I say, do you know me?'

Mr Patel assured James that he'd never met him, but that Delphine had briefed him. James frowned.

'Briefed you?'

'Yes, Lord Harrington. It is my understanding, because you are contacting me, that Miss Brooks-Hunter has met an untimely death. Is that correct?'

'Good Lord! D'you know about this?'

'I am knowing very little, Lord Harrington, but it may suit your task to visit me in the next few days. Are you able to arrange such a meeting?'

James said that he could and, while they were on the line, Mr Patel set a date for that coming Sunday, and hoped it didn't interfere with any worship James had planned.

'Well, if I miss one service I can always catch another,' he replied. 'However, my wife and a friend are coming to Petticoat Lane this coming Sunday, so it would suit me if I drop them off first and then come to you. Are you sure that's convenient?'

'That is most satisfactory, Lord Harrington.'

'Good show.'

'I am looking forward to meeting you.'

'Likewise. I say,' added James, 'before you go, could I ask — what is it that you do?'

Although James couldn't see Patel, he sensed some hesitancy before the answer came.

'All will be revealed on Sunday,' he said.

'Ah, right-ho, don't want to pry and all that. Look forward to seeing you then.' Before he put the receiver down, Kushal spoke.

'Delphine told me that you were astute, trustworthy and have an enquiring mind. I believe you are proving that to me already. Until Sunday.'

The line went dead.

'Well, well,' James muttered as he replaced the receiver. Bert had disappeared into another room and, in his place, stood George.

'Who was that?'

James went through the names in the address book, the telephone call and the fact that this Patel chap could probably shed light on the mysterious Delphine and, possibly, the riddle.

'Yes, well, I'll have to talk to him, too, at some stage.'

'By the way he was talking,' replied James, 'I got the sense that he didn't seem to know much more than I do. But he did assume that as I'd contacted him, Delphine had met with an untimely end.'

'I'll come up with you.'

James squashed the idea straight away. 'Sorry, old chap, I know you've got a job to do an' all, but I want to meet him on my own. I'm happy to tell him you'll be in touch, though.'

George clenched his teeth. 'Well, thanks for fitting me in,' he said with a hint of sarcasm.

They smirked at each other and, after a quick scan around the room, James followed George into the hall, where two constables and Bert were making their way out.

James accepted a cigarette from Bert as they climbed into the Jaguar. Bert struck a match and lit both tips.

'You know, Jimmy boy, that lady 'ad class, but there's nothin' much there, is there?'

James agreed. The house would, most definitely, be worth something, but the contents amounted to little. Perhaps the house was all she had, and it would certainly be worth a fortune to the Jacobs family. But, if that was the case, why the riddle? All this talk about a fortune must be leading somewhere. He wound his window down as George pulled up alongside.

'I say, George, did you find any bank statements?'

'Only a couple, but I've already had a word with Mr Chapman down at the Westminster Bank. She just had the one account with £402 pounds in it. Nice sum, but not a fortune.'

'Certainly not for a lady of Delphine's apparent status. Did you get hold of the sister?'

'She's not listed as having a telephone. I've asked the local force to get in touch with her.'

'Where are you off to now?'

'I'm visiting Reg and Derek Jacobs,' replied George. 'I may be tunnel-visioned, but I can't see who else could've done this, especially bearing in mind their attitude to her on May Day. They're a big family, so it needn't have been one of the main players, if you get my drift. They could've asked one of the family to slip in and attack her.'

James pondered on this as George drove off. Bert wound his window down and exhaled cigarette smoke as James posed a question to him.

'Do you think the Green Man outfit meant something?'

'I don't think so. It s'posed to represent new life, fertility, the welcoming of spring,' replied Bert. 'All nice stuff, really. They don't normally go around killing people — that's not part of the myth.'

'Yes, as I thought. So that just leaves one reason, doesn't it?'

Bert concurred. 'That's right. We said it on the day, mate. The killer had to wear something — '

'Otherwise she would have recognised him. And she did recognise him, I'm certain of that.'

Bert rubbed his cheek, perplexed, and turned to James.

'But the Jacobs lot could've done this at any time. They're family, so why wait until the fair? Why not come 'ere, break in, make it look like a robbery and kill 'er right 'ere?'

'So that suspicion is directed at more people?' suggested James.

'I dunno. It's not straightforward, that's for sure.'

Bert was right. None of it made sense. Here she was, living on her own; why wait until the Spring Fair to kill her and potentially be seen doing it? James turned the key in the ignition and pulled the starter button. There must have been over two hundred people at the fair. Was there anyone else there, apart from the Jacobs family, who wanted her dead?

'This whole thing is a riddle, Bert. The more I think about it, the more confusing it becomes. There's a fortune to find, shady family members, and a murder that didn't need to be in public view. Unless, of course, something came up that meant having to kill her quickly.' He put the car in gear. 'I believe, my friend, that our Miss Brooks-Hunter had an interesting past, don't you?'

9

Lunch on the terrace at Harrington's proved to have been a splendid idea and James, Beth, Stephen and Anne enjoyed a contented silence as the rays of the sun warmed their faces. Adam quietly fussed around, clearing away the duck pate on toast appetiser and replacing this with a crystal jug of Pimms, with large chunks of apples, oranges and sprigs of mint floating on the top.

'This r-really is a most civilised way to spend lunchtime,' said Stephen happily.

Anne agreed as she smiled affectionately at him. 'To think, you could have been teaching a class of noisy five-year-olds had you not decided to be a vicar.'

'God m-moves in mysterious ways.'

Beth agreed as she stirred the fruit in her glass. 'It's strange, don't you think, the way life has a habit of working out? Of all the places you might have gone to, you came here.'

'And jolly good that you did, too,' James added. 'I hope that you will continue to stay with us.'

Stephen said he'd do his best to be around for a long time. Anne put her sunglasses on.

'Well, the children are incredibly happy here. Village life is so community-minded, don't you think?'

'Cavendish and Charnley are,' said Beth. 'I couldn't speak for Loxfield though.'

Everyone groaned — only too aware of the awful Alec Grimes affair that had involved a couple from Loxfield. James squirmed in his seat.

'I'm afraid that had you gone to Loxfield, your views on village life might have been somewhat different. Not much community spirit over there. Charnley, though, is very similar to Cavendish.'

'But,' Beth said, 'they don't have you to chivvy them along with all the social events. There's a lot to be said for having a Lord of the Manor in the village, especially one interested in local folklore and customs. I know they're an endangered species these days; but, if they're active like James is, it can make all the difference.'

Adam arrived with their main course: fresh trout stuffed with white crab meat, surrounded by new potatoes and fresh asparagus. The chatter subsided as everyone tasted Didier's latest creation. After a few minutes, Anne put down her cutlery and sipped her drink.

'Are you any further forward with your mystery man?' she asked.

'I haven't gotten anywhere really,' said Beth. 'My jaunts around the village don't seem to be hitting the mark with him. He occasionally stops to look at something and then shakes his head. I'm hoping that when we speak to the people at the Mission in Bethnal Green it will shed some light on things. Perhaps they can go into a little more detail about where he came from, how long he's been here, friends, that sort of thing.'

'Do you th-think it likely you'll get anywhere with it?' asked Stephen. 'He doesn't seem to recall a-anything.'

'I'm not giving up,' replied Beth. 'He's such a delightful man — so well-mannered, well-spoken and agreeable.'

James swallowed a mouthful of trout and patted his lips with his napkin. 'Beth is loath to give up or return him to the East End. If he's still here in a couple of weeks, we're going to have to start thinking about where to house him. Summer's around the corner and we are pretty well full from June onwards. He can't keep that room for much longer, even though he's lending a hand.'

Anne cut into her fish. 'I saw him working on the old stables earlier. Is he doing that in return for a room?'

'He is. And he's had the most wonderful idea. James and I were thinking of just renovating the stables, but GJ had a brainwave.'

Anne and Stephen tilted their heads expectantly while Beth motioned for them to wait while she finished chewing her food. James volunteered the information.

'Trouble with having stables is the cost. We'd have to have a good dozen horses to make it work, but along with that comes a massive outlay for hay, bedding, equipment, instructors, not to mention the vet's bills. It really seemed like throwing money into a bottomless pit. These days, we have to temper our budget with a little prudence.'

'So,' Beth continued, 'GJ suggested an artist's studio, where guests can learn to paint or draw. Or even do some sculpture or pottery.'

'How lovely,' Anne exclaimed. 'I've always wanted to be able to paint water-colours. Perhaps I could learn, and this is such a marvellous setting.'

Stephen agreed. 'W-what with the river, the Downs and the sea views, this is a perfect location.'

'Absolutely, old chap,' said James, leaning forward. 'We also have the added bonus of it costing very little to set up. We're still having horses, though, but on a sort of loan basis. The farm over at Rottingdean has horses stabled there. We're setting up a deal with the owner to hire them for pony trekking. That way, we have the service but not the expense.'

Stephen agreed that it made sense. He took in the surroundings. 'W-where is GJ today?'

'Drawing, would you believe,' said Beth. 'He's sitting down by the river sketching as we speak. He's really very good. That's how this idea came about. He draws all of the time and he's extremely talented.'

Stephen dipped his head with interest and told Beth to continue encouraging this creativity as it might help to unlock his past. 'Th-these things may help to jog their m-memories back.'

'Do you still have room for me on Sunday?' asked Anne.

'Of course,' Beth said. 'It'll be fun.'

Stephen took on the expression of a child who'd had his favourite toy taken away. 'I — I can't believe you're going to m-miss my sermon.' He turned to James. 'At least James will be there.'

James' sheepish wince gave him away. 'Oh sorry, old chap, but I'm being the duty driver. I'm dropping them off at Petticoat Lane and then going to meet up with this Patel chap.'

Stephen's mouth opened wide. Anne told him to stop seeking attention.

'It's only for the morning, Stephen.

We'll all be back for the evening service.'

James reminded him that it was the first time they'd been absent since he arrived and their reasons were sound.

'After all, we're trying to solve poor Delphine's little mystery and the identity of GJ. I'm sure our Lord will be happy to learn of our good deeds on the day of rest.'

'I-I'm sure he will, but could you enlighten me? Who is this chap Patel?'

Between mouthfuls, James went through the details of his visit to Delphine's house, the address book and the telephone call to Kushal Patel.

'He seems a well-educated man and he's lived in some exclusive areas. I'm rather looking forward to meeting him. He seemed to know all about me.'

'Well, sweetie,' said Beth, 'it appears that Delphine had you in mind for solving this riddle a long time ago.'

'Yes. Old Bateson said that she'd chosen me after that affair with Alec Grimes — more about my stubbornness in not letting go. Do you think she'd thought of me before that?'

Anne slid her plate away. 'I suppose she could have just known you from what you do in the village. I mean, all of these events you organise and marshal, perhaps she just saw you as someone who gets things done and, being a Lord, trustworthy.'

James loved Anne's naivety. If only she knew how many lords who weren't quite on the straight and narrow. He rested his elbows on the table. 'I wonder if the sister will come up? When's the funeral, Stephen?'

'P-police still haven't released the b-body yet. Once they do that, I can make arrangements. Delphine didn't state where she wanted to be buried, just the hymns she wanted sung. I wonder if the sister wants her d-down there in Cornwall?'

'She may well do,' replied James. 'If I remember rightly, Delphine wasn't from Cavendish originally. I seem to recall her coming here in the early thirties.'

Beth agreed and thought that it was around the time they'd married. She added that, even back then, Delphine had been a little reclusive. 'A shame when you think of what a character she was. I'd have loved to have known her better.'

'Well,' James said as he prompted Adam for the bill, 'we may know her a little better after my visit to Richmond on Sunday. Are you all ready? I'd like to pop to the library to find out a little more about the Green Man.'

Beth gathered her things. 'Anne and I are going for a walk around the grounds. We'll make our own way back.'

'Splendid. Do you want a lift, Stephen, or are you joining the ladies?'

They knew full well that the ladies would discuss fashion, decorating and all those things that didn't really interest them and Stephen quickly opted to accompany James.

★ ★ ★

He parked the Jaguar by the village green and both he and Stephen commented on how the arrival of spring had brought Cavendish to life. The gardens in the terraced cottages opposite were a riot of colour; apple trees blossomed and the sweet smell of hyacinths and Lily of the

Valley perfumed the air.

'It c-certainly is the most attractive season.'

'You're quite right. But we have the villagers to thank for that, of course. Just about everyone in these cottages is a keen gardener. Come spring and summer, it'll be like the Chelsea Flower Show here, especially the gentleman on the end, there — his front garden is full of the most beautiful flowers and shrubs. And at the back, well, I think he supplies the greengrocer with most of his vegetables.'

'I must have a word with him. I'm about to do some p-planting and I'm not sure what I'm doing.'

'He'll put you right, I'm sure.' James grabbed the key from the ignition. 'Right, I'm off to the library — do you want to join me?'

Stephen declined the invitation, preferring instead to take a chance to speak with the gentleman in the end cottage. 'D-do I know him?'

'He's at your services most weeks,' said James. 'Sits at the back. Always in a battered old trilby and walks with a shepherd's crook.'

'Ah yes. Mr . . . '

'Bennett.'

'D-dog's name Blackie?'

'Correct.'

Climbing out of the car, Stephen let out a long groan. James followed Stephen's gaze and saw the unwelcome figure of 'Bruiser' Jacobs marching toward them, shouting and gesticulating. James frowned quizzically, cupped his ear to indicate that they couldn't hear a word of what he was saying. Bruiser strode silently until he stood eyeball-to-eyeball with him.

'What you poking yer nose into our affairs for?'

Stephen nipped around the car to join James, who replied, 'Mr Jacobs, I have nothing to do with your affairs. If Miss Brooks-Hunter has requested that I be involved in some way, then involved I shall be. But, I assure you, I don't intend to rob you of your inheritance, if that's what you're thinking.'

'You got money comin' ou' yer ears. If you ge' a penny off of 'er, you won't 'ave it fer long.'

'Are you threatening me, Mr Jacobs?'

'I'm just sayin', tha's all — you don't need 'er money. She's our family, not yours.'

'I'm sure where I'm involved it will be to do with the village. She was, as you may or may not know, very fond of living here.'

Bruiser grabbed James' lapels. 'I'm watchin' you. Just remember tha' and don't fink I believe your little private chat wiv tha' solicitor bloke was about no stupid folk day. You're 'iding somefink.'

Stephen went forward and twisted Bruiser's free arm up behind his back. Bruiser squirmed and let go of James.

'I-I do think you n-need to stop being such a bull-headed idiot,' said Stephen. 'I-if you were a more decent person, then James would no doubt discuss the rhyme — '

Bruiser slammed Stephen against the Jaguar. 'You lay a finger on me again I'll knock yer 'ead off, vicar or no vicar.'

'I say, buzz off, Jacobs,' said James. 'I'll make sure the police are informed about this outburst. You're not doing yourself any favours, you know, especially as Delphine appears to have been murdered.'

Bruiser shot an evil look at James, then spat on the ground and marched off. James turned to the vicar. 'I say, are you all right?'

Stephen assured him he was fine and smoothed his hair back.

'Stephen, you've no need to fight my battles. I may resemble a piece of streaky bacon, but I'm pretty handy when I need be. I used to box in the RAF.'

'Me too! But for the Army.'

They laughed. 'Well, between the two of us, we could probably beat him,' said James.

'H-he is a pretty hefty man, isn't he?'

'And certainly has a bee in his bonnet about me knowing the family secrets. I wonder what he's got to hide?'

'Th-thank heavens he didn't pick up on me talking about the rhyme,' said Stephen. 'So sorry. It sort of slipped out.'

'Yes, I must admit, I nearly kicked you myself,' replied James with a smile. 'Still, as you say, he didn't seem to notice.'

Stephen headed for Mr Bennett's cottage, while James locked the Jag and began walking toward the library. He pondered about the extraordinary outburst from Bruiser. Had he driven all the way into Cavendish to confront James? He didn't live anywhere near the village so was it worth the journey? Was he representing all the Jacobs family, or was there an ulterior motive? What exactly was the story between Delphine and this bunch of hooligans?

He simply couldn't believe she had any connection with them whatsoever. And if there was a connection, why did she feel the need to include them in her estate? Why not just cut them off? He stopped in his tracks. Perhaps she had been blackmailed? What was it about her that had made her so vulnerable?

'Lord Harrington?'

James spun round to see GJ smiling at him.

'Ah, hello there! I thought you were painting, or drawing, or something.'

'I was. I came into the village for a walk and a browse and saw you ahead. Did you want some company?'

'I'm actually just off to the library. Did you want to come, or do you fancy a quick pint in the Half Moon?'

GJ's eyes widened at the offer of a pint and James steered him across the green. As it was mid-week, the pub afforded a number of places in which to sit and James motioned GJ toward his favourite spot by the window overlooking the green. Donovan, who was wiping glasses and stacking them on the shelf above the bar, looked up in surprise.

'Not your usual drinking time.'

'You're right and I wasn't planning this detour. But when the sun is out, Donovan, one can't help but breathe the sweet smell of hops and taste the nectar of a Sussex ale.'

'Said like a true poet and make no mistake about it.' Donovan's gentle Irish lilt sounded almost melodic. The landlord flung the tea towel over his shoulder. 'So, what is it you'll be having?'

'Two pints of your South Downs bitter, please.'

With the promise they'd be delivered to

the table, James went to join GJ.

'So, young man, do you have any of your memory back yet?'

GJ massaged the back of his neck. 'I'm afraid not. Is it an awful imposition of me to stay? I'm really not a fraud but I honestly can't remember. If you want me to go back to London I will. I'm going to have to go back at some point. There's only so many odd jobs I can do for you.'

'You seem pretty genuine to me,' replied James, 'and Beth is determined to help you.'

'And your friend Bert, too. I can't thank them enough.'

'Did Philip, our doctor, have a word with you about this amnesia business?'

Donovan delivered the ale as GJ uttered an eager 'Yes' to James' question. He went on to describe how Philip had put the probability of this down to an accident.

'Apparently, if you've had a knock on the head and you then can't remember anything, you can lose your memory for just a few seconds, or even a few weeks. Sometimes, whole years can be lost.'

James swigged his beer and offered his cigarettes. GJ declined. James lit his and watched a wisp of smoke rise to the ceiling. 'So, it's likely you had a blow to the head,' he continued. 'You then end up at a Mission in the East End and you stay there for several years. Didn't the police put out a search for you?'

'If they did, they didn't find me,' replied GJ.

'But your parents must have been worried sick. Perhaps they still are?'

GJ gave a melancholy shrug. 'It would be lovely to have everything back. Not just my memory, but the people in my life as well. That's why I had to stop by your place. It was the first time I'd seen something that actually looked familiar.'

'What about your drawing? How do you suppose you've remembered how to draw so well? Beth says you're a master.'

The young man laughed. 'I wouldn't say that. Doctor Jackson did say there was a difference in memories. I can't remember what he called it now, but when you get amnesia it doesn't affect physical memories. So, if you learnt to ride a bike, you can still ride one. Similarly, I know how to draw and I can still draw. But ask me what I first drew, I can't tell you. But, the good news is that I've recognized something. That, apparently, will probably unlock more memories as time goes on.'

'Interesting.'

'I'm sorry I missed the Spring Fair,' GJ continued. 'It was so lovely to lie down on a comfortable bed with gorgeous pillows, I fell right off to sleep. I did peer out of the window when I felt a little better. Everyone seemed to be having a good time. But you had a lady collapse, I understand?'

'Yes, an elderly lady. I found her down by the river. Not an accident, unfortunately. It would appear that someone knocked her over the head and strangled her.'

The young man gave an incredulous stare and asked what sort of person would do that. James said he wished he knew, although his subconscious immediately blamed the Jacobs family. He gulped down the last of his pint.

'GJ, I really must get on. Having a beer wasn't in my schedule. You sit here, by all means.'

'Sorry, didn't mean to keep you.'

'Nothing to be sorry about, old chap. It was me that suggested it, don't forget.'

James bid GJ, Donovan and several villagers a cheery goodbye and made his way to the library, where Charlie Hawkins was sitting, feet on the table, munching a cheese sandwich. After a quick chat about the weather, their respective offspring and the upcoming folk festival, James focussed their attention to the matter in hand.

'The Green Man. Do you have any info on him?'

Charlie assured him he had plenty and led him through the converted cottage to the section on folklore and local customs. He headed toward one particular cabinet.

'This is all the folklore stuff we have. I've got some books in the reference library that shouldn't really go out of the building, but I'll make an exception for you. Tell me what you're looking for exactly and I'll go and check those out for you.'

'Splendid,' replied James. 'Anything that could be seen as remotely sinister about the Green Man.'

'Is this something to do with the attack on the lady? I heard that someone was dressed up. Jack Hedges told me he had his costume nicked.'

'That's right. It may be nothing, but I just wanted to check to see if there was anything relevant to the costume. Help George out, if I can.'

However, after an hour of searching, reading and scrutinising, both men discovered that the Green Man was anything but sinister or threatening. As Charlie turned to go, James quickly called him back. 'Do you know anything about solving riddles?'

'Me! Not likely. I've never been terribly good at that sort of thing. Why?'

'Oh, no reason, really. Just something that sparked my interest a little while ago.'

'Shame Miss Brooks-Hunter's no longer with us.'

James' ears pricked. 'Why's that?'

'I didn't know her well,' replied Charlie as he tidied some books, 'but I do know she loved crosswords and working out clues. I heard a rumour that she used to be a code-breaker or something. Do you need anything else?'

James shook his head and murmured a thank you. He ambled out of the library, deep in thought. George's car slowed up alongside him.

'What day does Mrs Jepson clean for you?' George asked.

James checked his watch. 'She's probably there now. She said she was coming later today. What do you need her for?'

'A couple of questions about when she did her stint as a fortune-teller.'

'Ah yes. Beth and Anne are probably there by now. You could do with a cuppa, couldn't you?'

'I wouldn't say no. I'll follow you up.'

On the drive home, James tapped the steering wheel with his finger. First there was a rumour of Delphine being a spy and now there was talk of her being a code-breaker. Rumours and myths were often based on some sort of fact. Could it be true? Could the gentle, refined and lady-like Delphine really have been mixed

up in some sort of wartime espionage?'
He gave a slow, satisfied nod. This really
was becoming exceptionally fascinating.

10

George steered Mrs Jepson to a chair as Beth placed a tray of Darjeeling and freshly-made lemon sponge on the coffee table between them. Mrs Jepson, at first, refused the offer of a seat, insisting that she'd prefer to stand. George gritted his teeth and James suppressed a smile. Mrs Jepson was strict about her social status and being asked to make herself comfortable in their lounge wasn't right in her book.

James stepped in and gently coaxed her to an armchair, while convincing her that they'd be delighted if she would join them for tea. With open and friendly persuasion, he managed to demolish the class barrier that occasionally separated them. She perched on the end of her chair and clasped her handbag close to her. Finally, she placed that on the floor and accepted a dainty cup and saucer from Beth. In the meantime, George had prepared his pipe and was already enjoying the first few puffs.

'Right, Mrs Jepson, this shouldn't take long. You remember you were acting as the fortune-teller at the fair? Miss Brooks-Hunter came to see you, I believe? I really wanted an account of your conversation with her, if you remember. Can you do that for me?'

'Well, yes, of course,' she replied. 'But she weren't there for long, so I don't know if what I've got to say will 'elp much.' She looked at James. 'Do you?'

James ignored George's silent exasperation and offered his cleaner some encouragement. 'I'm sure it'll be a great help, Mrs J. The chief inspector here can't pin all his questioning on one thing. He needs to build up a picture. So, the more information he has, no matter how trivial, the better. D'you see?'

'Oh right, yes. Well now ... ' Mrs Jepson pointed at George. 'You brought her over, d'you remember? I don't know what time it was — early afternoon, I think. Anyway, she popped her head into the tent and asked if I was free. I said yes and asked her to take a seat. I'd got a crystal ball in the middle of the table, that's all I was doing really. I can't read the tea-leaves or do Tarot cards or anything. Don't know why I offered to do it really; I'm not a psychic or anything.'

George gave an encouraging smile. 'That's fine, Mrs Jepson, we're not questioning your ability. I really just want to know what you said to the lady and what she said to you.'

Mrs Jepson chewed her lip. 'Well, she sat down and asked me to tell her about her future. They all do that, you know, ask what's in store. Well, I don't know, do I? So I just said the same as I say to all of 'em. I mean, it's just a bit of fun, isn't it?'

Beth took a seat next to her. 'And how exactly did you phrase it?'

'I changed it a little because she's quite elderly, so I couldn't really tell her she'd have a long and happy life, could I? But I did say that she'd live out her days in a lovely home with her friends around her.' She twisted her wedding ring back and forth. 'But she didn't, did she?'

Beth patted her hand. 'That wasn't

172

your doing, Mrs Jepson.'

George relit his pipe. 'And how did she react?'

'Oooh, now that was odd,' replied Mrs Jepson. She took a quick sip of tea. 'Normally, everyone says how nice it is to be told that, but she straightaway shook her head. 'No,' she said, 'that's not right.' She even commented that I weren't very good.' Mrs Jepson's expression took on a horrified look. 'She thought I was a real fortune-teller.'

James put his tea down. 'Don't worry yourself about that, Mrs J. What else did she say? Did she hint at something that might happen that day?'

George's lips tightened. 'Don't lead the witness, James.'

Mrs Jepson's eyes opened wide. 'Oh, yes. Yes. You've just reminded me. Yes she did. She said that she'd be unlikely to live many more days. Then she got up and put some pennies in the collection box. She sort of giggled and said 'don't take any notice of me'. Well, it took me by surprise, I can tell you. You shouldn't go around saying things like that.'

'And then she went?' George asked.

Mrs Jepson nodded. George felt for more tobacco and thanked the cleaner for being so helpful. She placed her tea on the table and thanked Beth and James for their hospitality.

'I really must get on,' she said. 'I have the bedrooms to do yet and it's getting late. Got my John's dinner to put on.' She scurried off to complete her duties.

James reached across for a slice of lemon cake. 'Well, George, there's no denying she foresaw this. Delphine, I mean, not Mrs J.'

George agreed, remembering the comment that Miss Brooks-Hunter made when they first met. 'Something about it being fortunate to have a Detective Chief Inspector — do you remember?' he asked.

'My word, yes, I'd forgotten about that. To be honest, she said a few things that were quite odd when I was showing her about.'

'Can you remember what and, more importantly, to whom?'

James rifled through the many memories and experiences he'd filed away about that particular day as Beth poured more tea. George waited patiently as James brushed some fluff from his trousers.

'Right, I remember a few possibly significant moments. I have to say, the initial thing that struck me was that Delphine wanted to come in the first place. I believe she'd been once before, but that must have been twenty years ago. I know that because the twins were only a few months old then. She particularly wanted to come, she said, to enjoy herself. But the reason this struck me as odd was that this was the first time — and the last, I hasten to add — that we'd booked the Jacobs lot for the fair. Isn't it strange for her to have wanted to come on this particular year, when her own relatives would be here? Particularly bearing in mind the bad blood between them.'

He quickly summoned up another memory.

'And did you notice, darling,' he continued, 'when we had lunch? She was a sprightly lady but, every so often, there seemed to be a touch of sadness about her.'

Beth agreed. 'Almost melancholy. Just for a second, and then she'd be back to her old self. She came over like that when she spoke of her sister.'

George scribbled in his notebook as James asked if the sister had made an appearance.

'Not yet,' replied George. 'It's like the dark ages down there. No crime, so hardly any police. She lives in a remote area; often out walking, apparently. They've put a note through her door asking her to contact them urgently. We're fine to release the body for the funeral, so I hope they get in touch soon. Anyway, did you notice anything else?'

'Yes I did. One thing I thought particularly peculiar,' replied James. 'We were strolling around the place, having a wonderful time, and she said 'I do hope nothing will happen today'. It sort of took me by surprise. I mean, here we were on a beautiful spring day at a lively social event and she came out with that. By the time I'd thought to ask what she meant, she'd changed the subject.'

'But sweetie, it's unlikely she would

have expanded on it, anyway,' said Beth.

'Yes, I'm sure you're right. And when we approached the fairground rides, the reaction of the Jacobs brothers was an eye-opener, I can tell you. There's certainly some history there.'

He sat bolt upright.

'I've just remembered something Jackie Connor said. She didn't mention any names, but I'm sure this referred to Delphine and the Jacobs. She said that Reg Jacobs was a rather rough individual, but he was worse that day. This was after Delphine was found. I asked if there was anything I could do. I thought perhaps someone from the village had upset him. But then she said that you can't put the history of one family right in a day.'

They gave one another questioning looks. George closed his notebook and finished his tea.

'It's one of the Jacobs, isn't it? I'm sure of it,' he said. 'But I've got no proof whatsoever. They're all backing one another up.'

James stood and wandered across to open the French windows. 'George, I believe that this all harks back to the past. Something happened a long time ago that led to Delphine's murder. I think solving this riddle may also help solve your murder.'

Beth lay back on the sofa and crossed her legs. 'What about all this business about being a spy or something during the war? Do you think that has any truth to it?'

'Perhaps,' said George. 'Stories like that often have truth at their heart.' He tipped his head at James. 'Like you say, you may be able to dig some stuff up while you're trying to solve the riddle.'

James scratched his head. 'I believe so. I certainly think this Mr Patel will shed some light on things. He seems to have been the only constant in Delphine's life over the years.'

'When are you seeing him?'

'This Sunday.'

'I'll pop up there myself in a few days but in the meantime, find out what you can and tell me everything, no matter how irrelevant you might think it is.'

11

James yawned as he dropped Beth and Bert off at Petticoat Lane. Rising at 6 a.m. was not, he decided, a pleasant way to begin a Sunday morning. He much preferred a leisurely start; tea in bed and a scan through the papers. But Beth wanted to explore the market and Bert insisted that getting there at 8 a.m. or before would be perfect. As they didn't know how long they would be, they told James they would return to Cavendish by train.

Anne, unfortunately, was forced to remain at home, as both Luke and Mark had succumbed to tonsillitis and were in need of their mother's nursing skills. She'd whispered, with a glint of mischief to James, that she thought it was a ruse on Stephen's part to ensure at least one of them attended his Sunday morning service. As a consolation for missing out on the morning, Beth promised to bring back some dress material for her.

Arriving at the market, he wished Beth and Bert well as he dropped them off, before driving to the other side of London. He snaked the Jaguar through the suburbs of Ham and Kew and up a steep and winding hill, past white stone mansions and three-storey red-brick homes sheltered behind ancient oak trees. His eyebrows rose as a gleaming Bentley turned onto the road ahead of him. Further up the hill were the magnificent iron gates that opened into Richmond Park, the largest Royal Park in London.

He remembered bringing Beth here when they were courting because it offered such a variety of landscapes and grassland. He knew the royal connection went back to King Edward's reign in the thirteenth century, when it was known as the Manor of Sheen. Throughout the centuries its oak trees had grown sturdy and tall and the red and fallow deer roaming the heath were, he was sure, descendants of those wandering the pastures in the 1600s.

Veering to the left, he crested the hill and arrived at The Terrace, a long gravel promenade that afforded the most splendid views of the Thames and beyond. He knew this to be a vista protected by an Act of Parliament and what a beautiful sight it was too. He parked and reached across to the glove compartment for a small notepad, which he flipped open. Checking the address, he was satisfied he'd parked in the right place.

His eyes scanned the wonderful architecture and his gaze settled on Kew House, a bay-windowed three-storied house built, James guessed from the style, during the eighteenth century. Collecting his thoughts, he locked the car, crossed the road and trotted up three steps to ring the bronzed doorbell. After some time, he rang the bell again. He waited and checked his watch. Perhaps he was early.

He heard footsteps scurrying along the hallway and finally the door opened. A young Indian man of around twenty years of age bowed.

'Lord Harrington?'

James instinctively bowed back as the young man invited him in.

'Lord Harrington, please forgive us.

My grandfather has an early visitor this morning. I am Dipak, by the way. Kushal Patel's grandson.'

James extended his arm to greet the striking-looking Indian and allowed himself a few moments to enjoy the decor. The immense hall was a treat for the eyes and he wished that Beth could have been with him as she would have loved it.

Black and white floor tiles, polished to within an inch of their lives, extended to what he believed to be the kitchen area. To the side of him was the first of three mahogany staircases that led to the upper floors. Oyster-coloured wallpaper lined the walls and, on a dark oak table, stood a tub of tulips of the deepest yellow James had ever seen.

Dipak opened a panelled door and motioned for James to step through.

'My grandfather will not keep you waiting long, Lord Harrington. May I bring tea for you?'

'That's most gracious, thank you.'

Dipak left him in a small office furnished with a selection of armchairs and occasional tables. He studied a water-colour of an action-packed game of polo against the backdrop of India. Further along he examined an oil painting of the London docks and suddenly wondered how Beth was faring.

* * *

Beth stood alongside Bert, with parcels of material under her arm. Aside from fabric, she also carried a shopping bag full of goodies and wore a satisfied grin on her face. The chaos of the bustling market was all around them and her senses were bombarded by noise, smells and colour. Parrots squawked in large cages, small monkeys dressed in jackets and hats posed for pictures, stallholders yelled the prices of their wares and the aroma of food lured her in all directions.

A blind man played an obscure tune on an accordion and a small boy did a tap-dance to accompany it.

They passed a stall selling stockings and Beth handed over some money for several pairs. Next door, a man did his best to sell her some shoes and further along, a grapefruit was thrust into her face, which she politely declined. They moved away from the crowds and onto the pavement.

'What a shame Anne couldn't make it,' she said doing her best to stay close to Bert. 'She would have loved it here. I hope she'll be happy with this cotton. And Bert, I didn't realise you knew so many people.'

'Well, your Ladyship, this is my stamping ground. Born and raised 'ere, so I've known most o' this lot since we was kids.'

'I can believe that.' She hugged the package of material. 'Most of these things came at quite a discount.' She pecked him on the cheek. 'We must do this more often.'

Bert groaned and tipped his head to the building opposite. 'Come on — I need a cuppa and this 'ere's the place we're gonna get it.'

'A church?' asked Beth in surprise. 'But won't they have a service going on? And churches don't do refreshments — well, not those I've been to.'

Bert led her across the street. 'Not a church, your Ladyship, a Mission.'

Beth turned. 'Oh! *The* Mission — where GJ lives.'

Delighted by this revelation, she followed him through the front door and into a large hall. Inside were a number of men and women sitting at benches, eating breakfast and drinking tea from chipped mugs and cups. Some glanced up to see who the strangers were but most barely noticed them; they were more interested in their food than anything else. Beth sidled closer to Bert.

A young man in his mid-thirties came across to greet them. Dressed in worn flannel trousers and a green sweater with a hole in it, he opened his palms.

'Hello. Can I help?'

'Yes, please,' replied Beth. 'We were wondering if we could speak with the person that runs the Mission. Could you direct us to him?'

'Well, you're looking at one of 'em,' said the young man. 'I help run this with my mum. She's out the back cooking breakfast. Would you like some?'

Bert immediately said he would. Beth gawped. How much could he eat in one morning? But then, she realised she wouldn't mind a spot to eat after the early start; the hustle and bustle of the market had given her an appetite.

They followed the man through to the kitchen, where two women rushed from one place to another frying bacon and eggs, grilling toast and washing up.

'Mum, we've go' visitors.' He turned to Beth. 'By the way, my name's David. This is my mum, Gladys, and over there's my wife, Nancy.'

'Cor blimey,' Bert gawped. 'Gladys Smith. I didn't know you were still up 'ere?'

Gladys' arms opened as wide as her smile. 'Ber' Briggs, as I live and breathe!' she said. 'I ain't seen you in years.'

'Blimey,' he said, 'you don't look any different.'

Gladys was around the same age as Bert. Her greying, red hair was curled into a loose bun. She wore a little foundation and lipstick and, beneath her wrap-around apron, was a floral dress.

They gave each other a long hug while Bert explained that he now lived in Sussex, but was often up at the markets around the East End. 'I can't believe I ain't seen you before now.'

She nudged him. 'Still sorting out yer dodgy deals?' She roared with laughter as Bert shuffled on his feet sheepishly. 'I knew it. I 'ope you've got time for a catch up, darlin'.'

'For you, Gladys, the world.'

'I'll get these breakfasts out and we'll 'ave a chinwag.'

David grinned and held an old wooden chair out for Beth. Bert took his cap off.

'This 'ere is Lady Harrington,' he explained. 'And, as your mother has already announced, I'm Bert Briggs.'

The mention of a titled lady sent everyone scurrying and apologising for the mess. Beth held her hands up, insisting they carry on as normal.

'I'm only a Lady because I married into the family and, to be honest, he hates people bandying that title around. Please, call me Beth. I'm from Boston, in America, and really don't deserve any special treatment. As Bert said, we've come up from Sussex.'

'Well Beth,' said Nancy, drying her hands. 'Would you like a bacon sarnie or the full English?'

Beth felt that a bacon sandwich would be lovely, along with a cup of tea. Bert rubbed his hands, opting for the full English with fried bread. David went across to the tea urn.

'Sorry, we don't have any cups left, only mugs.'

Bert took them from him. 'Not fussed, me old cock. As long as they've got tea in 'em, that's fine.'

David joined them at the table. 'So, wha' brings you 'ere? Oh, I s'pose you've been down the market?'

Beth said this was one of the reasons for coming up, but the main reason concerned this very Mission.

'Really?' said David. 'I didn't fink we made much a mark on the map. We're just a struggling Mission for the 'omeless — unless you're 'ere to give us a fantastic donation?' he said, grinning cheekily.

'David!' Gladys said attempting to clip

his ear. David ducked his head and winced.

'Sorry.'

Beth laughed. 'Please, don't be embarrassed. I'm not here to donate, I'm afraid — although, of course, we'll give a little by way of a thank you. We're hoping you can help us with some information.'

Their requested breakfasts were placed in front of them. Bert grabbed his knife and fork and took over the story from Beth.

'You've got a fella stopping here, been 'ere for years — young bloke with blond 'air and a posh accent.'

'Jim!' the three mission workers chorused.

'D'you know where he is?' asked David. 'We thought 'e'd had an accident or somethin'.'

'Nothing like that,' said Beth. 'He's with us, in Cavendish. I found him living in the remains of our stable block.'

David, Gladys and Nancy listened intently as Beth recounted how she'd found GJ and what he'd been doing since. Gladys praised the heavens that GJ was well and said it was like a weight being lifted off her shoulders. Nancy stood behind David as he cupped his mug.

'I went round some o' the local 'ospitals,' he said, 'even called the police. They didn't wanna know -'im being 'omeless, like. They just assumed he'd gone off somewhere else. But Jim's not like that, you see. I'm glad he's all right. Is he comin' back?'

Gladys tugged her son's arm. 'Leave 'em be, David. Let 'em eat their food. We've still got breakfasts to do for them ou' there and there's washing up to be done.'

Beth was keen to carry on talking but understood that their homeless people took priority, so reluctantly watched them carry on. Bert swallowed his first chunk of crispy fried bread and groaned with ecstasy.

'Blimey, that's good.' He slurped his tea. 'Wonder 'ow Jimmy boy's gettin' on?'

★ ★ ★

As James came to the end of a magazine article he was reading, an elderly gentleman swung the door open.

'Lord Harrington?'

Kushal Patel approached, introduced himself and greeted James like an old friend. He invited him through to the room opposite — a large, high-ceilinged lounge that gave views over The Terrace and beyond.

'Do please sit by the window,' he said. 'Tea is on its way.' He winked at James. 'Indian Darjeeling, of course.'

'Of course,' James said feeling very much at home. There were some people whose voice and face matched perfectly and this was one of them. Kushal Patel was around the same age as Delphine, and as spritely. Deep brown eyes gave the impression he knew the history of the world, and his welcoming and gentle demeanour could have melted an iceberg. Unusually for an Indian of his age, he was very Western. He wore wool trousers, a white shirt, a chunky cream cardigan and a pair of tartan slippers. He was exceptionally well-spoken and, judging by the books on the shelves, well-read too.

James made himself comfortable and thanked Kushal for making him so welcome. His host installed himself opposite and cleared the small coffee table between them. He registered James' interest in the various novels and magazines.

'You are a reader, too, Lord Harrington?'

'When time permits, Mr Patel. But, I have to say, I haven't read a good deal of these since my schooldays.'

'I am learning much of my English from reading these books,' replied Mr Patel.

'Your English is very good,' said James. 'You went to school in England?'

'I attended school, initially, in Bombay, but my father sent me to England at the age of ten to board at Winchester. I look upon England as my home, Lord Harrington. It is many years since I have returned to Bombay.'

'Your family, presumably, are all here?'

'What is left of them, yes,' replied Mr Patel. 'My wife sadly died many years ago. My son and his wife are living in York. Dipak, their son, is staying with me for a few days.'

The huge door leading from the hall opened and Dipak entered, carrying a large wooden tray. He placed it on the table between them, bowed and took his leave. Kushal's slender fingers agitated the leaves with a silver spoon.

'Before getting down to this business, Lord Harrington, I would prefer it if you were to call me Kushal. Salutation is too formal for an acquaintance of Delphine.'

James agreed that informal terms were more in keeping and insisted that Kushal drop 'Lord Harrington' from his vocabulary and simply call him James.

Over tea, they slipped into a polite discussion that took in numerous topics; their wives and families, the merits of living in the town versus the country, and other safe topics. James sat back and admired the view.

'You certainly have an enviable outlook, Kushal. You must spend a lot of time admiring it.'

'Ah yes, the famous view from the The

Terrace. Many a poet and painter has been hypnotised by its beauty. I believe it was Charles Moritz who wrote most eloquently about it in his *Travels in England*. 'The terrace at Richmond does assuredly afford one of the finest prospects in the world. Whatever is charming in nature or pleasing in art is to be seen here.' A rather handsome description, don't you agree?'

'I do indeed,' replied James. 'Have you been here long? I noticed a number of contact details for you in Delphine's address book.'

'I have lived in this house since I retired at sixty-five. Before that I have, as you say, moved about. I have always wished to settle here and I am delighted that I am doing so now.'

'Do you get any trouble from people about your background? I know people from certain walks of life can be rather prejudiced.'

Kushal gave him a knowing smile. 'It is, occasionally, a problem, but I am thinking that this is not my problem. I know where I am welcome and where I am not. The

Englishman states that his home is his castle and I agree most profoundly with this. When the door closes on the outside world, I am very much at home.' He placed his cup and saucer on the table. 'But now, James, I am thinking we have spoken enough of niceties. I believe you really wish to begin speaking of Delphine.'

12

Kushal reached behind him and picked up a manila folder from his desk. He slipped a pair of spectacles on.

'I have much history with our mutual acquaintance. Myself and Delphine go back to around 1916 and we worked together on many projects.' He peered over his glasses. 'There is much I cannot speak of, but some information I can share. I am asking, however, that you be most discreet when discussing this.

'Delphine Brooks-Hunter was born in 1883 to an unmarried couple. The third of three illegitimate children. The mother came from a wealthy background; her parents used to reside not far from here, in Kew.' He steepled his fingers. 'Did Mr Bateson provide an overview of the family rift following the birth?'

James went through the details as he knew them; the two sisters had remained together, while the brother went to the father's family. His host closed his eyes and commented on how dreadful the whole affair must have been.

James agreed. 'But the mother and father presumably stayed together for a while,' he said. 'They must have done to have had three children.'

'Ah yes,' replied Kushal, 'but such behaviour brought much shame upon the family. Arrangements were made to . . . ' He searched for the appropriate phrase. James pre-empted him.

' 'Cover up' is the phrase I believe you're seeking, Kushal. Do I take it that the family went on an extended holiday and came back with their offspring, or made out they were at school abroad or something?'

Kushal bobbed his head from side to side to confirm the assumption. 'The times are changing, James, but even now such a thing is frowned upon in respectable families. This is most especially where my culture is concerned.' He presented James with a sepia photograph of a young lady.

'Ah ha,' said James. 'I may not have

known her then, but you can't mistake those sparkling eyes. What a stunning lady our Delphine was.'

'She was certainly a very striking woman,' replied Kushal. 'This was taken in 1901, when she was aged eighteen.'

'Do you have a picture of her sister?'

Kushal held his palms up in despair.

'Unfortunately, I have yet to meet the sister. After all of these years, there are so many secrets I am not privy to. I am sometimes thinking Delphine did not wish me to meet her. Skeletons in the closet, I believe is the phrase.'

James confirmed that it was, indeed, the phrase and wondered what the skeletons could be. Could the rhyme reveal everything? Jackie Connor's statement about family history rushed into his mind. He returned the photograph.

'So, Kushal, let's get down to the nitty-gritty. We're not here to discuss her family history, are we?'

Kushal shifted in his chair and gave James an earnest look. 'What exactly do you know about Delphine?'

'I have to confess — very little. My

knowledge is that she's lived in Cavendish since around 1930 or perhaps two or three years later. I'm not sure of the exact time of her arrival; not sure if she was ever married or had children. I'm fairly sure that her mother's family were sufficiently well-off to spare her having to work.'

Kushal gestured for him to continue.

'Well, that's about it, really,' said James. 'I mean, you hear rumours and all, but — '

The Indian perked up. 'What rumours are you hearing?'

James waved dismissively. 'That she was some sort of spy. Nonsense, really. Village gossip. Unfortunately, we have a few of that type in our green and pleasant land, and some of them live in Cavendish.' He had immediately thought of the Snoop Sisters.

'That is the nature of the human being,' said Kushal. 'We are naturally inquisitive and want to know the why, the how, the where. We listen to the tone of a statement and detect humour, anger or sarcasm and we question, always question.' He met James' gaze. 'But you are dismissive of such rumours. Why?'

The words Kushal spoke resonated with James. It was true and he, himself, was an inquisitive and questioning person. The very fact that he was sitting here at the request of Delphine proved that. She'd chosen him because of that trait. And now here was Kushal questioning why he would dismiss these rumours.

His host's steely gaze bore into him and realisation dawned. He uncrossed his legs and put his tea down. 'Are you telling me . . . you're not serious! Delphine, a spy?'

Kushal carefully selected a slice of Victoria sponge and took a mouthful as James struggled to comprehend the news.

'But . . . how? I mean, who for? Where?' He slumped back in the chair and ran his hand through his hair. 'When?'

'She has been a spy since the Great War.'

'Good Lord.' James' jaw dropped. 'I can't believe it.' He knew he must have looked incredulous. 'Are you able to elaborate, or is it one of those confidential things?'

Kushal licked the crumbs from his lips.

'I am able to tell you who she was working for and where, but I am not able to tell you on what. The secrets of government must be remaining a secret.'

'Of course, that goes without saying,' replied James. 'Well, it would be thrilling to learn what she did do. She always struck me as a sporting sort of gal. But, a spy . . . ' He chortled at the thought of it. Kushal referred to the paperwork.

'She began working for this government in 1912. Secretarial work mainly but always pushing for a more adventurous position which she eventually gained during the Great War. Britain and Germany were most fearful about spies. You may know that there were many men executed in both countries; some without evidence to support such an action.'

'What on earth possessed her to enter such a world?'

'Excitement, Lord Harrington. Marriage and children were not for her; the Suffragette movement was active and she embraced a desire of being equal among men.' Kushal admitted he found it all quite unbelievable. 'That's when I first met her and, even then, I could see that she was the most extraordinary person.'

'And what is it that you do, Mr Patel? I'm still in the dark with that one. Or is that confidential?'

'I am a therapist. A psychiatrist, if you like. The human being, no matter what gender you are, is a delicate flower. Delphine witnessed many atrocities during her work, as did many of her male counterparts. It was my role to mitigate those memories — debrief her, if you like — and make her strong again. She spoke perfect German you know and spent weeks, sometimes many months, in Berlin.'

'So, she was presumably accepted as a German?'

'Yes, undoubtedly yes. She had a false name and travel documents and travelled across the borders frequently.'

'A double agent?'

'No. She never worked for the other side. But the Germans accepted her as German. She spoke freely about a fictional aunt here in the United Kingdom, about life over here and what the British were doing. So they liked to think she was giving information without thought, but the information she was revealing was carefully managed.'

'Carefully managed? Are you saying that the British couldn't trust her, or was it purposefully managed?'

'Most certainly the latter. Delphine was a huge patriot of this country and put her life at risk many times to serve it.' He poured more tea. 'But I am telling you something, Lord Harrington. In all of those years, from the Great War until 1950, not one person in the territory of our enemies ever knew. She was that good.'

'And coming to you, a psychiatrist? Was that a regular thing?'

Kushal's head bobbed from side to side. 'Most certainly, yes. When Delphine first arrived here, she had witnessed death and torture on the grandest scale. She should not have seen such violence in those tender years. It affected her, initially, but — forgive my ego — my methods are good and soon she is visiting, regardless of whether it was necessary or not.' He pointed at James' chair. 'She would sit there, where you are now, for many hours observing this wonderful view and, together, we would play chess — here, on this very table. Do you play chess, Lord Harrington?'

'I certainly do, although I'm no expert,' replied James. 'I'm sure Delphine played with a far more interesting strategy than I ever could.'

'Like chess, Delphine was most complex. Although I knew her for many years, I never really got to know the real her. I always thought she held secrets that even her closest ally would never know. But I loved her for her strength, her humour, her courage. She was truly one in a million.'

James agreed that she was and remarked how fortunate it was that the pair of them had known her. Kushal studied him.

'You are now having the unenviable task of deciphering a rhyme?'

'Oh Lord, yes. You know about that, do you?'

Kushal indicated that he did, but had no idea of the contents. He only knew that it would lead the person solving it to a huge fortune.

'Delphine became a most rich lady. She had no need of money. She and her sister were secure, financially. Their parents died many years ago and left them with a substantial income. She chose her salary in material goods — paintings, antiques, that sort of thing. She had the most exquisite taste. I am speculating that these items are not at the Coach House?'

'You speculate correctly,' said James. 'There's not a lot there at all. Nothing that suggests that she was a spy and certainly no gifts of value; in fact, no real material things of any worth. The paintings she has are pretty run-of-the-mill. Not an antique in sight as far as I can see. But I'll get an expert in, just in case.'

Kushal frowned. 'She would not be sending a riddle if these items were in plain view. No, Delphine is exchanging these items for something else. That is for you to find out.'

James stated that riddles really weren't his thing.

'Riddles,' Kushal continued, 'are there to confuse. You must study the language she is using. The language may have many meanings. Do not assume; open your mind to the improbable and study each line as a separate entity. Do you have help in solving this riddle?'

'I've summoned the help of my wife and three close friends who can be trusted with the crown jewels themselves.' James felt in his pocket and brought out a piece of paper. 'Can I show you a copy? You may pick up on something I haven't.'

Kushal studied the rhyme, expressed some surprise and returned the slip of paper to James. 'I have not been to the Coach House, but I cannot fathom it at the moment. I will most certainly contact you if something springs to mind. She clearly thinks you will solve this, so I wish you well with your endeavours. You have met the other side of the family?'

James groaned. 'Oh Lord, yes. I can't believe they're related, I really can't.'

'Mmm, Delphine had no time for them, yet they are having some sort of hold over her. It is regrettable that she was not more forthcoming with her life story.'

There was a tap at the door. It opened and Dipak peered round.

'I'm sorry Grandfather, but — '

'Let me through, young man.' A buxom, formidable lady in her late forties strode into the room. She wore, in James' opinion, a hideous cerise floral hat and a lavender tea dress with a lemon cardigan. Her thunderous face added another clash of colour. Woe betide anyone who crossed her, James thought to himself.

He stood up. Kushal did so in his own time.

'Mrs Crabtree,' he said politely, 'I am in a private meeting and I insist that you wait in the drawing room.'

Mrs Crabtree came closer and glared at James. 'You have an appointment?'

'Well, yes, actually.' He checked his watch. 'Are we running over, Kushal?'

'You are,' replied the lady. She spotted the name printed on the manila folder and scowled. 'That woman! You're discussing Miss Brooks-Hunter?'

Kushal's firm grip on James' forearm

stopped him from responding.

'My business with this client is private and it is being none of your affair. Kindly remove yourself from this room.'

She almost spat at the folder. 'Scarlett O'Hara. That's what she should be called.' She turned on her heels and marched out, followed by an apologetic Dipak. Kushal turned to James.

'I'm so very sorry. She is a little unbalanced and has been referred to me. Please accept my apologies.'

James held his hands up. 'Not necessary, old chap. She knew Delphine, though?'

'It would seem so.' Kushal collected the papers together and was clearly not going to expand on the subject. 'Now, if you will excuse me, James, I must not keep her waiting.'

He steered James out to the hall and took his hand. 'You will call me, please. Update me on your progress. I am interested to learn where this will lead. And I am very much hoping they find who took her life.'

'I'll keep you updated with everything,

Kushal,' replied James. 'Thank you for your time.' He nodded to the drawing room door and lowered his voice. 'Good luck with your next client.'

James went across the road and plonked himself down on an empty wooden bench to gather his thoughts. What an eventful morning that had been. He now had more questions than answers. And fancy Delphine being a spy! What sort of secrets had she passed on? What escapades did she get up to in Germany? Did the Jacobs family know she was a spy? Was that the hold they had over her? And what about Mrs Crabtree? She clearly knew, or knew of, Delphine. What did she mean, Scarlett O — Hara?

He searched his pockets for a cigarette. Skeletons in the cupboard, Kushal had said. But how many skeletons? So far, there appeared to be a graveyard full of them. He turned to study the house. It's a shame that Kushal couldn't discuss Mrs Crabtree? He clearly didn't want to take the conversation any further and professional ethics would have prevented him from doing so. He stretched back and crossed his legs. He wondered whether he should wait and catch Mrs Crabtree when she emerged.

After a few minutes, a Rolls Royce Silver Cloud drew up outside Kew House. James stubbed his cigarette out and observed the activity at the front door. Dipak Patel bowed his head slightly as Mrs Crabtree descended the steps into the waiting car. In a loud voice she instructed her driver to proceed to her home to Wimbledon. James quickly delved into his pocket for a pen and paper and jotted down a few notes: Wimbledon, Silver Cloud registration number WKD 344, Crabtree, Mrs.

Well, James thought, what she lacked in fashion sense, she made up for in her choice of car. He wondered if there was a Mr Crabtree.

He checked his watch. Beth and Bert would be making their own way home by now. He wondered if they'd had much luck.

13

While James was spending an enlightening morning with Kushal, Beth and Bert had planted their feet well and truly under the table at the Mission. Indeed, Beth found it so difficult to watch everyone running around cooking and serving and suchlike that she decided to lend a hand herself. David, Nancy and Gladys worked tirelessly around her as she washed and dried the dishes.

Bert, meanwhile, wandered around the main hall and seated himself with the tramps and itinerants. He engaged them with a degree of interest in their lives, while showing them the photograph of GJ that he'd taken on the day they'd found him.

Beth glimpsed over her shoulder and through the serving hatch. So far, she'd seen enthusiastic men and women who clearly knew the young man, others who appeared completely blank and a good many who greeted Bert like a long lost friend. She decided that their friend must know half the population of the East End. She wiped perspiration from her brow and decided that she should have worn something more suitable. A circular skirt and twin-set jumper wasn't the best outfit to wear in these circumstances. David ambled across to her, wiping his hands on a towel.

'I 'ave to say, Lady 'arrington, it's really good o' you to get stuck in like this. We didn't mean for you to get so involved.'

'It's been an honour and a privilege to help,' she replied. 'I think everyone should do this once in a while. It reminds you how lucky you are to have a roof over your head.' She watched the men and women as they finished their breakfasts. 'Where do they go now?'

David took a deep breath. 'On the streets. Some beg; some do a bi' of busking. Some, I'm sure, get up to no good, but . . . ' He shrugged.

'I guess if you're desperate, you'll do anything,' said Beth.

David threw the towel over his

shoulder. 'Yeah, that's true. Some of 'em come back 'ere to stay if we've got room.'

Nancy joined him and quickly thanked Beth for her efforts. 'Makes up for Jim not being 'ere on a Sunday.'

Beth gave her a questioning look and Nancy elaborated.

'The reason he's stayed 'ere for so long is 'cos he helps out, like you've just done. Cleans the floors, washes the dishes, does the laundry, fixes and mends, that sort of thing.'

'So how long has he been here?'

Nancy and David looked at each other and then at Gladys.

'A good few years, love,' Gladys said. 'Came 'ere in the summer of '52. Couldn't 'ave been more than fifteen or sixteen. Oh I know that's like a grown up but he was vulnerable, not used to life on the streets and he'd been living rough for a few months before that.'

'And he had no memory of who he was? Even then?'

'Not a sausage, luv. We told the local bobby, but no one claimed him. I don't even know if they tried. Most people that age are workin', so there's no great urgency for the police.' She took the tea cloth from Beth's grasp. 'Time you 'ad a rest.'

David opened the door from the hall to a stairwell. 'Would you like to see 'is fings?'

Beth expressed an eagerness to view anything that might assist with her quest to help GJ. She then followed David up a narrow wooden staircase to a dormitory above the kitchens. There were three rooms upstairs, quite sparse and each housing around eight beds with a locker for each by its side. She shuddered. How awful to think that life could be reduced to a bunk and two shelves in a cupboard. She supposed it was better than being on the streets, though. David led her to the far corner, where a neatly-made bed overlooked the main road leading into Petticoat Lane.

'He certainly keeps his area clean,' she remarked.

'Yeah, he's always kept 'imself clean and tidy, and he's well-mannered. Makes a change to some you get in 'ere.' David motioned for her to carry on. 'I'll leave you to it. If there's anyfing you think he'll need while he's with you, I s'pose you'd best take it.'

Beth promised to let him know about anything she took away.

'Can you let Bert know I'm up here?'

As if on cue, Bert ambled into the dormitory. 'Oi, oi, Nancy said you'd come up 'ere. Find anything?'

'Just starting. Why don't you give me a hand?'

Bert joined her, opened the cabinet to the side of the bed and viewed the contents. 'Not gonna take long, is it?'

As the sound of David's footsteps retreated, Bert piled the belongings from the cupboard onto the single bed.

'Mainly magazines.'

'Did you have any luck with your fact-finding over breakfast?' asked Beth.

Bert screwed his face up and explained that nothing much had come out of it. Everyone seemed to know GJ because he'd been at the Mission for so long, but no one knew where he'd come from.

'But everyone spoke well of 'im, you

know. They're all right pleased that someone's taken 'im in.'

Beth made a face. Taken him in! She wondered if she'd made the right decision about letting him stay. What if she never found out who he was? What would she do? She couldn't send him back up here again, no matter how hospitable they were. Perhaps they could find him work at Harrington's? He had a lovely demeanour. He could be a waiter or something. Anxiety crept in. Oh dear, she'd have to discuss this with James. No matter how gracious and accommodating he was, he probably had the same concerns.

Beth peered under the bunk and discovered a small, beaten-up suitcase, which she pulled out. She brushed off a layer of dust and opened it. Inside were well-worn jumpers; most appeared too small for the GJ she knew. She wondered if they had belonged to him when he first arrived. There certainly didn't seem to be anything recent in there. When was the last time he'd opened this?

Pushing everything to one side, she discovered a packet of charcoal pencils and a drawing pad. She leafed through it.

'Oh my goodness!'

'Wha'?'

Beth placed the open pad on the bed and heard Bert mutter 'Cor blimey!'

'These look a little like the views at Cavendish, don't you think?'

Bert flicked through the sketches. 'No two ways about it. That's the valley dipping down to the coast — it's even got the church spire in the distance. And look at tha'? That's the edge of the forest that runs alongside your gaff.'

Beth perched on the edge of the bed and examined the drawings. He was clearly a talented artist, especially of landscapes. Although they were not as polished as those she'd seen him do lately, the talent was there for all to see. If he were taught these skills, who taught him? Would a teacher remember him? But where would she search for the teacher? His accent reflected high-class schooling — nothing like the schools you found in the East End. She flicked to the last page.

'Oh look! Who's this?'

Bert frowned, studying the picture of a

woman around forty or perhaps a little younger, wearing a rather pinched expression. 'Dunno. Not sure I wanna know, neither — she reminds me o' those matrons you get in 'ospital.'

'Perhaps this is his mother?'

'He would 'ave mentioned the drawing then, wouldn't 'e?'

Beth sighed. 'I suppose. Perhaps he forgot he had these drawings here. I mean, they were at the bottom of his case, and it doesn't appear as though he's opened it in years.'

Nancy appeared in the doorway. She fastened a loose strand of her hair back into place. 'Sorry to bovver you, yer Ladyship. We was wondering if Jim was coming back? Only that bed's lying empty and someone could make use of it, even if it's just for a few days. We'd never turf Jim out, it's just . . . well, you know.'

Beth took her hand. 'I know, Nancy. Why don't I ask him when we get home? He has an open invitation at our place while we're trying to trace who he is, and I couldn't be so harsh as to throw him out when I've come this far.' She waved the sketchpad at her. 'And here I am with what may be a vital clue.'

Nancy joined them at the bunk. 'Oh, the drawings. I didn't know 'e still had 'em. He's a brilliant drawer, ain't 'e? He's done some o' the people in the Mission — we've go' 'em downstairs in the 'all. D'you wanna see 'em?'

'I'm more interested in this one,' Beth held up the portrait of the lady. 'Do you recognise her? Could she be his mother?'

Nancy took the drawing from her, studied it for a while, then slowly shook her head. 'I've never set eyes on her. As far as I know, 'e don't remember nuffink about his mum. He's never spoken about any family. She's never been 'ere, though; and I'm 'ere all the time with David and 'is mum.'

Bert closed the cabinet doors and prodded the drawings. 'Any chance we could take these with us?' he asked.

'Don't see why not,' she replied.

Beth tidied the area up and the three of them made their way downstairs, where Beth enquired whether the Mission had a telephone. Nancy pushed the chairs under the trestle tables.

'Nah, sorry. We've got the phone box on the corner — just down the road there.'

'Not to worry,' replied Beth. 'I'll get word to you about how long GJ will stay with us. But he'll be with us for at least a couple more nights if not more so please do let someone have that bed.'

Nancy said she was glad he hadn't come to any harm. David joined them. 'Got everyfing you want?' he asked.

Bert held the sketchpad up. 'Yeah, we're taking this with us — see if it jogs 'is memory a bit.'

'You'll let us know wha' you find, won't yer?'

Beth took her purse out and gave him two £5 notes.

'No arguments, please,' she said, as David was about to protest. 'I'd like to donate this to the Mission. And, of course, I'll keep in touch. I'm sure Gentleman Jim will be the first to visit with any news.'

David and Nancy thanked Beth and Bert and wished them all the best with their efforts. Gladys hurried through the hall and wrapped Bert in a bear-hug.

'Cor, blimey, it's been good to see yer, me ol' cocker,' she said. 'Don't you leave it so long next time.'

'I'm always up 'ere love,' replied Bert. 'I just didn't realise you was in 'ere. I'll pop in next Sunday morning. I'll be round the market as normal.'

After a fond farewell, Bert flagged down a taxi and the pair of them journeyed to Victoria Station to catch the train home.

⋆ ⋆ ⋆

James swung the Jaguar onto the drive and parked at the front of the house. He hauled himself out of the confines of his car and stretched his arms high above him. The journey from London had been a long one and he was looking forward to a cup of tea and some sustenance.

In the hallway, he shouted out a quick hello. Beth opened the door from the kitchen.

'Oh sweetie, you're back. I thought you might be a little longer. We've only just got here ourselves.'

He kissed Beth on the cheek. 'I'm gasping for a cup of tea, Beth. Is the kettle on the boil?'

'It certainly is. Bert's on the patio drinking his. Why don't you go and join him? I'll top the pot up.'

'I'll quickly get changed into something a little more casual. Can I have some cake, too?'

Beth grabbed the cake tin and called out. 'Did you have a successful trip?'

James turned at the bottom of the stairs. 'More an interesting one, I think. How about you? Any news on our mystery man?'

'Like you — interesting.'

'Good. We'll have a good catch-up — '

The doorbell rang frantically. James trotted across and opened the front door.

'Stephen!' he gasped. His friend stood before him, nursing a bruised cheekbone and a cut lip. 'What on earth happened to you?'

'Bruiser Jacobs, that's what h-happened.'

14

James ushered Stephen through the house and out onto the patio, where Bert leapt to his feet.

'Blimey, what 'appened to you?' He snatched out a chair for Stephen, who gratefully accepted a seat, while he nursed his sore lip.

Beth arrived with a tray of fresh tea and a fluffy Victoria sponge. She caught her breath on seeing Stephen. 'What on earth happened?' she asked.

Stephen told them Bruiser Jacobs had collared him after the church service. James frowned.

'He was actually in church? Does he attend church?'

'Jacobs, I-I believe, does not attend any religious ceremony,' replied Stephen. 'If he does, I'd b-be surprised. No, he was actually w-waiting for me outside.'

He winced and put a hand to his cheekbone. Beth reached up and turned his face to study the bruising. 'Have you been to the hospital?'

Stephen had, he told her, been seen by the nurse at the cottage hospital. She'd assured him that no bones were broken and the cut lip would heal in a couple of days. As Beth poured the tea, she advised the young vicar to buy some witch-hazel.

'It brings the bruise out quicker,' she explained. 'Actually, I have some in our medicine cabinet, so remind me before you go and I'll give it to you.'

James pulled his plate toward him and cut into his cake. 'So, this Jacobs chap was waiting for you when you finished?'

'Y-yes. I had a chat with everyone as they filed out and, once e-everyone had gone, I went to go back and tidy up. He sort of came out of nowhere.'

Bert scratched his head. 'But what's 'e want with you?'

'Yes, I was about to ask that,' said James. 'He's not still annoyed with you for standing up to him, is he?'

Stephen almost snarled. 'I could have punched him — he's such a vile man. But, he's enormous, isn't he? You can't go

224

pushing people about l-like that. And it doesn't pay to have your parishioners witness their vicar engaged in fisticuffs.'

A murmur of agreement went around the table. Stephen, with some difficulty, took a sip of tea, avoiding the cut on his lip. 'Un-unfortunately, he'd cottoned on to my little *faux pas* from our previous altercation.'

James closed his eyes as Bert and Beth asked for clarification. He went over the unsavoury meeting with Bruiser by the village green and how Stephen had displayed another side to his character when faced with violence.

'Our Stephen put up a good show, but nearly let something slip.' He instinctively lowered his voice. 'He mentioned the riddle.'

A collective 'Oh' prompted Stephen to apologise. 'I-it just came out. That's the trouble wh-when things get heated. You can let your tongue run away with you.'

'So 'e knows about this 'ere riddle?' asked Bert.

'W-well, yes and no.'

James' quizzical frown prompted Stephen to apologise.

'He sort of grabbed me by the collar and asked what I meant about a rhyme. I said I-I didn't know what he was talking about and that he must have misheard or s-something.'

'And that's when things got a little rough?'

Stephen felt his lip and nodded. Bert pushed his flat cap to the back of his head.

'So, bottom line is, 'e don't really know anythin'.'

The vicar's face lit up. 'No, I-I suppose he doesn't.'

'Even so,' said James, 'I'm not convinced that he'll give up that easily. Have you let George know about this?'

Stephen confessed that he hadn't, preferring only to discuss it among friends. 'I didn't know w-whether telling the police would inflame the situation even more.'

'Well, all the Jacobs family are suspects,' said Beth. 'He may have killed Delphine, so we can't take this threat anything less than seriously. I think you should let George know. Don't forget, the last person who attacked you was a killer.'

'H-how could I forget?' He said. Several months back, he and Anne had only just arrived in the village and become involved in the investigation into the death of Alec Grimes. He'd never forget it. Hallowe'en, of all nights, when he'd been hit over the head by that awful woman, Diana. He shuddered.

'A-am I destined to be attacked every time there's a mystery to solve?'

James laughed and slapped him on the knee. 'I wouldn't imagine so, no. But Beth's right. Bruiser Jacobs is a shady character — you need to let George know. Give him a call from here if you like. How's Anne taking it?'

Stephen gave him a sideways glance. 'Well, she's concerned, of course. Angry with Jacobs.'

'But?'

'But, like you, c-certain that one of the Jacobs family is a murderer. She's the one who told me to come over here to t-tell you.'

'She's as bad as James when there's a mystery to solve,' said Beth.

Stephen assured her that he needed no reminding of that fact. He gently bit into his slice of Victoria sponge and licked the crumbs from his lips. 'I'll call George before I leave. B-but, before I do, tell me, were your adventures worthwhile?'

James, Beth and Bert looked at one another, wondering where to start. Beth thought it only fair that James should spill the beans about his trip, especially as his visit related to such an unpleasant death. James settled back in his chair and outlined his discussions with Kushal Patel; from the glorious setting of his residence to the cloak and dagger escapades of Delphine Brooks-Hunter during both wars. His audience listened, spellbound.

'So those rumours in the WI tent were true?' said Beth. 'She *was* a secret agent?'

'It appears so, yes.'

He went on to say that no one seemed to know anything about the sister. Even Kushal hadn't met her. Bert rapped on the table to stop him.

'D'you think she exists, this sister of 'ers?'

James gave an assured nod. 'Of that I am sure. George has been in touch with the local constabulary in Cornwall and they've located her house. She's just not there.'

'Sweetie, do you think they were on good terms?' asked Beth. 'We're assuming they got on, but perhaps they were enemies? Perhaps she has something to do with Delphine being killed, especially as she's not at home? Could she be here in Cavendish? Could she have been at the fair?'

'I never even thought of it like that. I have to admit that I've been so taken with Delphine's character and spirit, that I've been somewhat blind to any potential faults she might have had.'

'Jimmy boy,' said Bert, 'you didn't know 'er well enough to know 'er faults.'

'True,' replied James. 'George certainly has an investigation on his hands. I don't envy him having to trawl through the family archives to discover the reason behind her killing.' A lightbulb flashed in his head. 'I've just remembered something.'

'What is it?' asked Beth.

James quickly detailed the closing moments of his visit with Kushal and the interruption by the rather rude lady who had likened Delphine to Scarlett O'Hara.

'S-Scarlett O'Hara? Whatever f-for?'

'I don't know. I've never really thought about what sort of woman Scarlet is.'

Beth brushed a hair from her eyes. 'Well, I've seen *Gone with the Wind* and read the book. In both, Scarlett was a strong woman, never one to abide by the rules. She could be quite manipulative; attractive to men, but at the same time incredibly beguiling.'

'Well, I can imagine Delphine being all of those things,' replied James. 'Perhaps that's what she meant.'

'But James, if she was accusing Delphine of being like Scarlett, she must be talking about her negative attributes — being manipulative, wilful, stubborn.'

'Mmm. Well, anyway, Mrs Crabtree, her name was. Hideous woman. No dress sense, but clearly well-off. Lives in Wimbledon and gets chauffeured about in a Rolls. She may not have met

Delphine, but she obviously knew of her. I say, you don't think she's the sister, do you?'

Bert pulled a face. 'Not if she's middle-aged, Jimmy boy. Delphine was in 'er seventies. The sisters were palmed off to the mother early on so there can't be an age difference.'

'Well, my friend, regardless of who this woman was, I've got a note of the car's registration number and I know she lives in Wimbledon, so I may get George to track her down. She could be of some help where solving this riddle is concerned.'

'And w-what of our mystery man?'

Beth's eyes lit up. 'Oh, Bert and I had the most wonderful time.'

James listened to his wife described their visit to the East End and how marvellous it had been to explore Petticoat Lane. She broke off halfway to retrieve some material that she'd purchased for Anne. She peeled back the brown paper wrapping to reveal beautiful summer cotton with a white background and huge pale blue roses.

'I hope Anne likes it. I've seen her in this blue before — I think it'll suit her.'

'I-I'm sure it will,' Stephen replied.

She then placed on the table the sketchpad they'd found in GJ's belongings.

'We're going to have to interrogate GJ about these drawings.' She opened the pad and displayed the first sketch.

'I say,' said James, 'that's the view down to the sea from the edge of the forest.'

Beth's eyes were wide with excitement as she flipped over the next two or three, each of them instantly recognisable as local landscapes. James asked if she knew when they were drawn.

'I think quite some time ago,' replied Beth. 'These were at the bottom of a dusty old suitcase; it was full of clothes that wouldn't fit him now. It proves to me he's from around here or he knows this place better than he thinks.'

Bert took the pad and flicked through the pages to the last drawing.

'This is the drawing you wanna be looking at. It's the only one 'e did that isn't a landscape.' He held the drawing up. 'Bi' of a battle-axe, if you ask me.'

James gasped. 'Mrs Crabtree!'

15

James made his way through the bar of the Half Moon toward George, who was supping the top half inch of his pint. Above the chatter, Donovan's voice called out.

'Will you be wanting a drink, your Lordship?'

'Absolutely! A pint of whatever you feel warrants my attention.'

'Right you are.'

James raised his hand in thanks and slipped into the booth opposite George. Outside on the village green, a game of rounders was being set up between the girls and boys. Mark Merryweather was pacing out the pitch and deciding where the bases should be. Georgina Porter followed behind, dropping a jumper wherever he pointed.

Donovan delivered his drink. 'A pint of Golden Harvest. Will you be wanting anything else?'

'No, that's fine, Donovan. But have one yourself.' He handed over some money and raised his glass. 'Cheers.'

' 'tis early in the evening for me,' replied Donovan. 'But, as you're offering. Cheers.'

James took a sip of ale and looked at George. 'So, my friend, how goes the world of sleuthing? Are you any further forward with the Brooks-Hunter murder?'

George drew his attention away from the children and reached inside his jacket to retrieve his notepad. He flipped it open and scowled.

'It's a ruddy slow process, James. Those Jacobs stick together like wet clay. One of 'em's responsible, I know. But they're giving each other alibis like there's no tomorrow. I've found that with fairground folk before.'

'Mmm, they strike me as having a huge network of support,' replied James. 'If one's in trouble, they all rally around and back one another to the hilt. Commendable in a way, but not if someone has committed a crime.'

George agreed. 'We've had a few of the Jacobs family in before for stealing — you know, shoplifting, that type of thing, but they tend to be the youngsters. I don't think this is anything to do with them — this is Reg and Derek's territory.'

'Ah yes, and that cousin of theirs, Bruiser. Did Stephen call you about our little fracas the other day with the said Bruiser?'

'Yes, he did. What do you make of it?'

'Well, I was there, George. Can't imagine that he was there for anything else but to accost us — or, I should say, accost me. Wanted to know why I was included at the meeting with Bateson. We told him to shove off. I say, did you know that Stephen's pretty handy in the boxing ring?'

George indicated that he did, but quickly added that the vicar perhaps wasn't good where quick thinking was concerned. 'He let slip about the riddle, I understand?'

James' finger slid round the rim of his glass. 'Unfortunately, yes. And you know he had an altercation with Stephen just yesterday. Damned thug. What does Bruiser have to say for himself?'

George eased back and gazed out onto the green. He squinted in the brightness of the low evening sun.

'Claims he wasn't anywhere near the fair that day. Went on about Reg and Derek being the guvnors and they didn't need him there. Claims his family never leave their rides. Don't know how he can confirm that if he wasn't there, but he's not the sharpest tool in the box. And he says the attack on the vicar was unfortunate, that he never meant to do it.'

'What about Delphine? What does he know about her?'

George flicked through his notes and quoted word for word. ''She's a stuck-up cow who did nothing to help us. Not a bloody penny she gave us and she's worth a mint. And now she's gone and she's still not giving us a thing. We've struggled all our lives. Snobby bitch.'' He snapped the notebook shut.

James supped his ale and watched the children playing. They'd sorted their teams out — girls versus boys and the game was now under way. Why did the Jacobs clan feel they were due an inheritance? Why did Bruiser think Delphine owed him something? What had happened to make him think that way? Would he kill to get what he wanted? He turned his gaze to George.

'If she's worth a mint, then where on earth is it?'

'I think that's your job, isn't it? Why don't you pop back to the house and have a good nose about? You only really spent time in the drawing room. By the way, what happened with your visit to the Indian chap?'

James went through the details of his meeting with Kushal and updated him on the status of GJ. He clicked his fingers. 'I say, you couldn't do me a favour, could you?'

'As long as it's a legal one.'

'I need to track someone down.' James described his meeting with the formidable Mrs Crabtree, her comments about Delphine and the fact that GJ appeared to be connected in some way. He dug into his trouser pocket for a piece of scrap paper and handed it to George.

'Car registration's there. Rolls Royce

Silver Cloud. She lives in Wimbledon. Could you tell me exactly where in Wimbledon?'

George winced. 'Not really part of your remit is it? You're not an official investigator.'

'But it's part of *your* investigation! I've just given you a link between Delphine and Mrs Crabtree. You're just following it up to eliminate her from your enquiries. That's the phrase, isn't it?'

His friend slipped the paper into his pocket and said that he'd see what he could do. They finished their beers.

'You staying here?' asked George, grabbing his trilby.

'No, I'm popping round to see Charlie Hawkins. Beth's there at the moment discussing the folk day. D'you want to come?'

'Thanks, no. I'll get off and check on your Mrs Crabtree. May need to have a chat with GJ too. Are you sure he was in the house when Delphine was at your fair?'

'I'm absolutely certain. Beth, Anne, Philip, even Harry and Oliver popped their head around the door every so often and not once had he disappeared.'

George's expression was one of resignation as he left the pub. James felt for him. It must be difficult trying to sort the wheat from the chaff in a murder enquiry, especially when it involved the likes of the Jacobs family. At that moment, he didn't envy him his task.

★ ★ ★

Charlie Hawkins' house was only a hundred yards from the pub. His small terraced cottage overlooked the green and, next door in the end house was the library, where he was the sole employee. As always, the welcome at the door was cheery and chirpy and his two children, Tommy and Susan, raced to greet James and update him on their very important news.

'Tommy trod in dog pooh,' Susan stated as her brother giggled beside her.

'It's really stinky,' Tommy added with a proud look on his face.

Charlie playfully admonished his children then ushered them back to the garden and invited James to join him and Beth in the back room. James loved the back room at Charlie's. Although small and cramped, it provided a view of his gloriously colourful garden with a swing in the middle for the children. Charlie, who had lost his wife to pneumonia, was not only the librarian, but a bookworm of the first degree. Accordingly, the shelves were filled to the rafters with tomes of various shapes and sizes on all sorts of topics; from gardening to physics, historical tales to futuristic fantasy, comedy to crime. James waved a hand around the room.

'You know, you should extend the library into your lounge, Charlie.'

'Yeah, I know, there's a lot here, isn't there? I keep meaning to 'ave a clear out and make some room, but I can't throw 'em out.'

'Well,' said Beth, 'why don't you put them in the library? Keep a note of what's yours and, if you ever move, you just take them with you.'

Charlie replied that he was considering this and had drafted a letter to the council for permission. He invited James to sit down and picked up a large glass jug.

'Home-made lemonade. The kids made it — d'you want some?'

James grinned; he could see Tommy and Susan peering in from the garden to witness if he would actually try their concoction. On confirming that he'd love some lemonade, they yelled with excitement and ran back to the swing.

Comfortably seated in an old armchair, James stretched his legs out. 'So, how goes it with the folk day?'

Beth placed her palms together enthusiastically and updated James on the day so far.

'Bob Tanner, of course, is our folk expert, but he couldn't make it today. But, he has sent over some recommendations and Charlie has some good ideas, too.'

Charlie scratched his head. 'Yeah, I thought about expanding it a little. You know we always have a stage on the village green and have various acts going on throughout the day?'

It was the same every year and, James

commented that he didn't really want to change the format too much. 'It works well, don't you think?'

'Well, it does; but this year, we're having two stages. The green's big enough for a platform at both ends and people could visit whichever takes their fancy. If we have completely different sorts of music on at the same time it means that, if you don't like something on one stage, you could go across to the other.'

'But if it's all folk, how are we going to provide different sorts of music?' asked James.

'That, sweetie, is where Charlie has had a brilliant idea.'

'Bob managed to get quite a variety of acts this year, some from other countries who are over here touring the big festivals,' explained Charlie. 'So, we could have our Morris team in one area and Peruvian dancers in another. Traditional singing on one stage, more modern stuff on the other.' He shot a hopeful grin at James. 'What d'you think?'

'I think it's an absolutely splendid idea. Only one problem I see.'

Beth and Charlie enquired what that could be.

'Time. We've only got a few days now to finalise everything.'

Charlie and Beth quickly explained that, while he'd been gallivanting around doing his 'Lord of the Manor' duties, Bob Tanner and Charlie had booked singers, dancers, musicians, storytellers and folklore historians, so it really was just a matter of filling in the gaps and working out a schedule.

'Do we have something for the children?' asked James.

'We do. We've got a Punch and Judy show, plus old-fashioned games, you know, like the hoop and stick, skittles, that sort of thing. Donovan apparently knows a really good clown and he's in the process of booking him. And we have a singer who knows lots of children's songs, so there'll be a special concert, just for them.'

'How absolutely marvellous. Who's the singer?'

Beth and Charlie smirked at each other and this wasn't lost on James.

'Come on, you two. This is obviously someone I know.'

Beth brought her hands together and grinned. 'Mr Bateson.'

'Bateson! The solicitor! Are you serious?'

'Never more so. He knows lots of songs. Well, you know he sings at the local folk club?'

James assured her he knew only too well, but he'd never pictured Bateson entertaining children. But then, he did resemble an eccentric professor and he could imagine the man being quite fun to be around. He shrugged.

'I'm sure it'll be wonderful. And we have the big ceilidh in the evening?'

'Yeah,' said Charlie, 'and guess who we've got for that?'

'I thought Bob Tanner's lot were leading it?'

'He is. But a friend of his is doing a spot in the middle of it.' Charlie waved James closer as he whispered. 'It's got to stay a secret otherwise we'll have the whole of Sussex descending on us.'

James frowned and cocked an ear. But,

much to his annoyance, Charlie simply grinned like an idiot.

'Well, come on man! Spit it out.'

'Lonnie Donegan and his Skiffle Group.'

For once in his life, James was completely speechless. Lonnie Donegan was *the* man of the moment; the king of skiffle who'd had hits across the world with his revamped American Blues and jazzed-up folk songs.

Beth flicked her hair back. 'Isn't it fantastic? Only the three of us know. And Bob Tanner, of course, but we've sworn one another to secrecy. This has to be solely for the Cavendish residents, so no telling.'

James assured them of his utmost discretion. Charlie reached over and grabbed some sheet music.

'And I'm singing, too.'

James studied the sheet music placed before him; 'A Brisk Young Sailor' and 'The White Rose'.

'I didn't think this was your sort of thing, Charlie.'

He replied that it wasn't. 'But Miss

Brooks-Hunter asked me to sing them.'

Both James and Beth stared at each other. James returned the sheet music. 'When did she ask you?'

Charlie reached behind him to grab an envelope, which he promptly handed to James. 'Funny thing — I had this letter from her. Postmarked the day she died — just asking me to sing these songs on the folk day. They apparently mean something to her.'

James slipped the letter out and read through it. 'Has she written to everyone?'

His friend looked as if he were completely in the dark and then James remembered that Charlie didn't know about the riddle, so made out that she'd written to him about the fair and quickly moved on.

'Lonnie Donegan, eh? That's a real coup, isn't it? I hope he doesn't want paying — we could never afford him.'

Charlie assured him that Lonnie was doing it as a favour to Bob. 'Apparently, they go back a long way.'

Satisfied the plans were going well, James and Beth made their excuses to leave and bade Charlie and the children goodbye.

They strolled along the pavement by the village green. The evening sunshine warmed their faces and the laughter of the children on the village green sent a sentimental tingle through them. They sat on a wooden bench to watch them play.

'Sweetie, it seems like only yesterday that Oli and Harry were playing ball here.'

James patted Beth's hands. 'Yes, time certainly does fly by, doesn't it? And now they've spread their wings and are making their own way in life.'

Beth snuggled up to him. 'What did George have to say for himself?'

'He thinks I should have a proper rummage around Delphine's house re the riddle. He thinks I haven't looked through the house properly.'

'He's probably right. You and Bert only retrieved the address book.'

'He wants to speak with GJ too, especially now we can link the three of them together.'

'Well, he'll have to wait. GJ decided he

wanted to walk along the downs and camp out. He said he'd be back in a day or two.'

'You know we can't keep him in the lap of luxury at Harrington's, Beth. We need to think about where he's going.'

'Oh, he's already moved his stuff back to the stables — just for the time being. I think he's a little embarrassed that he can't pay his way.'

James gazed at the sky. He hoped that GJ wasn't involved in this business over Delphine. He'd grown quite fond of the man. And, he needed to stop thinking about GJ and put his mind to this riddle once and for all, but he didn't know where to start. If there was a 'mint' to be had, was it staring him in the face? Perhaps the place was full of antiques?

'Who do we know in the antiques trade? You know, collectables, valuations, that sort of thing?'

Beth answered straight away. 'Your cousin, Herbie.'

James couldn't believe he'd forgotten the most obvious person. 'Herbie, yes, of course. Why didn't I think of him?'

Herbie Harrington rarely visited Cavendish, preferring to stay in the centre of London where he could immerse himself in old buildings, museums, galleries, antique shops and markets. Villages, he said, were incredibly boring with not enough going on. The only time James ever saw him was if he visited the Lanes, a popular area in Brighton.

The Lanes were famous for their cobbled alleyways, packed with tiny shops filled with antique jewellery and furniture. The said cousin had been an auctioneer for Sotheby's, but found it to be a tedious role. Now, he hired himself out as a valuation consultant for the well-to-do and did very nicely at it.

'Mmm, good old Herbie. If I offer him lunch and a jaunt down to the Lanes, d'you think he'll take a gander at Delphine's place?'

'Give him lunch at Harrington's,' replied Beth with a grin, 'and he'll do what you want — you know what an appetite he has.'

James squeezed her hand. 'I'll call him when we get back.'

16

Herbie Harrington's face flushed a deep red as he heaved himself out of James' Jaguar and straightened the jade green waistcoat of his checked suit. He reminded James of an overweight dandy with his slightly effeminate manner and pomposity. Being among lords and ladies was grand enough, but Herbie often behaved as if he were the King of England. His chubby fingers wrapped around an ever-present hip flask as he sipped the contents.

'Cognac, you can't beat it,' he said in a cut-glass accent.

James checked his watch. They'd spent the morning strolling around the Lanes and picked up one or two delightful antiques. Lunch at Harrington's was a somewhat tedious affair, as Herbie had chosen to witter on about himself with no thought or care for anyone else. It was now two in the afternoon and Herbie had already demolished a bottle of Claret over lunch and bored James and Beth to tears with how much better everything was in London. When James had invited Beth along to the Coach House, she quickly feigned a headache and mouthed a silent apology to James. Now, here he was with his awfully condescending cousin and the prospect of another couple of hours in his company. He unlocked the door to the Coach House.

A musty smell greeted them; the sort of odour that announced this was an empty house in need of life and love. Herbie blustered in after James and surveyed the hall with a sneer.

'How quaint!'

James held his tongue and wondered how Herbie had become such an obnoxious individual. He didn't recall the man having been such an oaf when they were smaller. James pushed the lounge door open.

'Why don't we start in here, Herb? Good a place as any?'

Herbie's huge frame appeared to glide effortlessly into the room. For such a heavy man he was amazingly light on his feet. His cousin moved purposefully from one area to another, picking up what few ornaments there were, checking hallmarks, styles and veneers. He peered at paintings, examined the furniture and leafed through various books, records and magazines. Finally, he stuck his nose up.

'Nothing, dear boy.'

'Are you sure?'

Herbie peered at him with a haughty air. James shrugged and invited him to cross through to the study. He watched as Herbie went through the same routine. If this had been anyone else, he'd question their knowledge simply because of the speed he did things. However, one thing he knew for sure — Herbie might be a pain in the neck but, where antiques and collectables were concerned, he certainly knew what he was talking about.

After attending boarding school near Chichester, he had progressed to Cambridge to study the History of Art and, during that time, made some useful connections with those in the antiques business. To be fair to him, he had worked hard and studied for several years to become one of the most respected people in the business where valuations were concerned. It was a shame that with his aloof attitude he distanced himself from many potential clients.

He worked the room as the professional he was; knowing exactly what to look for, where to examine hallmarks and signatures and indeed whether any item even deserved a cursory glance. In twenty minutes, Herbie had swept through the ground floor with precision and accuracy. He flopped down on the sofa and waved an empty hip flask at James.

'I take it you are going to refresh me, James. Valuation is thirsty work.'

'Absolutely, old chap. I was just admiring your speed and skill. You certainly know a thing or two about your subject.'

'I do and, unfortunately, no examples of it are here. I thought you said this lady was well-to-do?'

James found the drinks cabinet and poured them both a sherry. 'Oh, she is . . . was. She was a delightfully elegant lady of immaculate taste.'

Herbie sneered as he accepted his sherry. 'Well, the items here are of no value whatsoever. Pretty, yes; tasteful, yes. But valuable? No.' He waved a beckoning hand. 'This rhyme . . . riddle, or whatever the ditty is called that you mentioned — do you have it?'

James placed his glass down. He hadn't meant to tell Herbie about the rhyme; it had come out mid-sentence during a chat as they wandered through the Lanes. He retrieved the riddle from his pocket and, with strict instructions that Herbie should tell no one, he handed the paper over. His boozy eyes scanned it and, again, the top lip sneered.

'Why didn't she just write a letter? This is drivel. What a mundane life she led if she had to write this sort of thing to liven it up. Did she harbour dreams of being some sort of heroine? Amelia Earhart or Mata Hari? Pah!'

James let out a laugh. Mata Hari was the famous female spy of the Great War. If only Herbie knew! His cousin glared at him, swigged the sherry down in one go and marched upstairs to the two small bedrooms built under the eaves. He called back to James.

'I trust you'll get me on the ten to four train?'

'Of course,' he said as he gulped his sherry down and followed his cousin up into the first bedroom. If he could get him on an earlier one he would. He'd had about enough of his pomposity for one day.

'Tch,' was the only sound emitted from Herbie as he surveyed the room and its contents. 'One thing I will say for her,' he said, looking at the bed linen. 'Dorma bedding — very nice.' He brushed past James and into the second room.

'Ah-ha!'

James rushed inside. 'I say, have you found something?'

Herbie held up a small glass bowl. 'This is rather delicious. Lalique, French Art Nouveau. Not worth a fortune, dear chap, but in auction would fetch the price of a car.'

He replaced the bowl and picked up something small. James peered over his shoulder.

'The Roaring Twenties, dear boy. A delightful cameo encrusted with diamonds. This would buy you another car, should you desire.'

'Herbie, I don't receive any of this — it goes to the estate. I need something that is worth a mint and fits with the riddle.'

Herbie swept past him and peered into the bathroom. 'Then you're wasting your time.' He looked up and groaned. 'Loft — you don't want me to go up there, surely?'

James eagerly told Herbie that he did. After what he'd found in the loft when investigating the murder of Alec Grimes, he wasn't going to overlook this one.

However, after some difficulty getting up there, the loft proved to be merely the resting place of a Christmas tree and a box of children's toys, neither of which were of any value. James passed them down to Herbie.

'May as well have everything to hand,' said James. 'I wonder if our primary school teacher would be interested in the toys?'

'Give them a good wash first — they're filthy.'

James placed them on a small occasional table as Herbie returned to the lounge and helped himself to a large slug of sherry.

'Dear boy, I rather think this old girl had a screw loose. I'd not bother about seeking a fortune. Apart from those two pieces up there, she has nothing of value here.'

James put his hands in his pockets. Should he tell Herbie about Delphine's tales of espionage? No. It was a pound to a penny that his cousin wouldn't keep it to himself. It would be all over London before the end of the day and, no doubt, embellished beyond recognition. He jumped as the front door burst open.

'Where is it?' hollered a female voice.

James rushed into the hall to be confronted by Jackie Connor.

'I say, what on earth are you doing? Barging in here as if you own the place.'

Herbie peered round the door frame as Jackie stabbed a finger at James.

'Me? I've more right to it than you. She was family — you ain't. I've more right than you to be 'ere.'

Herbie waded in. 'You, dear lady, are more suited to the zoo than this historic coach house.'

James quickly stepped between the two as he glared at Herbie. 'Excuse my cousin, Miss Connor. I'm sure he didn't mean to offend.'

'I'm sure I did, dear boy. But, if you must be conciliatory, don't mind me.' Herbie then returned to the sherry bottle in the lounge.

'What is it you want, Miss Connor?' asked James.

To James' horror, Derek Jacobs strode in behind her, kitchen knife in hand. 'Wha' we want, your Lord 'igh and mighty, is the rhyme. That's why you're 'ere, ain't it?'

James closed his eyes in frustration and held his hands up. He wished he'd never told anyone about it. 'Your aunt gave me the task of solving it, and solve it I will. I'm afraid you won't bully me into parting with it.'

His heart skipped a beat as Derek came toward him. 'You wouldn't want anyone to get 'urt, would you?' said Derek.

'It's no good you threatening me,' replied James, trying to keep his voice level. 'You know the story where the will is concerned. If there's any foul play, you won't see a penny. Now, clear off before I call the police.'

James held his breath as Derek lunged. The knife pressed against his neck and Derek's breath was hot on his face.

'Jackie. Search 'is pockets.'

Jackie's hands deftly searched James' jacket pockets and brought out the only item she could find — his wallet. Derek snatched it from her and leafed through three five pound notes before finally spotting a piece of paper. He pulled it out, quickly scanned it and held it up triumphantly.

'So, you don't 'ave it on yer? Yer lying toe-rag.' Derek pushed the slip of paper into his pocket and threw the wallet back at James. 'Come on, Jackie, we'll see who gets to the treasure first.'

James' heart thumped with rage. Damn it! He rushed to the telephone, picked up the receiver and hammered the cradle.

'Are you calling your detective friend?'

said Herbie, studying his nails. He'd been watching with mild curiosity from the lounge, but seemed to feel no inclination to come to James' aid.

'I would do if the phone wasn't cut off. Blast and damnation.' He turned to Herbie. 'Come on, I'll drop you at the station and call him from home.'

Herbie retrieved his fedora and glided out of the house. 'I wouldn't worry, dear boy. The two of them looked as if they shared the one brain cell between them. If you can't solve it, I'm sure they won't, either.'

James appreciated Herbie's loyalty and support. He was probably right, but it wouldn't hurt to keep George informed. Perhaps he could put some sort of watch on the house.

True to his word, the following morning George had arranged for a policeman to stand guard. However, by the time he'd arrived, the rose garden at the front of the Coach House resembled a freshly ploughed field.

★　★　★

James and Beth, hands on hips, surveyed the scene. The pretty garden surrounded by a box hedge resembled a rubbish tip, with earth strewn across the lawn and roses uprooted. Anne retrieved a spade from the back of the car.

'I think we can save these roses if we dig them back in now. What d'you think?'

Beth's eyes lit up. 'I think you're right. Do you have another spade?'

'No. But I do have a trowel. It's in the car.' Anne turned on her heels and marched purposely toward their Austin 30.

James wandered around the borders and studied each vandalised rose. There were about a dozen plants in total and, after a quick deliberation, he was satisfied that they had not found Delphine's fortune. It would appear that the plants had been ripped from the ground, and the earth beneath the roots had been disturbed. Beth and Anne, now armed with garden tools, made a start on replanting. He called across.

'I'm taking a look inside. Won't be long.'

For an instant, James wondered if they had broken in to the property as well as destroyed the garden, but it was clear they hadn't. Herbie was right; they didn't have a clue what they were searching for and had taken the riddle too literally. But a rose is a prominent feature. He took out the original copy of the rhyme. Thankfully he'd held on to this one. The word 'rose' was spelt with a capital. Could that be a name instead of a flower? He didn't know of anyone by the name of Rose in the village. No one of that name had been mentioned in any conversation.

He wandered into the drawing room and leafed through Delphine's address book. No Rose there. Easing himself down into the wing-backed chair he rested his head back. The chintz wallpaper was full of roses. He pursed his lips. Damned roses were everywhere. A gentle tap on the door brought him out of his thoughts.

'Ah, hello George,' he said absently.

'We've got Derek Jacobs and Jackie Connor down the station about digging up this garden.'

'And?'

'They swear blind they'd nothing to do with it. Can't prove anything. No witnesses. It's got to be them, but unless I've got some proof, there's nothing I can do. Unless, of course, you want to put in a charge for assault.'

James winced. 'Not particularly. I don't want to add fuel to an already burning fire. What about mud on the shoes and all that?'

'Couldn't find anything.' George flopped into the chair opposite. 'That Bruiser bloke was there this morning when we picked 'em up. Perhaps I should've brought 'em all in.'

'They're all capable. Any footprints left here?'

'No. Funny that — I thought they might have been a little careless and left something, but the earth was all turned over. Covered their tracks well.'

'You're pretty sure this *is* the Jacobs family and their lot?'

'Absolutely,' replied George. 'I haven't got any other leads. I just need proof. I'm pretty sure one of 'em killed Delphine.

They obviously dug the garden up, especially as they nicked that riddle from you. You sure you don't wanna press charges for threatening you?'

James gave a vigorous shake of the head. 'No. No, I don't. I'd much rather they think they've got away with everything than start angling for minor charges.' He pushed himself out of the chair and examined the painting on the wall. 'That looks like the front garden, doesn't it?'

George joined him and peered at the picture. He leant forward to read the signature. 'Can't make that out. Looks like initials — S C or S G something or other.'

'No matter,' replied James. 'This isn't getting us anywhere. I say, did you have any luck with that Crabtree woman?'

George gave a brief nod. 'Yes. That's an interesting one.' He felt in his pocket and brought out a slip of paper. 'Before I part with this, I'm going to give you an order and you've got to promise to stick to it.'

James waited. George lowered his voice.

'Mrs Crabtree is one Mrs Hyacinth Crabtree, sister-in-law to one of the top men in MI6. Her husband works there, too, but at a much lower rank.'

James let out a whistle of surprise. George thrust the slip of paper at him. 'If you go and see her, you're to be subtle and diplomatic and speak to her only about your task. Do I have your word?'

James read the paper with a Wimbledon address. MI6. This was getting more mysterious by the minute. He steered George out to the hall.

'This is too unbelievable, don't you think? Delphine Brooks-Hunter is a spy and now we've discovered that this Crabtree woman is related to people in MI6. And who's in the middle of all this? GJ. All three of them link together in some way and, as an extension to that, so do the Jacobs family.'

'About the GJ link,' said George. 'Do you think this Crabtree woman is his mother?'

'No, no, I don't think so although I have no proof of that.'

George felt for his pipe. 'Are you

absolutely sure he has amnesia? It's odd that he pitches up the day the old lady is killed. If you ask me, he's as shifty as that Jacobs lot. In fact I might see if there's a link between those two.'

'Absolute rot,' replied James. 'Jackson's diagnosed amnesia and GJ is a genuine sort.'

'You're too trusting by half, James.' With that, George recited what seemed like an endless list, counting on each finger as he did so. 'How easy is it to fake memory loss? How convenient that he suddenly pitches up at your place at the time of the fair? How convenient that Reg and Derek Jacobs and Delphine are all there on the same day? How convenient that this GJ knows Mrs Crabtree? Odd that Delphine's killed the day he's in the area.'

George summed it all up by announcing they had absolutely no information on GJ, his background, enemies, etc. 'For all we know, he may be a spy himself.'

James chewed his lip. He was right, of course. It was all too coincidental that everyone involved in the murder and the mystery of the riddle were connected in some way. He waved the slip of paper at George.

'Well, there's only one thing for it,' he said. 'I have to have a firm talk with GJ. I think he's back today or tomorrow.'

'He better be,' said George. 'I don't like the fact that he's suddenly gone AWOL. If you see him before me, I want to get one thing clear before you do anything.'

James gave him his full attention.

'When you speak to him, you speak to him about the rhyme and Mrs Crabtree. You *don't* speak to him about Delphine's murder. That's my area. Stick to the task given to you by Miss Brooks-Hunter. If I hear you've veered off the subject, I'll arrest you. Understood?'

James clicked his heels and saluted. 'Yes, sir!'

17

The stream glinted in the sunlight as it meandered through the grounds at Harrington's. The gentle trickle of water across pebbles brought a sense of calm and tranquillity. A kingfisher studied its flow from a protruding branch, while an otter scurried along the riverbank and out of sight.

James, kitted out in fishing waders, focussed on the float bobbing up and down in the shallows. His companion for the day, GJ, had returned as promised and had set himself up a few yards away, sketching the area with a set of coloured pencils. He reached down for the tartan flask and spoke softly to James.

'Do you want some tea?'

'Splendid idea.' James waded back to the clearing, placed his rod on a rest and settled down in his fishing chair. 'Did Beth pack something to eat, too?'

GJ laughed as he picked through the

items. 'She must think we're away for a couple of days. We have everything — sandwiches, pork pies, tomatoes, all sorts. What d'you fancy?'

'I'll have one of those pork pies and some mustard.'

James explained that their local butcher, Graham, made the pies and that the meat came from the smallholding he'd started. The diced and tender pork was wrapped in fresh aspic jelly and encased in the crustiest pastry imaginable. He smeared a section with mustard and took a bite. Holding it up triumphantly, he declared that you couldn't beat a good quality pork pie. GJ mirrored him by complimenting the cheese.

'Yes,' said James, 'that is rather tasty, isn't it? It's made down the road, you know, at the Rottingdean farm.'

'The place with the horses?'

'That's the one. We do a fair amount of business with them where the food is concerned. Didier orders most of our cheese from them now. That one you're eating makes a particularly good cheese sauce.'

GJ enquired if this was relevant to the

Harringtons' Welsh Rarebit that Beth had spoken about.

'Ah yes,' James responded. 'You'll have to taste that and see what you think. We put the same sauce over cauliflower, too. I'm not a great lover of cauliflower, but if you shove on some of Granny's sauce, it becomes the jewel in the crown.'

'Perhaps you should do a cheese and wine party?' suggested GJ.

'I say, what a splendid idea!' James filed the notion away to discuss with Beth. In the meantime, he had a more pressing exchange that he'd been putting off. 'GJ, I need you to be straight with me. Do you mind me asking a few rather impertinent questions?'

GJ shifted his chair to give James his full attention. 'Of course not. I've been living off your hospitality for long enough and you and Lady Harrington have done so much for me. It's the least I can do.'

'I'll get the impertinent question out of the way and my reason for asking. The question is, do you really have amnesia?'

James noted the surprise on GJ's face. 'Well, yes . . . of course,' he replied, flustered. 'Why . . . what . . . do you not believe me?'

'Had to ask, old chap, and here's the reason why.' James stretched a hand down and retrieved the sketch pad that Beth had found from his belongings in London. GJ gawped.

'Crikey, I haven't seen that in ages,' he said. 'I'd forgotten I still had it.'

James opened it to the picture of Mrs Crabtree. 'The lady that was killed the day we found you and your old gal here are linked in some way.'

GJ nearly choked on his tea. James leant forward. 'And I believe you may be connected to both of them.'

'You don't think I killed that old lady, do you?'

James held his hands up. 'Personally, no, but my friend George will be questioning you because of the link, so be prepared. My interest is solely to do with your relationship with the said lady in your drawing — Mrs Crabtree.'

'Crabtree . . . ' GJ gazed at the picture. 'It's so long since I've seen this sketch. I'd forgotten all about it.'

James repeated the name and allowed time for it to sink in. If one could view the internal workings of the brain, he felt sure the cogs in GJ's mind would be whizzing around like whirling dervishes. After a while, a spark of recognition flashed across the young man's face.

'Hyacinth! Hyacinth Crabtree.' GJ strained to remember. 'Yes, yes: Mrs Crabtree — I lived with her.' He stared at James in amazement. Then a broad smile. 'She's the one who brought me up.' He shook his head in disbelief and stared at the picture. 'I think I called her Auntie.'

James remained quiet, hoping that the young man would continue to remember.

GJ screwed his face up, trying desperately to retrieve lost memories. 'Yes! Yes, I remember now, I called her Aunt. Aunt Hyacinth. And she was married.' He looked to the sky for inspiration. 'What was his name?' The cogs spun again. Round and round. 'Hyacinth and . . . oh God, what was it. Peter. That's it. Aunt Hyacinth and Uncle Peter!' He laughed. 'My God, I can't believe it. Have you found her?'

For what seemed the hundredth time, James went through the details of his visit to Kushal and the appearance of the bombastic Mrs Crabtree.

'Was she like that with you?'

GJ was quiet for a while, obviously trying to come to terms with his memories. Eventually, he gave a wry grin.

'I don't know. I do think that I may have been an inconvenience but I don't know why. Perhaps I was in the way. I don't feel any warmth toward her at the moment.' He cut off a chunk of cheese. 'Uncle Peter.' He repeated the name several times. 'I have vague memories of getting on with him. I think.' He stared at the stream. 'I remember having nice clothes and a school uniform. I don't know what school or where it was though. But I don't ever remember having bedtime stories or being cuddled or anything. Perhaps those memories will return now they've been jogged.'

James couldn't imagine the Mrs Crabtree he encountered being at all maternal and he felt for him. One thing never missing in the Harrington household was love and affection. And he would never have dreamed of allowing Oliver or Harry to go to sleep without a story. He placed the sketchbook on the ground.

'They live in Wimbledon. Did you live there? Do you remember it at all?'

GJ nodded slowly and said that it sounded familiar, but he couldn't be certain. 'I *think* I went to school in Wimbledon.'

'Do you know anyone who works for MI6?'

The young man appeared startled by the reference. He frowned. 'No, should I?'

James shrugged as GJ reached down for the pad and studied the drawing of Hyacinth Crabtree.

'Why didn't she try and find me? Not that I want to go back. I've got my own life now. May not be much, but it's mine.'

'Perhaps she did,' replied James. 'Does any of this help with knowing how you lost your memory?'

'I wish it did. Lord Harrington, how does Aunt Hyacinth come to know the lady that was killed here?'

'Good question. I don't suppose your Hyacinth had a sister?'

'Not that I remember. I think she was an only child. What was the name of the lady that died?'

James glimpsed Beth walking toward them. 'Delphine Brooks-Hunter.' He scrutinised GJ for a glimmer of recognition, but none came. The young man got up and opened a garden chair for Beth. She brushed a hand down the sleeve of her cardigan.

'This is infuriating. That shrub growing down by the river, it's so sticky. It leaves a residue on everything it touches. This was clean on today and I'll have to wash it again.'

'I know the shrub you mean,' said GJ. 'I don't think it's the shrub itself. I think it may have mealy bugs on it. They're the cause of the residue.'

'Oh well that's helpful to know. Can I get rid of mealy bugs?' Beth asked.

'Yes, you can,' replied GJ. 'It's unusual to get them outside but, if you're going to get them, it's generally in southern England. I would cut the shrub right down and use some sort of plant wash. That should do it.'

Beth beamed. 'You really know a lot of

things for someone so young. How did you know that?'

GJ shrugged. 'I'm sure it'll come back to me. Where is the shrub? I can cut it back for you, if you'd like.'

'It's in the clearing, where we found poor Delphine.'

'Well, you show me where that is and I'll treat it for you.'

Beth helped herself to some lemonade and said she'd show him once she'd had some refreshment. Meanwhile, James revealed that Mrs Crabtree was 'Aunt Hyacinth' and that she belonged to GJ.

'Well, we're not entirely sure if she is a true aunt or one of those ladies you *call* aunt.'

She put a hand over her heart. 'Well, sweetie, that's incredible.' She reached for GJ's hand. 'Isn't that good news?'

GJ and James shared mutual cautionary looks, which Beth noticed straightaway. 'What is it?'

'Well, darling, GJ here doesn't think he got on that well with the said Aunt Hyacinth. So, it's good news that he can remember, but he's not too keen on returning to the fold.'

'But it will help get your memory back,' she said to GJ. Her eyes opened wide in anticipation. 'Why don't I take the Jaguar and give GJ a tour of Wimbledon?'

James knew better than to dampen what was actually a good idea. GJ sought his approval and he shrugged, gesturing that it was entirely up to the pair of them what they did.

'I have a folk day meeting and want to get together with Bert about something, so the pair of you can do as you please.'

Beth tucked her hair behind her ears. 'That's settled then.' She turned to James. 'What are you doing with Bert?'

James looked innocent. 'Oh, nothing much.' Seeing Beth wasn't convinced, he added, 'He just mentioned meeting for a pint, that's all.'

After a delightful picnic and with three trout bagged for lunch, they made their way through the woodland where Beth pointed out the offending sticky shrub. GJ promised to cut it back for her then headed off for the stables. James and Beth returned home. As they entered the hall, the phone rang. James lifted the receiver.

'Ah, hello, George. Everything all right?'

'Yes, everything's fine. I've just been chatting with the Reverend Merry weather. Thought he ought to know first. Delphine's sister, Juliet Brooks-Hunter, has told us that she wants the funeral to be held in Cornwall. She wants it to be a private affair — no guests, just her and the local vicar. She's refusing to see me, but I'll get one of the locals to pop round and ask her a few questions.'

James scratched his head in confusion. 'But Delphine spent most of her time in Sussex. Why on earth cart her down to Cornwall?'

'No idea,' replied George. 'This Juliet woman seems a little odd. Doesn't want anyone to see her. Didn't speak with me, just got someone to pass the message on.'

'Can we send flowers?'

'I suppose. Get in touch with Stephen, he'll tell you who's organising everything.'

James replaced the receiver and immediately picked it up again. Checking his address book, he dialled the number for the Half Moon pub. Kate Delaney answered.

'Ah, hello Kate. James here. I say, you don't happen to know if Bert is on your premises, do you?'

'He certainly is. Do you want a word?'

'No, just keep him there for ten minutes. I need him to assist me with something.'

Kate assured him she would. He hung up and swung round to see Beth standing in the doorway with her hands on her hips.

'James, what are you up to?'

He walked over and kissed her forehead. 'If you must know, I'm paying a visit to Reg Jacobs.' He put a finger on Beth's lips. 'And before you admonish me, I'm not investigating the murder. This relates to the riddle and may help sort out the mystery of our young man.'

As James grabbed his car keys, Beth called out after him. 'Just be careful.'

He waved a farewell. He didn't think she had anything to worry about. Having Bert with him might actually force Reg Jacobs into being a little more co-operative.

18

Using his binoculars, James peered through the windscreen of his Austin Healey. Reg Jacobs lived in a caravan on a piece of rough ground on the outskirts of Brighton. The Jacobs family, including the Trents and Connors, resided alongside one another in trailers, all of which were in various states of disrepair. Bert lit a cigarette.

'Jimmy boy, d'you think this is a good idea? I know you wanted a bit o' muscle, but I can't fight the Jacobs clan if they get nasty. They'll 'ave all sorts up there, not just muscle.'

James squinted through the lenses. 'As far as I can tell, there's no one around. We may have had a wasted journey.'

'Does Bruiser live 'ere?'

'I'm not entirely sure.' James scanned further up the field where the fairground machinery stood securely fastened under green tarpaulins. He placed the binoculars on the rear seat.

'Well, I don't intend going in with all guns blazing,' he said. 'We'll be polite and, if things start getting out of hand, we'll dash off pretty damned quickly.'

He started the engine and edged the Austin forward, steering her off the main road and onto the dirt track leading to the site. A curtain twitched in the far caravan. James turned the car around, mindful that it would help to be parked in the right direction should they need to make a dash for it. They got out of the car and observed the trailers. An eerie silence loomed over them. Although it was a pleasant day, weather-wise, James shivered — it all felt rather unnerving.

The door to the far caravan opened and Reg Jacobs stood in the entrance. He was a similar height to James with wavy grey hair combed back. A faded anchor was tattooed on his forearm and his fingers were stained with tobacco. Although grey, his eyebrows remained dark.

James swallowed his nerves and instinctively stood tall to help give him some confidence. 'Ah, hello Mr Jacobs.'

Bert stuffed his hands in his pockets,

grunted a greeting and followed James up the incline. Reg jumped down from the trailer and wiped his hands on a filthy tea towel. He glowered at the pair of them.

'Wha' you doin' 'ere?' His eyes darted around the site. 'You been watching us? Waiting for them to go?'

James held his palms up and assured him that he'd been doing no such thing. 'To be honest, I didn't know whether anyone would be here. It's getting toward summer — you probably have a lot of work this time of the year.'

Reg shrugged and picked up a bottle of beer from just inside the trailer. He took a swig and scraped his sleeve across his mouth. 'You're 'ere now. Whatcha want?'

James felt a tension he hadn't realised was there. 'Simply to talk, Mr Jacobs. Can we sit down and do this pleasantly?'

Jacobs frowned. 'Or what?'

Bert sidled up to James. 'Or nothing. He's being polite, if it didn't escape yer notice.'

Jacobs shrugged again, kicked a couple of upturned tea chests and told them to take a pew. He collected two more beer bottles and held them out to Bert and James. Bert used his key-ring to flip the tops off. James detested drinking from the bottle but, mindful of keeping tempers on an even keel, accepted it from him.

'Mr Jacobs, I have to tell you that it's not my intention to stop you claiming what is rightfully yours.'

Reg said nothing.

'I hardly knew Delphine,' continued James. 'The first I knew about any of this fortune business was after she died. To this day, I have no idea why she chose me to help. But choose me she did, so we're both stuck with it.'

Reg remained still.

'Thing is, Reg, I'm on the same side as you. Simply trying to get to the truth, so that Delphine can rest in peace and you can claim whatever's due to you.'

Reg glared and took a step toward him. 'She should've known better than to mess with us Jacobs, stuck-up bitch.' He pointed to his wrists. 'We've got the same blood running through our veins. What made 'er so special?' He came so close that James feared things would get nasty.

'You think she was charming, sophisticated, don't ya? Well, there's another side to 'er that no one saw.'

Jacobs then appeared to regret what he'd just said and James wasn't slow to pick up on it.

'What side would that be, Reg?'

Reg swigged his beer and told James to keep his nose out. 'It's family business. Nothin' to do with you.'

James eyes went heavenward in exasperation. 'But, surely if it helps to solve matters and get to the bottom of things, it would be best if I knew. Whatever you tell me goes no further. You have my complete assurance on that.'

Reg studied him and shifted his attention to Bert. He tossed a nod at him. 'And you? How do I know I can trust you?'

Bert pushed his cap back and scratched his head. 'You don't. You don't know me from Adam, but I ain't a squeaky clean member of the Cavendish community. I'm an East Ender, who does dodgy business with the likes of you all around the south-east. I've done time and I don't grass on anyone.'

James stared at him. Done time? When on earth did that happen? He proffered a quick smile at Reg. 'There you have it. A lord of the manor who can be trusted with anything and an ex-con whose life wouldn't be worth living if he turned out to be a grass.'

Reg scanned the area, over-zealous in scrutinising every nook and cranny for movement. Finally, he relaxed and focussed on the rim of his beer bottle. 'Did you know that my aunt was a spy?'

James closed his eyes in frustration. 'You have to give me more than that, Reg. I discovered that ages ago.'

'She spent a lot of time in Germany. She spoke fluent German. She smuggled plans and orders out. I dunno how she did it, but she did. She must've been workin' with someone else. She was always mixing with the German officers — even met Hitler, I 'eard.'

James couldn't help but think how remarkable she had been, to have come face to face with such an evil man and seemingly fool him and his entourage.

But nothing Reg said was new and he told Reg as much.

'There must be something else, Reg. Didn't she ever say anything to you?'

Reg leapt up and smashed his empty bottle against the caravan. Splinters of glass rained to the ground. Bert tensed, ready to put up a fight.

'She said nothin'. I know she mixed with the Nazis and their like; went to parties with society toffs. Loved it, she did, made her feel special.' He ran his hands through his hair. 'Then she'd come back 'ere with gifts. Not gifts for us. Oh no, gifts she'd 'ad given to 'er by the government. *Our* government — for services rendered.'

Bert stood up and offered him a cigarette. 'What sort o' gifts?'

'What sort of gifts? Not a box a bloody chocolates and some flowers, I can tell you that. Oh no, works of art, first edition books, expensive watches and clocks. Thousands o' pounds worth of antiques and collectables. The 'ouse was full of 'em.' He lunged forward and grabbed James by the collar. 'Where's it all gone?'

Bert pulled him back. 'Clobbering 'im won't get you anywhere.'

Reg snarled at Bert. 'It'd make me feel better, though.' He pushed James back in his seat and faced Bert. 'And that bloody rhyme is the key to it all.' He glared at James. 'And you've got that. Who's to say you won't solve it and nick the lot?'

James had heard enough. He pushed himself up from the tea chest and eyed Reg.

'What absolute rot. If you've got nothing to do but accuse an already wealthy man of stealing from a delightful old lady, then we've wasted our time. I was hoping that we might be able to work together and solve this between us, but you're clearly focussed on disrupting my efforts as well as your own.' He brushed him aside. 'I'll carry on without your help. It'll just mean that you'll get your fortune, if you're due it, later than hoped.'

Reg hollered. 'I don't know any more than you do.'

'I'm sorry, Reg, but I don't believe you.'

'Well, ask that fella of 'ers, then.'

James stopped in his tracks. 'What fella?'

Reg studied his shoes and shuffled uncomfortably. 'No one.'

'Are you talking about Kushal?'

'Kushal? Wha' sort o' name's that?'

James decided that Reg was altogether too shifty. Did he really not know Kushal? He'd put on a good act if he did. He pushed again for information, but Reg put the barriers up, swearing blind that it was family business. Clearly, he wasn't going to say anything more. James studied the man and decided to throw a name at him.

'What about Mrs Crabtree?'

Although it was tiny, James recognised a flinch when he saw it. He'd have missed it if he'd blinked, but it was there, he was sure of it. Here, at last, was a trace of recognition, albeit fleeting.

'Never 'eard of 'er. Who's she?'

James handed his full beer bottle to Reg. 'Come along, Bert, we're not getting anywhere here.' He turned to Reg. 'If you do think of anything, you know where I am.'

When he reached the car, he called back. 'And remember what I said earlier. I am on the same side as you, Reg. I'm not here to swindle your family. Perhaps you could tell that imbecile cousin of yours, Bruiser. He seems intent on threatening all and sundry.'

On the drive back to Cavendish, Bert swigged down the rest of his beer. 'He's holding back.'

'Yes, isn't he just?' replied James through gritted teeth. The man had really got under his skin. 'But what's he holding back? If it's not the spy business, what is it?'

'I wonder who that fella is he was talking about?'

'And he knew Mrs Crabtree. Or he's certainly heard of her.'

They drove in silence, each lost in their own musings. James had so many thoughts going round his head he felt his brain would melt. If his instincts were correct, Reg honestly hadn't heard of Kushal, so that couldn't be the man he was referring to. Had Delphine been having some sort of secret liaison? Had she been having an affair? And Mrs Crabtree — where did she fit into all of this? A moment of inspiration came. He slammed his foot on the brake and the Austin skidded to a halt. Bert planted his hands on the dashboard.

'Bloody 'ell, Jimmy boy! Whatcha playing at?'

'This mystery man of Delphine's,' said James. 'Do you think he could be quite high up in the government?'

Bert, still getting over the shock of the sudden stop, shrugged. 'How should I know?'

'Reg Jacobs knows of Mrs Crabtree. Whether he's met her is neither here nor there, but he knows about her, that's something I'm sure of. Mrs Crabtree is married to someone in MI6, whose brother is one of the top people in the same organisation. She likened Delphine to Scarlett O'Hara.'

'You think that's the fella?'

'Don't you?'

'It 'adn't crossed my mind, no. You're taking a leap, Jimmy boy. Bit of an age difference. That Mrs Crabtree you reckon is around the fifty-ish mark, didn't you say?'

James restarted the engine. 'It's no good, Bert. I'm going to have to pay our Mrs Crabtree a visit. I'll give her a call when I get home.'

'Drop me off at my accountant, will you?' said Bert.

James almost ran into a tree. 'Accountant? Do you have an accountant?'

His chum expanded. 'Turf accountant, Jimmy boy. There's some good 'orses running at Epsom.'

James grinned and steered the car toward the village. 'By the way, I didn't know you'd been in prison? When was that?'

'I 'aven't. I just visited a mate, but I weren't gonna tell Reg Jacobs that.'

*   *   *

After dropping Bert off at the bookies James went straight home, where he found a gaggle of villagers discussing the folk day preparations. Around the patio table were Stephen, Anne, Charlie,

Professor Wilkins and Beth, who rose to greet him with a kiss.

'We're having a quick update on the folk day. We wanted to make sure we have everything arranged. Can you join us?'

'Absolutely. I'll get myself a drink first.'

Anne waved a bottle at him. 'We've pushed the boat out and opened some wine.'

James pulled a chair up alongside her. 'Splendid. Pour away, old thing.'

Stephen helped himself to a cracker and a slice of stilton. 'I — it's all coming along quite nicely,' he said. 'Do you do this every year?'

'Every year without fail,' James replied, reaching across for his own cracker. 'I can't actually remember a time when we didn't do it.'

Beth topped her glass up. 'We even carried it on during the war. Do you remember, darling?'

'That's right, we did. Thought it'd be good to keep the traditions going and it turned out to be a roaring success.'

Professor Wilkins, who headed up the historical society, expressed his interest.

Although he was a serious-minded and cantankerous individual, if there was anything offered that meant continuing tradition and history, he was a great supporter.

'I think it's good to have two stages this year,' he said. 'Who decided that?'

'Nothing to do with me,' said James, reaching for some more cheese. 'I think it was Beth, Charlie and Bob Tanner between them. Jolly good idea, though, don't you think? Music at one end, dancing down the other, something happening in the middle — no time to get bored. Do we have everything arranged?'

Beth, who was the other side of Anne, moved in to examine the schedule in front of them. 'We're starting at two o'clock on the village green. We have two Morris sides coming, our own Cavendish troupe and the Chanctonbury crowd. We've also got a ladies' clog team from Lancashire.'

'How are we going to hear the clogs on grass?'

'They're gonna be on the cobbles outside the pub,' said Charlie.

Anne continued. 'The Morris teams are rotating and, in between times, we have a group of Bavarian folk dancers. They're touring at the moment and Bob managed to book them for the afternoon.'

A murmur of anticipation went around the table.

'On the singing side,' continued Anne, 'we've got the residents from the Cavendish, Lewes and Brighton folk clubs. The Stewart family, who sing four-part harmonies, have offered their services late afternoon and, of course, we have a surprise guest.' She made an attempt to get James to spill the beans.

'C-come along, James,' Stephen egged.

James pretended to button his lips. 'Sorry, but I am sworn to secrecy. It's a friend of Bob Tanner's and I think he, or she, will bring the whole event to a satisfactory end.' He turned to Professor Wilkins. 'What were you organising?'

Wilkins crossed his legs and clasped his hands together. 'I've secured a traditional Punch and Judy man. One of the best. I've also persuaded our teacher, Mr Critchton to run a competition for the children — skipping, hop scotch and a game of chess for the older kiddies.'

Stephen reached for another cracker and commented on how lovely the cheese was. 'Th-that reminds me. Wh-what about food?'

Beth invited Anne to disclose the plans. She sat up, as excited as a three-year-old.

'Absolutely scrummy treats,' she said. 'Mrs Keates is making some divine quiches — mushroom, cheese and onion, bacon and tomato. Graham has put the hog roast on hold and, instead, he's going to make some home-made sausages and fried onions to put in rolls. The WI are making a selection of cakes. Rose and Lilac Crumb are making something called a lemon meringue cake.'

'Mmm,' said James, closing his eyes. 'Lemon meringue cake! That sounds absolutely delicious. Rose and Lilac Crumb are doing that?' He stared at Beth. 'Are they quite well? It's not like them to get involved in such a spirited way.'

Charlie smoothed his hair back. 'I got chatting to them in the library the other day. As usual, they were having a moan about the folk day, saying it's the same old thing. I told 'em they should get involved and that, at their age, they must have some songs that were passed down to them.' His eyes lit up. 'And they did. They started going on about songs their dad used to sing. So, I've given them a fifteen-minute slot on the stage.'

Chuckles rang out and James applauded. 'What a splendid idea! If they're the centre of attention, they can't moan, can they?'

'A-and now they're singing, they want to do b-baking, too. Amazing.'

'Lemon meringue cake,' said James, licking his lips. 'Sounds wonderful. D'you think they'll give us the recipe, darling?'

'If you sweet-talk them,' replied Beth. 'Are you doing your lemon pudding?'

'Absolutely. The folk day wouldn't be the same without a handful of lemon puddings.'

James made a mental note to dig out the recipe and buy some lemons. Such a simple dessert, but one that melted in the mouth.

Anne gazed at him. 'You really are a

man of many talents, aren't you? Is this another one of Grandma Harrington's recipes?'

James smiled. 'It is indeed.' He rubbed his hands together. 'So, we have hot and cold food, cakes, drinks, games for the children, stages set and an audience waiting to be entertained. The only thing we need now is good weather.' He pointed to the sky and caught Stephen's eye. 'Can you put in a good word for us?'

Stephen grinned and assured everyone that he would send his prayers up. And, with that, they decided to finish things off. Beth gently tapped an empty glass with a spoon to silence everyone.

'Our last meeting is the day before. We're to meet at the pub at one o'clock on Friday. Everyone involved in organising must be there to help set up the stages and bunting and we'll have one final study of the running order.'

'I say,' James said, 'who's compéring?'

Anne finished her wine. 'Donovan is doing the singing stage and Charlie's offered to introduce the dance acts.'

Professor Wilkins mumbled that he

would arrange those events he'd organised. Beth and James gave each other a subtle grin. James knew how hard that would be for Wilkins — a grumpy individual with little ability to deal with people. He wondered if he might actually scare the children off.

'Right,' James announced, 'that's settled then. I'll see you all on Friday, if not before.'

Their visitors left in dribs and drabs. When she closed the door on the last of them, Beth wrapped her arms around James' neck and hugged him.

'This is going to be a marvellous day. I do hope the weather holds out for us.'

'Mmm, me too. I say, you don't fancy a run out do you?'

'Sure, where to?'

'I rang Mrs Crabtree before I came through earlier. I've arranged to visit later this afternoon.'

Beth gave him a knowing look. 'Is this about GJ?'

'GJ, Delphine, spies and espionage — the works,' replied James. 'I thought it would be nice for both of us to be there.

She's a somewhat formidable woman and having you there may help matters. Plus, of course, you've spent more time with GJ than me. Are you game?'

Beth assured him that she was, most certainly, game.

'There's no time like the present. Let's make a start and, if we're early, we can always have tea in Wimbledon. It's a delightful town.'

'Splendid. I can brief you on my visit with Reg Jacobs.'

'Give me something to whet my appetite,' said Beth.

'I must get changed first,' replied James. He trotted up the stairs and called back down, 'One thing I can tell you, however, is that I believe Delphine may have been having an affair with Mr Crabtree.'

Beth's eyes almost sprang out of her head. 'What? How did you come to think that? If Mr Crabtree is the same age as his wife, that's quite a difference.'

James shouted down his agreement and proposed that he was probably being stupid. He appeared at the top of the stairs.

'In a way I hope I'm wrong as it will make our reception a little frosty. The woman is scary enough and I'm not looking forward to this encounter one iota.'

19

Mrs Crabtree lived in a classic 1930s semi-detached house with bay windows and a long front lawn. If James remembered correctly, this type of home usually had two large bedrooms, one small box-room, an upstairs bathroom and a coal bunker at the rear. The road on which the house stood was a busy thoroughfare leading south to Kingston and north to Kew. All of the exteriors of the houses on the street were identical -brick built with terracotta tiles under the upstairs windows. James parked directly outside and he and Beth surveyed the house. He slid an arm across the top of the passenger seat.

'For some reason, I was expecting something more substantial. After all, I did see her getting into a Rolls Royce and, I have to be honest, a Roller doesn't really fit with this particular house.'

Beth agreed. 'Perhaps they're not as well off now and she can't bear to give up some of the niceties of life.'

As he held the door open for Beth, James reminded himself that his own family were in the same position. Moving from the Harrington estate to their more modest home had involved a complete change in lifestyle and budgeting. It was, most certainly, an immense undertaking and a huge decision to up sticks from the ancestral home. But, in the twentieth century, family-owned manor houses were few and far between and their own finances meant that changes had had to be made. Luckily, the Harringtons' decision to enter the 'tourist' trade meant that, not only did they keep the manor house, but they also made a profit from it — so it was an action many other landowners were now contemplating.

They walked up the path, neatly bordered by pansies and tulips. James rang the bell and viewed the garden, all the while with a feeling of apprehension running through him.

The front door opened and Mrs Crabtree, dressed in a tweed suit, invited them in. She indicated they should go through to the front room, where she'd already prepared tea. James offered his hand.

'Lord James Harrington, and this is my wife, Beth.'

James didn't like to throw in the 'Lord' card, but sometimes it helped when dealing with people who pandered to notions of status, and Mrs Crabtree certainly fell into that bracket. However, her smile failed to reach her eyes and he couldn't imagine it ever doing so.

He and Beth were together on the sofa as their hostess poured tea and then perched on the armchair opposite. She didn't look comfortable in her demeanour and her eyes focussed on the tray. This was a reluctant hostess; no cake or biscuits. They would have to proceed with caution.

'Mrs Crabtree, it's really very kind of you to see us. We're trying to clear up a few things our end about Miss Brooks-Hunter and — '

Mrs Crabtree huffed at the name. James glanced at Beth and continued.

'And we're finding it difficult to move forward. You'll remember that we met briefly at Mr Patel's residence and you appeared to know, or know of, Delphine. Thing is, I'm at my wit's end trying to resolve an issue and I think you may be able to help.'

'Why on earth do you think I can help?' Mrs Crabtree replied haughtily. 'You surmise this from a chance meeting in Richmond. Preposterous!'

James felt a rare surge of anger rumble deep within him. He felt Beth's hand rest on his as she addressed Mrs Crabtree.

'Miss Brooks-Hunter died a few days ago,' spoke Beth, 'in suspicious circumstances. My husband's been asked to resolve some issues concerning her estate, but we've come to a dead end.'

The confirmation that Delphine was dead momentarily softened the hard-faced expression of the lady opposite them. She took a sip of tea and placed her cup and saucer on the table.

'What is it you want to know?'

'What do you know about her?'

'You were at Mr Patel's,' she said, looking at James. 'Surely he told you what she was?'

'I was given some information, yes,' he replied, 'but your interruption rather took me by surprise. What exactly did you mean when you called her Scarlett O'Hara?'

Mrs Crabtree's lips pursed tight. 'You'll need to speak to her family about that.'

'What family?' said Beth. 'She only has a sister whom we've yet to find, and the Jacobs family, who are decidedly stubborn when it comes to speaking with outsiders.'

'Pah! The Jacobs — you've met them, have you? Always after money but not prepared to work for it.'

James gritted his teeth. This wasn't getting them anywhere. 'Mrs Crabtree, we know that Delphine worked for the government. She was a spy and, I understand, a good one. We've heard a rumour that she was well paid.'

'Well paid! Extravagance. How our government could afford all of that for one woman beggars belief.'

'Why was she paid so well?'

Mrs Crabtree shrugged. 'Secrets, secrets, secrets. Why would I know?'

'I understand that both your husband

and brother-in-law work in MI6?'

Her glare bored into him. 'How did you know this?'

James decided he wouldn't beat around the bush. Clearly he had to be straight-talking with this individual.

'The investigations taking place are two-fold,' he explained. 'One is a criminal investigation led by Detective Chief Inspector George Lane. He advised me of the connection and may wish to speak with you. The second is a request direct from Delphine to resolve issues concerning her estate. It's vital that we learn about her past, her connections and her family. Now, Mrs Crabtree, are you willing to help us or have we wasted our time?'

An awkward silence descended. Mrs Crabtree gritted her teeth and her eyes darted here and there. Finally, she made eye contact.

'It's true. Gerald, my brother-in-law, and my husband, Peter, do work for a specific section within the government. Delphine worked closely with Gerald and his department during the Second World

War. She spent most of her time in Germany. He fawned on Delphine and she flaunted herself at him, like she did with all of the men there. She even had the nerve to tease my husband. Hussy.'

James felt Beth stiffen beside him.

'That's an awfully strong word,' she said. 'You obviously knew her well to form such an opinion.'

'I'm old-fashioned, that's all. She was older than me and should have known better — flaunting herself to married men!'

James scanned the room. On the shelf beside him he noticed a photograph of Mrs Crabtree and a man of around the same age. He reached across and turned the picture frame.

'You and your husband?'

She nodded once.

'No children?'

Mrs Crabtree bristled. 'No.'

James looked across at Beth, who reached into her bag and brought out the sketch that GJ had drawn of their hostess. She passed it across. Mrs Crabtree gasped and covered her mouth.

Beth studied her reaction. 'You know who drew this?'

For the first time since meeting the formidable Mrs Crabtree, James witnessed a chink in the armour; a vulnerability that he didn't think he'd find.

'Who drew this, Mrs Crabtree?' he asked gently.

She quickly regained her composure and refused to speak. James fought back the urge to raise his voice. Beth, sensing his frustration, patted his hand and opened her handbag. She brought out a small photo that she and Bert had taken of GJ and placed it on the table.

'This is a picture of the person who drew that picture, Mrs Crabtree,' said Beth. 'I found him sleeping rough in our old stable block. He has amnesia and we're trying our hardest to find out who he is and where he's from. He doesn't deserve to be kept in the dark.' She perched on the edge of her seat and they gazed at the handsome face staring out at them. 'He's been living in an East End mission for years and we found that drawing by his bed. It's one of the few things he's recognised. He now remembers your name and he thinks it was you that brought him up. Is that true?'

James and Beth held hands as Mrs Crabtree stared at the photograph. Pushing herself out of the chair, she opened a door to the sideboard and slid open a drawer, from which she extracted a card. Easing back in her chair, she offered it to Beth, who lifted the cover. A school photograph. Staring back at them was a young boy with a mop of blond hair. Beth showed it to James. It was GJ.

'Mrs Crabtree,' said James, 'it really is imperative that we get to the bottom of this. You appear very reluctant to give any details. What is it that stops you? And what is this young boy's name? How is he connected to you?'

Mrs Crabtree excused herself and went through to the hall where James could hear her dialling out on the telephone. He whispered to Beth.

'What d'you think?' he said.

Beth shrugged. 'I think it's all very odd,' she whispered back. 'Who d'you think she's calling?'

'I haven't a clue.' He studied the school photograph. 'That looks like the uniform for the boarding school at Westminster. I wonder if it is?'

'Why won't she talk?' said Beth. 'She seemed surprised by Delphine's death and this business about GJ hit her like an express train. Can you hear what she's saying?'

James cocked an ear in the hope of eavesdropping but couldn't catch more than a couple of random words. After a few minutes, Mrs Crabtree hung up and returned with a slip of paper in her hand. She hesitated at first, then handed James the paper.

'I was hoping that, after all this time, all these years, the truth would melt into a distant memory and no one would be bothered about all this.' She held her head high. 'I've nothing to be ashamed of. Delphine was a friend until . . . ' She stared at the paper. 'Anyway, that's where you need to go.'

James unfolded the paper. 'Somerset House?'

'I've called them — the people at the front desk will expect you.'

James checked his watch. 'What time do they close? It's almost five now.'

'They'll wait for you.'

She collected the cups and saucers and briskly ushered them into the hall, where she quickly saw them off the premises.

'Extraordinary,' said James as they walked to the car.

Beth agreed and held on to the slip of paper tightly. 'Somerset House is the place with all of the family records, isn't it?'

'Yes.'

'Do you think we'll finally establish GJ's identity?'

Starting the motor, James slipped the Jaguar into gear and steered the car onto the road to London. 'Let's hope so. I feel that we will experience the domino effect in that once one thing falls into place, the rest will follow. Fingers crossed, whoever we're going to meet there, can start the process off.'

20

Somerset House stood in all its magnificence on the bank of the River Thames. The size of Buckingham Palace, the huge, elegant structure with four tall pillars at its centre had been built on the ruins of the Duke of Somerset's Tudor pile. It now housed government offices, including family records.

Although it was still light, the doors had closed on the public and government employees had already begun their journey home.

But a handful of officials remained and, on learning their identities, a suited gentleman beckoned them in. He was a dapper man in his early seventies with a pencil moustache, a gracious smile and a smooth, educated voice.

'Lord Harrington, Lady Harrington, delighted to meet you. My name's Gerald. I'm — '

'Mrs Crabtree's brother-in-law,' interrupted James as he greeted him. 'You work here?'

'I have an office here, but my main port of call is further up the road.'

The gentleman flashed another grin and James noted a mischievous twinkle in his eye. They followed him into an office along the main corridor.

'You've met the fearsome Mrs Crabtree, then?' he said with a smile, indicating for them to sit down. James and Beth couldn't help but grin. He offered James a cigar, which he declined. 'What did you make of her?'

'Well, as you say — fearsome,' replied James. 'But why has she sent us all the way up here?'

'You want to know about Delphine, don't you?'

James knew that he and Beth must have looked surprised.

'I thought we were here about GJ?' said James.

'Who?'

'Oh sorry,' Beth said, realising that the initials meant nothing to him. 'GJ is the young man who turned up at our stables a few days ago.'

Gerald closed his eyes and let out a

resigned 'Ah.' James chewed his lip, undecided as to whether the question in his head would be too forward, but he couldn't help himself.

'I'm sorry, Gerald, but I need to ask a very personal question.' His host motioned for him to continue. 'Did you have an affair with Delphine Brooks-Hunter?'

Beth looked at him, horrified, and her gaze skipped between the two men. Gerald let out a titter.

'I did have a fling with Delphine in my younger days, but I am not the subject of Delphine's secret past. Not the one I believe you're interested in anyway.'

The door opened and an attractive brunette brought in a large, ledger-style book. She placed it on the desk between them and leafed through some pages until she reached the section required. Gerald thanked her and whispered something in her ear. She gave a curt nod.

'And when you've brought her, you can run along home,' he continued. She thanked Gerald and disappeared. Gerald slid open his bottom drawer and pulled out a bottle of sherry and three glasses.

He poured each of them a glass and slid them across the desk.

'If you'll permit me, I'll start with Delphine. She was a spy, you know.'

James forced interest. How many more times would he hear that?

'She was more prominent in this last war but she also made a significant contribution in the latter stages of the Great War, too,' continued Gerald. 'An amazing woman with a zest for life and a wonderful spirit of adventure about her. Did you know her well?'

'Not well enough,' said Beth.

'My wife's right, Gerald,' added James, 'but her personality shone through during our brief get-togethers.'

'Anyone who crossed Delphine's path couldn't help but love her,' said Gerald. 'Even Hyacinth . . . Mrs Crabtree got on with her, once upon a time.'

'Yes, what happened there?' asked James. 'We detected some animosity.'

'Delphine was a flirt — it was in her nature. Didn't matter what status you were, she would melt your heart. Gladys' husband, Peter — my youngest brother

— was somewhat smitten. She was much older than him of course but you can't help falling for charm and fun, can you?'

Beth grimaced. 'Oh dear.'

Gerald assured her that nothing untoward had happened. 'But the very fact that she caught his eye and he had flirted back made tongues wag, and my sister-in-law is rather a prude.' He gave them a knowing smile. 'No, Delphine's affairs of the heart were complex, to say the least, and I suppose you'd like me to spill the beans? That is, after all, why you're here.'

A pulse of adrenalin rushed through James. At last — someone who could shed some light on this infernal affair. He brought his chair closer to Beth's and held her hand as Gerald began.

'Although Delphine was a flirt and somewhat flighty, she was also studious and political. When the Great War loomed, she used her magnetism to wheedle her way into the top ranks of MI1, or the Secret Service Bureau as it was then. She'd studied languages and was fluent in German and she kept hounding the people there that she could be an effective agent.' He sipped his sherry. 'She started life simply in Intelligence and proved her worth time and time again. Her knowledge of the language and the country was an important factor. She insisted she become part of the action and, eventually, our people listened. Over the last year to eighteen months of the war, she ingratiated herself among the elite of Germany, particularly officers and government officials. She had the most beguiling nature and some of her followers unwittingly let slip a few secrets here and there. Those secrets found their way back here.'

James frowned. 'D'you mean she just went back and forth from there to London, without being challenged?'

Gerald twirled his moustache. 'All in good time, Lord Harrington, I promise not to leave anything out. When the Great War ended, Delphine returned to London. However, the government asked her to carry on with her activities. They'd been impressed with her, so she split her time between Germany, on the outskirts of Berlin, and Cavendish. Her home in Cavendish is also, I believe, out in the sticks?'

Beth shifted in her seat. 'To remain inconspicuous?'

'Exactly. I believe the residents of Cavendish saw Delphine as a bit of a recluse — never seen, never heard?'

James agreed that was exactly what they all thought. 'But when she did show herself, everyone loved her.'

'And that couldn't be helped — that was her personality,' said Gerald. 'She purposely remained a recluse, both here and in Germany. That way, if people didn't see her for weeks, no questions were asked. She'd say she was visiting relatives and no one would be any the wiser.'

'But surely, during the war, questions would be asked about her returning to England?' asked James. 'Surely she couldn't just come and go as she pleased?'

'You're right, of course. But, between the wars, Delphine did exactly that. She'd gained the trust of the Germans, and her identity papers, compiled by our government, were in the most excellent order.' Gerald poured another glass of sherry.

'But when the Second World War began, she anticipated problems and decided that she'd have to remain in Germany and smuggle secrets out.'

Beth stared open-mouthed. 'How on earth did she smuggle secrets out?'

James suggested the French rèsistance. 'They put their lives on the line every day.'

But Gerald shook his head. 'She actually concocted the most wonderful plan herself; so blatant, that she did it under their very noses.' He chuckled to himself. 'Quite extraordinary.'

James found this whole thing completely absorbing. 'Are you able to divulge this blatant plan, or is it something you can't discuss?'

Gerald rubbed his hands together. 'All in good time, Lord Harrington.'

James hid a smirk. This chap was clearly enjoying himself and obviously saving something as a finale. What it was, he hadn't the foggiest, but something told him that the best was yet to come. He swigged his sherry, boldly helped himself to another and topped up Beth's glass.

Gerald referred to the ledger in front of him. 'Now, how does this relate to your young man, GJ?' he asked.

He reached for a small magnifying glass and began studying the names listed in fine-tip pen down the left-hand margin. 'Our Delphine, as I've stated before, was a flirt, and beautiful with it.' He struck the book with the palm of his hand and let out a triumphant 'Hah' before giving James and Beth his full attention. 'Delphine was around the age of fifty in the mid-thirties. Things were beginning to rumble in Germany but war was some years away. But age didn't dampen her personality or her beauty. It remained with her. In some cases, I would say she became more attractive, as I believe Lillian Gish has over the last decade. A beauty that comes with wisdom and experience.'

James caught himself looking at Beth and had thought the same of her. She'd become more attractive as the years went by, likening her to her own style icon, Audrey Hepburn. Gerald continued.

'Delphine had a number of admirers in

Germany, and a lady with her spirit simply could not deny herself any fun.' There was a mischievous glint in his eye as he leant forward. 'In 1937, she had a six-month affair with a high-ranking German officer. Unfortunately, he was married. There was no long-term future in it, but the affair was an intense one. Not just a fling, if you follow me.'

James allowed his subconscious to digest the words. The assumption that it spat out, although absurd, he knew would be correct.

'The intensity of this affair.' James surmised, 'led to a son.'

Beth gasped as Gerald acknowledged his statement. 'Unfortunately, yes.'

'Well I never . . . '

Gerald grimaced. 'Quite. Times are changing. Perhaps she thought that at her age there would be no chance of conceiving but, unfortunately, she did. And to have a child out of wedlock is one thing, but to know that the father was a German officer, and married, spelt out all sorts of trouble for her.'

'This, presumably, was leaked by

someone?' suggested James.

'Do you think this was the hold the Jacobs family had over Delphine?' asked Beth.

'I think so, yes,' said James. 'In some ways, if this had happened in England, she would have behaved differently, but — '

'To a German officer,' Gerald interrupted. 'That was beyond the code of decency of a British woman at the time, even one who was risking her life with the work she was doing. We were increasingly sure at that time that we would inevitably slide into war with them. In the early thirties, there were a fair few Fascist sympathisers who hobnobbed with Hitler, a man who was very accessible. You recall the Mitford girl . . . '

James recalled it very well. A well-to-do British debutante who befriended Adolf Hitler and the Fascist movement. Gerald continued.

'Delphine's job was crucial but she let her emotions get the better of her. Her actions would be unthinkable to the patriots here in Britain. The Jacobs lot discovered this secret; how, I don't know but they threatened to make life very uncomfortable for Delphine.'

'In exchange for a share of her spoils?'

Gerald went on to explain that Delphine was handsomely paid with extravagant gifts. She, herself, felt she'd let both herself and her country down with this liaison, so she gave in to their threats.

James verbalised his thoughts.

'So she wrote the Jacobs family into her will. On condition that she died a natural death.'

'That's right,' replied Gerald. 'The Jacobs clan are not the nicest people I know. I've seen them from a distance. She didn't think they would wait for what might be years until she died. She was, after all, a very healthy lady destined to live for another twenty years.'

'So she took a risk and came to our Spring Fair?' said Beth.

'A risk, yes, but she'd planned it that way. I would imagine they'd been harassing her and she decided to push things along.'

'By getting herself killed!'

James shook his head. 'I get the impression with Delphine that she'd rather that than the truth of her affair be known.'

Gerald explained. 'Delphine was not a sit-in-the-country-doing-crochet type of woman. She was too old to be of any use to what is now MI6 — she'd been put out to pasture. I knew she wouldn't stand for that.' He cleared his throat. 'If one of the Jacobs family is responsible, she's transferred the scandal to them. If they *do* bring up the subject of a bastard son, who will believe them?' He stabbed the ledger with his finger. 'Especially considering what is written here.'

James couldn't hide his frustration. 'Gerald, we've been very patient. Are you going to tell us what this book is?'

The gentleman stroked his moustache and spun the ledger around to face them. James and Beth studied what appeared to be a birth certificate with an accompanying letter. James read them both.

'Born, 23 November 1937, Sebastian Gregory. Mother, Delphine Brooks-Hunter, Father, Walter Weiss.' He unfolded the letter. 'This is from . . . ' He stared at Gerald. 'Your brother?' After a short time, James muttered 'Good Lord' and passed it across to Beth. 'Your brother offered to put himself down as the father?'

'He did. Although nothing happened between them, he loved Delphine more than anything. He couldn't bear to see her ostracised for fraternising with the enemy. He offered to make what he thought was the right gesture.'

Beth emitted a silent *phew*. 'No wonder Hyacinth turned against her. I presume she had no say in the matter?'

Gerald's shake of the head reiterated the fact.

James frowned. 'So Delphine could have rejected the Jacobs' threat and cut them off completely?'

'She could have, yes,' replied Gerald. 'But she couldn't allow Peter to put his name on the birth certificate — she would not allow his name to be dragged into her secret.' A knock on the door sounded. 'Ah, just in time. Come in.'

The attractive brunette entered. 'I have her here, sir.'

Gerald leapt to his feet and clapped his hands together. 'Good, good! Show her in, show her in.' He chivvied James and Beth to their feet. They quickly followed him and, as the door opened wider, they stopped dead in their tracks.

'Delphine!'

21

Beth struggled to stay on her feet as James instinctively moved forward to scrutinise the lady in front of them. It couldn't be. The same eyes, the same features, the same stance. The lady tilted her head and extended her hand.

'My dear, before you have a heart attack, I'd best introduce myself. I'm Juliet, Delphine's sister.'

'Twins,' James mumbled.

'Identical.'

Once James and Beth had overcome their shock, Gerald steered them all back to the desk and ushered his secretary off the premises. Juliet stretched across for the bottle of sherry and asked for a glass. James allowed himself a quick smile. Not only was she identical to Delphine physically, but she appeared to have the same no-nonsense personality, too.

'I say,' James said, 'how long have you been in London?'

'I arrived the evening following Delphine's death,' replied Juliet. 'She'd explained everything to me; the delightful Spring Fair and how she'd be asking you to solve her irritating riddle. Have you, by the way? Solved the riddle?'

'No, I'm afraid not. I'm not terribly good at riddles. Are you?'

'Hopeless,' she replied with a twinkle in her eye. 'Delphine was, too. So don't think she concocted anything complicated, because she couldn't.' She let out a laugh. 'She could spy with the best of them, dear. But setting riddles was a time-waster for her and you'll find it quite tame.'

James felt a sense of relief enter the pit of his stomach. Perhaps he'd take another look at the rhyme when they returned home and the answer would be staring him in the face. He turned to Juliet.

'Did you see much of your sister when she was gallivanting around Europe?'

He noticed Juliet and Gerald smirk at each other. Juliet took a sip of sherry and settled back in her chair.

'We had a great deal of fun, Lord Harrington.'

Beth's ears pricked. 'Fun? How can spying be fun? And in Germany, for goodness sake! You could have been shot.'

'Could have been, yes, but we never came close, my dear. I suppose you would call me a decoy; Delphine's decoy. We hatched the plan between us back in 1916, when Delph first started working in Germany. She worked on her own during the Great War but it all sounded rather exciting, so I joined up with her during the last war — behind the scenes, so to speak — and helped out in a rather wonderful way.'

James' heart beat a little faster. Juliet crossed her legs.

'Do you like amateur dramatics, Lord Harrington?'

James glanced at Beth and back to Juliet. 'We're both heavily involved with the Cavendish Players, Juliet. So yes, we love it. Beth here makes the costumes for many of our plays.'

'How wonderful,' replied Juliet. 'I do so love a well-made costume. Do you manage quite well with the amount of material you need?'

Beth clasped her hands together. 'Oh yes, we have a second-hand clothing bank for most productions. But, if we're pushing the boat out and need something new, we have an excellent contact at Petticoat Lane.'

'How perfect for you. Petticoat Lane ... so diverse and, yet, so English.'

Like Delphine, Juliet seemed prone to drifting into a daydream of bygone days, but she quickly came out of it.

'Now, where was I? Oh yes, amateur dramatics. We had such fun when we were children, dressing up and pretending to be something we were not. It came naturally to us to extend that when we entered the world of espionage.'

Beth was swept away. 'Do tell, Juliet. It sounds enthralling.'

'Well, my dear, that is certainly one way to describe it. Our plan was, like Delphine's atrocious riddles, very simple. Delphine was the spy, not me. I went along as a bit-part player, coming in and out of the wings when necessary.'

James' curiosity was roused. 'How did that work?'

'I played Delphine's elderly aunt,' replied Juliet. 'My skills with costume and make-up are second to none. I learnt the art of ageing one's self from a theatrical company in the West End.'

Juliet held up a finger to stop proceedings and reached for her handbag. After a few seconds, she retrieved a black and white photograph and handed it to James.

'Is that you?' he asked.

The grainy photograph showed a lady of mature years with a wrinkled face and a lace shawl over silver-grey hair.

'It took some time to get the desired effect, but I think you'll agree that this is the face of an old woman.'

Beth puffed her cheeks in disbelief. She handed the photograph back. 'But how did this help Delphine?'

'Well, my dear, Delphine decided that, to be an effective agent, she needed to have the ability to travel back and forth to France from Germany and, where possible, England, without unnecessary questioning. So she gave herself a debilitating illness. One that cropped up every now and again that could only be cured with bed rest.'

Juliet's laughing eyes flitted from James to Beth and back again. 'Migraines. Headaches so bad that she had to take to her bed in a darkened room for days, with no noise, no interruptions, and no stress.'

James ran over everything in his mind, seeking an understanding of what Juliet was saying, but it still didn't make sense to him. 'Forgive me, Juliet, but I don't understand how this helped.'

'I visited Delphine frequently, so the Germans were used to seeing us together. But, every so often, Delphine would feign a migraine and they'd last at least a week.'

James gave a slow nod. 'So, knowing you and your sister's love of excitement and adventure, am I right in thinking that you swapped roles?'

Beth gasped. 'Swapped roles! But how?'

James reminded her of what Gerald had said. 'Right under their noses.' He wagged a finger at Juliet. 'You became Delphine.'

Juliet's beaming smile lit up her eyes as she rocked like an excited schoolgirl. 'Yes, yes. We swapped identity. Oh, we'd spend a few days shopping, or enjoying a dinner out and Delphine always escorted me back to my own rooms. There, I made Delphine up to be an old aunt and I became Delphine.'

'And you would return to Delphine's house with a severe migraine?'

'And spend the next week in bed in a darkened room.'

'While Delphine swanned off to France as an elderly aunt.'

Juliet's eyes opened wide and she grinned. Beth giggled. 'That's ingenious. And no one stopped her?'

'My dear, who stops a fussy old lady with a carpet-bag, distributing mint humbugs?'

James stood up and put his hands in his pockets. What amazing women these sisters were. What a wonderfully simple trick to swap identities.

Gerald, enjoying the revelations, topped everyone's glasses up and allowed the conversation to flow without any input from him.

'Now, Juliet,' said Beth, 'can you please tell us about Sebastian? I'm so desperate to see that young man settled.'

Juliet's sad expression spoke words. 'Oh yes, poor Sebastian. An innocent player who will never know his mother.'

Beth reached across to comfort her. 'But he can know the truth and get to know his aunt who, from what I've seen today, is his mother's replica in every sense of the word.'

Juliet brightened, confirming that this was most definitely what should happen. 'Sebastian was born in Berlin. His father was a high-ranking German officer, Walter Weiss. He was married with a family of his own. What Delphine was thinking of, heaven only knew, but I can't blame her for taking up with him; he was quite the matinèe idol and he knew it. I'm sure the baby was conceived during a rather drunken birthday party at a huge country estate outside Berlin. The place was full of officers and friends of Hitler and it reminded me of the early days in Berlin when the place was notoriously immoral. Our mother was the same, you know. Very Bohemian.'

James couldn't fathom it; he didn't

come from that sort of background and accepted her explanation more out of politeness than anything. Beneath it though he shuddered at the sense of shame inflicted on the Brooks-Hunter family. It appeared that the females in this particular family were risk-takers and damn the consequences. In a way, he admired them and felt there was a place for people like them. On the other hand, the pleasure of knowing that it wasn't his own family helped counter those beliefs. Lord knows what he'd say if Oliver or Harry got a girl into trouble. His stomach churned at the thought.

'Now,' said Juliet, 'Sebastian came to England a week after his birth, with me. Delphine knew she couldn't keep him. Doing so would cause trouble in all sorts of ways. She decided I was to bring him to England on the understanding that he went to a good home and that she would know where he was.' Tears welled. 'She couldn't give him up completely, you see; she wanted to see him grow.'

James was slowly beginning to understand. He nodded to Gerald. 'So your brother offered to adopt him?'

Gerald's expression told them everything.

'Is that why he recognised Cavendish?'

'Yes,' Juliet said. 'Peter would take him there on the pretence of fishing or walking in the country. Delphine always made a point of bumping into them.'

'How sad that Sebastian never knew,' said Beth. 'And to think they were at the Spring fair together on the day she died.'

They silently pondered the thought.

'Gerald, didn't your brother think to discuss this with his wife?' asked James.

Gerald winced. 'He worshipped Delphine like a goddess. He insisted that he and Hyacinth bring him up. She can be a difficult woman, Lord Harrington, but my brother was, and is, the head of the household. Peter was like a father to him. And Hyacinth? Well . . . '

Beth picked up on the hesitation. 'Hyacinth would, I'm sure, have disliked Sebastian because of your brother's feelings toward Delphine. I can't imagine she was a mother to him.'

'Not in the way we want a mother to

be,' replied Gerald. 'Oh, she fed him and clothed him. But there was no love, no bond. Peter was away a lot during the war, so that left Sebastian and my sister-in-law. Sebastian's relationship with Hyacinth deteriorated rapidly when he was about fourteen. They argued constantly and eventually he walked out. He was fifteen and they never saw him again. Peter tried to find him and, of course, he had the contacts to do so but the search was not successful. You can imagine Hyacinth's surprise when she discovered you discussing Delphine at Patel's house.'

'I most certainly can,' James said. It would have brought back all those memories she'd hoped had been buried. 'What was she doing at Mr Patel's?'

'Mr Patel was aware of Delphine's death. He had simply let the Crabtrees know that there might be some unpleasantness when the will was read. That Sebastian's identity would be revealed.'

'Of course — the will! I'd forgotten all about that. Surely Delphine would be giving everything to Sebastian?'

Juliet patted his hand. 'I'm sure it'll all

come out once this business with the Jacobs family is resolved. If I understand correctly, the will has yet to be opened.'

'That's right. Delphine said she would not divulge her will until her death was clarified.' James heaved a sigh. 'Hopefully, that won't be too long now.'

'And how is Sebastian?' asked Juliet with interest.

James held Beth's hand as she gave Juliet a summary of events; the discovery of GJ in the stables, his recognition of the area, the trip to the Mission, and the drawing of Mrs Crabtree. At the end, Juliet put her hands to her cheeks.

'My, my, what an eventful month you've had! And amnesia? I wonder how he got amnesia? Must have knocked himself out or something. But you say he's beginning to remember?'

'Oh yes,' replied Beth. 'And now we have a more complete story today, we can fill in the blanks.'

'And when the dust settles, perhaps you will allow me to visit my nephew?'

'I'm sure he would love that.'

James rubbed his hands together. 'You

must be our guest at Harrington's, Juliet.'

'That would be most agreeable and the sooner the better. But first, you must solve this confounded riddle that Delph set for you. I'd like everything settled before I bundle in and surprise my nephew.'

James' mind buzzed with tasks: update GJ — or rather Sebastian — with the day's events; speak with George about the murder enquiry and try again to solve the riddle. If they didn't do that soon, they'd never settle Delphine's will.

On the drive home, he said to Beth: 'I think now we have this information, I'd like to pay another visit to Reg Jacobs.'

'I hope that Bert will go with you,' she replied.

James reached over and stroked her cheek. 'Don't worry, I'll make sure he's there as reinforcement.'

22

James stood back as Bert hammered on the side of Reg Jacobs' caravan. He checked the field. Most of the caravans had left, along with the fairground equipment.

'I think the family must be in gainful employment,' he mused. 'I don't suppose Reg is here.'

Bert tried the door and it swung open. They pulled back warily. Bert switched into his 'better safe than sorry' mode and picked up a metal bar from underneath the trailer. James peered into the caravan. The day was a warm one and the stifling heat caused the smell of stale food to hang in the air.

'Why on earth do people hire these things during the summer? They're unbearably hot.'

'You only sit in 'em when it's raining, Jimmy boy.' Bert nudged James further into the kitchen area where he saw two unbroken eggs; one in an eggcup and one on the side along with two thin slices of burnt toast. James felt the kettle — it was still warm. The teapot stood ready with its leaves settled at the bottom. It certainly seemed that someone had left in a hurry.

James dabbed a finger down a cupboard by the seating area.

'I say, look at this, Bert. It's that sticky residue I was telling you about from that plant near the river.' He snatched a jacket up from the floor. 'Here, it's on this too. Down the sleeve here.' James held the item up and frowned. 'I've seen this before.'

Bert made his way to the bedroom at the end. 'Oi, oi. Man down!'

James hurried to join Bert, who was leaning over Reg. The man was sprawled on the floor. Bert heaved him over and gently slapped him on the cheek.

'Is he dead?'

Bert held up a frying pan. 'No mate, just concussed. Give us a glass o' water.'

James did as asked and watched Bert throw the liquid over Reg's face. Reg spluttered and slowly regained consciousness. He rubbed the back of his head and focussed on James, then Bert.

'What 'appened?'

'I think one of your gang 'ere whacked you good and proper,' said Bert. 'You don't 'appen to know who, do you?'

Reg eased himself up and rubbed his head. 'Nah. I was getting me breakfast. Dished it up and then came in here to pick up me paper. I felt the caravan dip when someone came in, but I didn't get a chance to turn round.'

James suggested they boil the kettle and at least have some tea. Bert, meanwhile, helped to transfer Reg from the floor to the bed.

'You wanna doctor, Jacobs?' he asked.

'Nah. I'll be all right. I'll 'ave the bastard that did this, though.'

After a few minutes, Bert brought Reg through to the kitchen area where James handed them two chipped and stained mugs of tea. He was loath to drink from anything so filthy and decided to abstain. He sat down opposite Reg and Bert.

'So, Reg, are you going to come clean about Sebastian?'

Reg tensed as he glared at James. 'How

the hell did you . . . '

But then a sudden weariness descended and his shoulders fell. 'I s'pose you 'ad to find out about 'im eventually.'

'You were blackmailing Delphine?'

Reg appeared astounded by the accusation. 'Nah, not me. I 'ad nothin' to do with 'er being killed. Nothin'.'

'But you were blackmailing her, yes?'

Reg averted his gaze to the floor. James allowed the silence to become an awkward one. Finally, Reg opened up.

'The whole family were trying think of a way to get money out of her. She let us 'ave a couple of 'undred quid here and there. But she came to me a few weeks before your fair. Private like, when the rest o' the family were workin'. She said she was gonna find Sebastian, bring everything out in the open. She reckoned people were more tolerant o' that sort o' thing now. She knew that it'd cause a fuss to begin with, but then life goes on and people forget about it. Then she said she was gonna change the will.'

'And?'

'I told everyone 'ere the nigh' that

'appened. I weren't bothered, to be honest, I'd 'ad enough of it. But a lot of 'em weren't 'appy, I can tell you.'

'So someone killed her to stop the will being changed?'

'It weren't me!'

James's fingers touched the residue on the cupboard door. 'What about this — this more or less proves you were there, Reg. This sticky substance is very rare. You can find it in the area along the riverbank where Delphine was killed.'

Reg jerked up, his eyes almost pleading. 'Well, I weren't there. I've got plenty of witnesses that'll testify I didn't leave my ride. Most of 'em being your villagers, by the way. That could've come from anyone — everyone comes in and ou' of this van.'

James thought so. As much as he despised the man, he believed him. Reg's attacker came into the caravan and knocked Reg out cold. Whoever it was perhaps felt that Reg was turning against them.

Reg sneered. 'I might seem like an 'ard nut to you, but I ain't. I try to do the right thing and told the family to do fings right. If we'd 'ave treated Delphine more like family, she would've seen us right, I'm sure of it. But some of 'em got greedy, started threatening her — they knew her weakness.'

James knew it, too. Sebastian; born out of wedlock to a German officer, handed over to a married admirer ready to take the responsibility. She'd rather be black-mailed than allow that to come out. Someone here had made threats that were counter-productive. Instead of giving in, Delphine had stood up to them.

She was right, too. Who would have taken any notice? Her parents were dead and her sister would have supported her. Peter and Hyacinth would be affected but, with the time that had elapsed, not overly so. Indeed, he thought Peter would welcome the opportunity to be reac-quainted with Sebastian.

'You know, Reg, I'm pretty sure that Delphine had already changed her will.'

Reg frowned.

'Well, why else would she ask that her death be investigated?'

'Search me.'

Then he began to laugh. James baulked at this change in behaviour and mirrored Bert's worried expression. What on earth was he laughing at?

'Sorry, but that's just typical of 'er. She's just got 'er own back. She's 'ad all that blackmailing business and now she's gonna do one of ours for murder from beyond the grave.' He shook his head. 'Priceless.'

James understood the man's thinking. There was clearly no love lost between Reg and some of his own family. And, did he detect a hint of respect for Delphine? Bert cleared his throat.

'We'd best get onto George. We're not gettin' anywhere 'ere.' He prodded Reg. 'You know who murdered 'er, don't you?'

Reg pushed himself up. 'None o' your business. I may not like 'em much, but family's family and I ain't a grass. And I ain't gettin' involved, so I'm off.'

'Off? Where?'

'Somewhere far away from 'ere. I ain't getting done for conspiracy to murder and I ain't giving a witness statement to the coppers. I'm off.' He glared at Bert.

'And don't you try and stop me.'

Bert was happy to step aside. James motioned for Bert to join him outside. Reg rested a hand on the door frame.

'I'd appreciate i' if you didn't tell my family you've been 'ere. I've been talkin' about going for a long while, so if I'm not 'ere when they come back, it won't be a surprise.' He heaved down an old army bag and started packing. 'You'll ge' your murderer. My lot ain't the brightest bulbs in the ceiling.'

'I say, where will you go?'

Reg slammed the door on them. James gave Bert a gentle shove toward the car.

'Well, I'll leave it up to George as to whether he wants to track that one down. In the meantime, I'd like to join Beth for dinner and see how Sebastian has taken the news.'

Bert jutted his chin at the trailer. 'Are you certain it's not 'im that killed Delphine?'

James stopped in his tracks. 'Do you know what, Bert? I am. I can't put my finger on it, but instinct tells me it's not Reg Jacobs.' He continued toward the car.

'And anyway, it's George's enquiry. My job is to solve the riddle.'

Bert slapped him on the back. '*And* it's the folk day tomorrow.'

James groaned. 'Oh Lord.'

'What's up, Jimmy boy?'

'When I booked the Jacobs lot for the fair, I booked some of them to come along and do the swings and merry-go-round.'

'D'you know who's coming?'

'I haven't the foggiest. But, with Reg disappearing, I've a feeling the whole gang will be there and I can't imagine they'll be in a particularly good frame of mind.'

23

With flaming June just a week away, the early summer sun warmed the village of Cavendish. The village green heaved with residents all straining to get a good view of the singers, dancers, puppeteers and musicians, who were putting every ounce of energy into their performances.

The majority of visitors had remembered to display an oak leaf for Oak Apple Day and James checked to make sure his own was visible. The last thing he wanted was children pinching his bottom and his being unable to retaliate. Judging by the odd shriek, a few girls and boys had discovered a handful of visitors who were unaware of the custom.

At one end of the green, a lively collection of Morris tunes were being belted out by an enthusiastic band. Accompanying them on a temporary boarded area were the Chanctonbury Ring Morris men. They wore shiny top hats adorned with beer mats and rosettes. Their bell pads jingled as they leapt energetically across the dance floor, playfully attacking one another with sturdy oak sticks.

A small notice-board outlined their history for those unfamiliar with folklore. James went over to read it. 'The tradition of Morris men is thought to have originated with the North African Moors, whose name evolved through 'Moorish' to 'Morris'. Many participants blacken their faces, therefore, in imitation of the dark-skinned Moors.'

Cavendish residents and visitors from neighbouring villages meandered around the various stalls surrounding the green. Traditional arts and crafts stands were beside the tombola. Individual stalls displayed all manner of entertainment from magic tricks to the traditional Punch and Judy show. Further along, a circus performer was teaching people how to juggle.

A ladies' clog troupe stamped a rhythmic dance outside the pub and, with the numbers involved, James likened it to an entire army marching in unison. Dorothy Forbes and her husband tried on a pair of wooden dance clogs and declared them most uncomfortable. Charlie Hawkins sprawled on the grass next to the dance stage, teaching his children how to play ninepin, a traditional game mainly found in pubs.

The Women's Institute ladies had set up stalls along the pavement between the Half Moon and the library and appeared to be doing a good trade with the staple delights of cake, scones and tea. The smell of hot sausages mingled with those of roast beef rolls and hamburgers. GJ, deep in conversation with Professor Wilkins, suddenly noticed him and waved. James returned a mock salute.

Alongside the Women's Institute, James saw Elsie and Mrs Keates, who'd decided to join forces and share a charity stall together. He made a mental note to pop by and see how his lemon pudding was being received.

At the far end of the green, James applauded as Rose and Lilac Crumb took to the stage. He wandered toward them, not quite believing what he was seeing. Never in a million years did he ever think he'd see the Snoop Sisters actually join in with a social activity. Normally, they would pitch up and take what was free and moan about the rest. But today, here they were, delighting their audience with frail, yet perfect, harmonies. Their song, 'Oats and Beans and Barley', a tune that James remembered singing many years ago in his school assembly, was certainly a foot-tapper. Beth linked arms with him.

'They really seem to be enjoying themselves, don't they?'

'I'll say. Perhaps we've discovered the secret of keeping them happy — actually put them in the spotlight.'

'We'd best make a fuss of them when they come off — try and keep that positivity going.'

James patted her hand. 'Mmm, good luck with that.' His gaze settled on the pub where Bert, Stephen and Anne were enjoying a drink on the make-shift seating outside. 'I say, d'you fancy a drink, darling?'

Beth said she'd love one, but was

intrigued by some of the acts performing around the green. 'The magician over there looks particularly good, so I'll carry on around here and do some socialising.'

James pecked her on the cheek and told her he would do the same once he'd obtained some refreshment. As he sat down, Bert handed him a beer.

'I got a spare,' he said. 'Thought you'd be coming over.'

James accepted the beer and wished everyone good health.

'I-I was surprised to s-see the fair people here,' said Stephen.

James groaned. 'Oh Stephen, don't remind me. I booked the swings for this bash when I booked them for May Day. Believe me, it's the last booking they'll have from me. I've already booked Lambs for next year.'

'At least they're just doing a couple of rides,' Anne said, 'and they don't seem to be causing any trouble.'

James cast an eye at the area. He'd hoped that it would only be a couple of the family attending but, as predicted, the whole clan had turned up. He silently cursed as he spotted one particular individual.

'Oh Lord, I didn't realise *he'd* be here.' He nudged Bert. 'Look who's with them.'

Bert scanned the crowd and his face hardened. 'Bruiser.'

Stephen's face paled. 'B-Bruiser? W-what's he doing here?'

'Nothing at the moment, old chap,' replied James. 'But keep your eyes open.'

Anne cast the giant Bruiser a fixed stare. 'If he comes near us, I'll give him a piece of my mind.'

James didn't take his eyes off the hard-nosed fighter. And then something caught his eye and things began to fall into place. Of course, that's where he'd seen it. He shielded his eyes from the sun as he scanned the crowd. 'I say, have any of you seen George?'

'He's about, Jimmy boy,' said Bert. 'I've seen 'im.'

James gulped his beer down and handed Bert the glass. 'Go and find George and tell him to keep an eye on me.'

Bert held him back. 'Oi, you're not doing anything stupid, are yer?'

James shrugged him off. 'I'm not doing anything of the sort — but I have an idea.' He strode off, aware of Bert's colourful language as he tried to persuade him to stay.

He positioned himself close to the swings, which were convenient for the singers' stage, and he stood idly with his hands in his pocket, ears focussed on the music, but his peripheral vision on Bruiser. A round of applause rang out as Charlie Hawkins took the stage. James adjusted his position slightly. Bruiser wouldn't be going anywhere for the next couple of hours as he was working; he could wait and James wanted to see Charlie do his turn. Stephen joined him.

Charlie addressed the audience a little sheepishly, not used to being the centre of attention.

'Thanks,' he began. 'I've got a couple of songs to sing. They were requested by a very dear lady who was, unfortunately, killed a few weeks ago. Many of you know her. Delphine Brooks-Hunter. She lived at the Coach House. Anyway, when we were arranging this little do, she asked if I would sing a couple of her favourite songs.' He rummaged in his trouser pocket and brought out a sheet of paper. 'Sorry, I do know the words, but I don't want to forget them, so this is just in case. The first song I want to sing is 'A Brisk Young Sailor'.'

He cleared his voice and, with a quick prompt, Bob Tanner began an introduction on the concertina.

James forgot about Bruiser and listened as Charlie's clear voice sang out.

'A brisk young sailor courted me, he
   stole away my liberty,
He stole my heart with a free good-
   will, I must confess I love him still.
Down in the meadows she did run, a
   gathering flowers as they sprung,
Every sort she gave a pull, 'till she
   had gathered her
apron full.
When first I wore my apron low, he
   followed me through frost and snow,
But now my apron is up to my chin,
   he passes by and
says nothing.'

James straightened. He turned to Stephen. 'Are you listening to this?'

Stephen came out of an obvious daydream. 'N-not really. It's a pleasant tune, but I sort of drifted off.'

As Charlie continued with the song, James pulled Stephen aside. 'That song, 'A Brisk Young Sailor', was requested by Delphine. It's all about having a child out of wedlock to a serviceman. Do you think this is another clue?'

'I-it's a bit belated, if it is. You already know about the son.'

'That doesn't matter, Stephen. The fact is, she was trying to tell us. What was the other song she requested?'

'I-I've no idea, I'm afraid. I w-wish I could remember now.'

George approached them with a pint of beer in his hand. 'I hear you've summoned me.'

'Ah hello, George. Yes. I've got your murderer for you.'

His friend almost choked on his ale. 'You've what!'

A round of applause rang around the stage.

'James, what *are* you talking about?' asked George.

'The killer — the one who coshed our dear Delphine to death. He's here.'

George's eyes darted from stall to stall. 'Where?'

'Just hold on a tick. I need to hear this next song.'

'Blast it, James,' spluttered George. 'Damn the next song. This is far more important.'

James baulked. 'I say, steady on old chap. The song may hold a clue to solving that riddle. Stick with me and all will be revealed. Our killer is oblivious to my suspicions, so he's not going anywhere.'

George scowled at him. 'I'll warn the constable. He's by the WI.'

'Tell him to stay out of sight and munch on a scone. We don't want our fellow getting jittery.'

James returned his attention to Charlie. But, no sooner had he done so, than a kerfuffle by the swings took his attention.

'I'm tellin' you, e's gone!' shouted a red-faced Jackie Connor.

'Gone where, that's what I'd like to

know,' Derek Jacobs snarled, throwing down a spanner. ''E must've found 'er money. Why else would 'e disappear?'

James nudged Stephen forward. Bruiser pushed himself up from an orange box and puffed out his chest. James mouthed a silent 'Phew'; the man was the size of a wardrobe. He glanced over his shoulder. Come on George, where are you when I need you. Ah, there you are. George had left the local constable at the edge of the green and was weaving his way back through the crowd. The Connors and Jacobs continued arguing as George sidled up beside him.

'What's going on?'

James whispered. 'Please don't interrupt what I'm about to do.'

He heard George curse him as he approached the warring clan.

'I say, Bruiser,' he said. 'That jacket you're wearing.'

Bruiser turned his massive frame and eyed James. 'Wha' about it?'

'Well, I notice you have rather a lot of that sticky residue on it.'

Bruiser looked down at the scruffy

sleeves of his jacket and leered at James. 'So?'

'Well, it's just that it belongs to a specific plant that's very rare around here. You don't see it much at all but I've got it on the estate at Harrington's.'

Bruiser's eyes darted back and forth at the gathering crowd. The argument amongst the fair folk ceased.

'So you've go' some on the estate. What's tha' gotta do with me?'

'I think it has everything to do with you,' replied James. 'You see, the only place it grows is down by the river. The spot with a small clearing. It's where I found Delphine Brooks-Hunter the afternoon she was attacked.'

Bruiser snarled. Jackie Connor edged back.

'Because I believe,' James continued, 'that you were there and you attacked her.'

Bruiser made an aggressive move toward him. 'That's a lie.'

'Come on, Bruiser, we both know you were there. Don't make it hard for yourself. No one else had that jacket on. It's too large for anyone else. You weren't at the actual fair, of course. No, you came in through the forest and waited for your opportunity. You discovered that Delphine was proposing to change her will and didn't want the family missing out on a small fortune. That's right, isn't it? You couldn't bear to see that money go to her rightful heir.'

Bruiser gritted his teeth. 'He don't deserve it. She gave 'im away. She promised us the money.'

James gritted his teeth and glared at him. 'You threatened her. You and your family intimidated a defenceless old lady and killed her out of sheer greed. You knocked out poor Jack Hedges and stole his Green Man costume and you left your jacket on that shrub while you did it. You may have disguised yourself, Bruiser, but the evidence is literally all over you.'

Bruiser's face turned purple with rage as he grabbed James by the shirt collar and wrestled him to the ground. James landed on his back with a thud and groaned. He felt Bruiser's hands around his neck; his throat constricted. Beth screamed as Derek Jacobs dived in to loosen Bruiser's grip, but Bruiser quickly tossed him to one side and returned his attention to James.

James began to lose focus. The world began to spin. A police whistle shrilled through the fog in his head and, as he began to lose consciousness, he heard the twang of a metal bar. The grip around his neck loosened. Bruiser slumped to one side. James struggled to breathe. Beth rushed to his side, quickly followed by Philip Jackson, who ordered everyone to give him room. He felt his collar loosen.

James turned and opened his eyes. Beside him, Bruiser rubbed his head in a daze, while George read him his rights and a constable handcuffed him. Standing over Bruiser, and holding Derek's huge iron spanner, was GJ, grinning proudly. The young man squatted down.

'Are you all right, Lord Harrington?'

GJ and Beth helped him up and he brushed himself down. He felt his throat. 'I think you saved my life, young man.'

'It's a life worth saving,' replied GJ. 'I'd like to think I would have made my mother proud.'

'Yes,' James said, 'I'm sure you would have.'

Bert emerged from the throng. 'Blimey, Jimmy boy, you all right?'

James' response was a half-hearted grimace. Stephen and Anne hurried everyone away, insisting that the folk day continue without further trouble. George helped disperse the crowd and ordered a constable to round up the Jacobs clan. With his faculties restored, James grabbed Stephen's arm.

'I say, Stephen, what was the other song that Charlie sang?'

Stephen mumbled that he didn't know. 'I-I didn't hear it. You dragged me h-here.'

Philip brushed some grass off James' back. 'It was a Cornish song, 'The White Rose'.'

James thanked him and tugged at George. 'Come on, old chap, we have to get to the Coach House. GJ, go and get the lyrics from Charlie. Can we all get in your car, Stephen?'

'By all, who do you m-mean?'

'You, me, GJ, Beth, and Anne. Bert,

would you mind keeping things rolling here?'

'As long as you fill me in on the details later,' he replied.

'Of that, you can be sure.'

George shook his head. 'Why you have to do things as a job-lot, I don't know.'

Anne pushed him along. 'Really, Chief Inspector, we're all eager to solve this rhyme, so stop complaining.'

She manhandled him toward their tiny Austin 30. George elbowed her away.

'We'll never fit in there!' he protested. 'Beth, James, you come with me. The rest of you, we'll meet you there.'

24

James and his companions gathered in the drawing room of the Coach House. All chose to sit except for George, who stood by the French windows; his hands clasped behind his back, taking in the view. A carpet of roses and hydrangeas swayed lethargically in the breeze. The branches of a gnarled apple tree reached out to the sky as goldfinches and blue tits flitted here and there, singing their chirpy songs.

The room smelt musty, which prompted Anne to get up and swing the doors open.

'This place needs airing,' she said briskly, returning to plump the cushion in her chair.

James sat at the desk and studied the walls. For some reason, the wallpaper attracted him, which was a surprise because it simply wasn't his thing; a chintz design, full of pink roses. He unfolded the piece of paper in his hand and placed it on the desk in front of him. He read the contents aloud.

'Fortune comes to those who search, beneath the Rose of rich red earth, A window through which Man can gaze, Encapsulates and clears the haze.'

GJ reached across and took the paper from James to re-read.

'Fortune comes to those who search. That simply sounds like an introduction to me. We're the people searching — or rather you are, Lord Harrington. And, if you search, well, you'll find a fortune.'

'Didn't someone say that D-Delphine wasn't actually that good at r-riddles?' asked Stephen.

'Yes, yes they did,' said James. 'Who was that?'

'That was Juliet,' said Beth.

'Of course it was. Wonderful spy, she said, but a terrible code-maker. She told us not to take it too seriously. That chappie, Patel, suggested we take each line as a separate entity.'

'Perhaps we should do that and not look for hidden meanings?' suggested Beth.

'I say, GJ, go through the rhyme again.'

The young man repeated the riddle.

James scratched his head.

'Beneath the Rose of rich, red earth. I'm no gardener, but the soil here isn't rich and red. If anything, it's clay and chalky. I don't think this fortune is buried under the roses.'

Getting up, he wandered past George and through to the garden where he trod a path around the borders. His friends looked on as he meticulously examined every flower planted and, using a piece of dead wood, turned the soil over. He returned to the drawing room.

'These are all red and pink roses, and it's far too risky to write a riddle about a plant that could potentially die.'

As he stood behind Beth, he fondled the back of her neck with his hand. 'You know, the songs that Delphine asked Charlie to sing were relevant to solving this mystery. The first one, 'A Brisk Young Sailor', was a clue to her own history.' He turned to GJ. 'That's all about a son born out of wedlock. The second was 'The White Rose'. Now, the words to that song, I think, are unimportant with the exception of the last verse.'

James felt in his pocket for another piece of paper. 'The words to this are:

'And now that you've left me my
  darling, from your
grave one single flower grows,
I will always remember you darling
  when I gaze on
that lily white rose'.

Anne sat forward. 'One white rose.' She scanned the room. 'But there aren't any white roses. What about elsewhere in the house?'

James shook his head. 'There's nothing flowery in this house except here. The answer is here and it's probably staring us in the face.' He asked GJ to repeat the third line.

GJ picked up the rhyme. 'A window through which man can gaze.'

Stephen's brow contracted in confusion. James took the rhyme from GJ and studied it.

'Sweetie,' said Beth, 'a window is a window — we're gazing out at a garden full of roses. There must be a white rose there somewhere. Is there a variety called the white rose that perhaps isn't white?'

James wasn't a gardener and said as much; but the general consensus was that it was unlikely.

He wandered around the room and finally stopped by the oil painting, which he stared at until his eyes glazed over. He moved closer and squinted. Once his eyes had focussed, he examined the painting and mumbled.

'A window through which man can gaze . . . '

Getting closer, his nose almost touched the canvas.

'Good Lord.'

Everyone turned in their chairs. Stephen joined him.

'W-what is it?'

'GJ, hand me the rhyme.' The young man quickly went across and pushed the paper into his hands. 'We didn't account for the capitals. We assumed the capitals were to start a new sentence; that the one for rose was to highlight a name, or that a rose was important. But it means something else.'

Anne fidgeted. 'Oh do tell, James.'

He handed her the rhyme. 'The capitals spell out a word; a word that could be interpreted as a window. F, R, A, M, E — frame.' He scrutinised the painting and beckoned everyone over. 'Come here and tell me that this isn't a single white flower, here in the bottom left-hand corner.'

Everyone gathered around James. They shuffled close, their noses almost touching, as they stared at one tiny mark on the canvas.

Anne gawped. 'It is! It's a white rose. I'm surprised you saw it, it's so small.'

Beth turned her attention to the right-hand corner. 'Who painted it?'

GJ staggered back. 'Oh my God.'

'I say,' said James, 'do you recognise it? Is it valuable?'

'Hardly,' the young man said. 'This is one of mine. I painted it. That's my signature.' He studied the image and appeared bewildered by the discovery. 'It's not a good painting. I must have done it years ago, when I was still living with the Crabtrees. They must have given it to her.' He winced in frustration. 'God, I wish I could remember. It's not my style to add a colour that doesn't blend in.'

'You didn't, GJ,' said James. 'I think she added it.'

'As a clue,' Anne added.

George took out his pipe. 'Perhaps the frame is worth something?'

GJ was quick to dismiss the notion and explained that this was a cheap frame from Woolworths. A collective groan went around the room.

'S-so we're no further f-forward,' said Stephen.

'Wait a minute!' James put the rhyme in his pocket. 'We're forgetting that we've now interpreted this frame as a window — so we have to go through the window. This little touch-up to the painting is like the key to the door. Whatever it is must be on the back or hidden behind.'

Anne and Beth almost leapt in excitement. 'Oh sweetie, come on! What are you waiting for?' Beth cried.

James heard an intake of breath behind him as he unhooked the painting from the wall. He stripped the paper from the back of the painting but felt a wave of disappointment flow through him.

'Nothing,' he said as he placed the painting on the floor.

George retrieved his pipe and wandered back to the French windows. Stephen, Anne, Beth and GJ exchanged disappointed shrugs.

Stephen flopped down. 'Th-that's that, then.'

Anne threw her hands up in frustration. 'Do you think we'll ever solve it?'

Beth rested her head on James' shoulder. 'Oh, James, you're so close. I really thought you'd worked it out. We must be missing something. Juliet insisted her sister was hopeless with riddles.'

'Mmm, well that speaks volumes where my brain power is concerned,' James said, leaning against the wall. He brought his hand up; his fingers gently ran over a section of the chintz wallpaper where the frame had been.

He started.

What was that?

He ran his hand over it again.

A bump, or groove.

Beth followed his gaze. 'What is it?'

He studied the wallpaper. 'Look here. There's another one. A tiny rose, here on the wallpaper. It's white. It's been painted white and . . . feel it. There's something there.' He turned. 'Does anyone have a knife?'

GJ rushed over to the desk as everyone, again, gathered around James. 'Here's a letter opener. Will that do?'

'Splendid.' With the handle firmly in his grasp, James cut into the wallpaper and gently peeled it back to reveal a small brown envelope.

Anne gasped. 'Oh goodness, I can't stand the suspense. What's in it?'

James's heart pounded. His hands shook as he opened the envelope and picked out a small key and a slip of paper. George took the key from him and turned it over in his hand.

'Looks like a key to a safe deposit box.'

James unfolded the paper and gave it to George. 'You're right. In the Midland Bank in Cavendish.'

'I'll get on to the manager there,' said George, 'see if he'll open the bank up for me.' He pointed to his audience. 'That's police business. No need for you to be there.'

'Jolly good,' said James, 'I don't want to miss seeing Lonnie Donegan at the ceilidh.'

'Lonnie Donegan!' said the group simultaneously.

James had the grace to appear sheepish. 'Yes, he's our surprise. He's giving us half an hour of his time, courtesy of his friendship with Bob Tanner.'

George assured the group that they would be the first to know what was in the safety deposit box as they scurried out to return to the village.

25

The view from the terrace at Harrington's was a vista to seduce any artist or photographer. Flowering meadows stretched into the distance and sloped down to the river; horses grazed on the fresh spring grass on the ridge of the South Downs; and beyond, through the dip in the valley, the English Channel sparkled.

The previous evening's ceilidh had been a roaring success and the surprise appearance of Lonnie Donegan had sent villagers into a frenzy of excitement. Although only booked for half an hour, Lonnie played for half the evening and had graciously posed to have his picture taken with the majority of residents.

On the terrace, Adam had prepared a large round table with fresh white cotton tablecloths, azure napkins and a centrepiece of beautiful Sweet Williams. James reached across for one of two bottles of white wine and poured himself, Beth and Anne a glass. Opposite, George did the same for Stephen, Bert and GJ.

Didier appeared at the entrance to the dining area, gave a slight bow and silently applauded.

'Lord 'arrington, congratulations on the solving the mystery of Miss Brooks-Hunter. She was the most charming of guests.'

James agreed that she was, most certainly, a unique lady.

'A lady,' he added, 'whom I believe was ahead of her time in every way.' He raised his glass and swirled the contents. 'Bottled in Sussex down on a farm near Heath-field; let me know what you think. A toast to Delphine.'

His guests chorused her name, sipped their wine and unanimously agreed that it was fruity and refreshing.

'I say, Didier, is the food ready? I'm really rather hungry.'

'*Oui, oui,*' replied Didier. 'I 'ave thinly-sliced roast lamb, the garden peas and Jersey potatoes with mint sauce and gravy.' He clicked his fingers at Adam. 'What are you waiting for, this is ready to serve — go!'

Adam quickly jumped to it and sped to the kitchen. Didier bowed again and wished them bon appétit. Bert settled back in his chair.

'So, are all the Jacobs family locked up, or just that Bruiser geezer?'

George put his glass down. 'Bruiser is our murderer, but we've got no evidence to charge anyone else unless I can nab them for perverting the course of justice. Derek Jacobs wasn't exactly forthcoming with his statement. The Connors deny knowing anything. They're probably all lying, but at least we've got the man who pulled the trigger, so to speak.'

'Th-that Bruiser chap was an awful bully,' said Stephen.

James smoothed his hair back. 'He certainly was. The first time I set eyes on him at Bateson's I thought he was a bad lot.'

'You did w-well to spot that sticky stuff on his jacket.'

'More luck than judgement, old chap. I was banking on his lack of intelligence if I'm being perfectly honest. I'm sure there are plenty of shrubs around here with the stuff on, but I had to play a hunch and make out it was a rare plant-disease and we had only one shrub on the estate liable to that infection.'

Adam, helped by a colleague, distributed dinner and placed gravy and mint sauce on the table.

'Do you need anything else, your Lordship?'

James quickly scanned the table. 'No, I don't think so, Adam. We'll let you know when we do.'

Adam made his way to serve other guests as Anne helped herself to gravy.

'What will happen to him?'

George waited for her to pass the gravy to him. 'The crime was premeditated. Up to the jury though. Hanging is pretty frowned upon now but if he doesn't swing he'll see the rest of his life in prison I'm sure.'

A murmur went around the table. No matter who the villain was, the punishment didn't bear thinking about. Bert pointed a fork at James.

'So, Jimmy boy, what 'appened at Bateson's?'

'Oh, do tell them,' urged Beth.

James sliced into a piece of tender lamb. 'Good news. As you know, Delphine would not allow her will to be read because she suspected her death would be suspicious. Turns out she had two wills written up. One in the event of a natural death and one if there was foul play. We, of course, opened up the latter. Anyway . . . '

He quickly munched on some potatoes and garden peas and took a sip of wine before continuing. 'The Jacobs receive nothing. Bruiser brought that to a halt the day he came here and coshed her. Everything goes to Juliet, the sister and, of course, GJ — or, should I say, Sebastian.'

Sebastian grinned. 'I've actually got used to GJ,' he said.

'I think it rather suits you,' said Beth.

'Juliet will be staying with us over the next couple of days,' added James. 'She's with Peter and Hyacinth Crabtree, reacquainting herself with them and giving them an update. She's decided to have the funeral here.'

'Yes,' commented Stephen. 'I-I believe she wants us all th-there to give Delphine a good send-off.'

George spooned more mint sauce over his lamb. 'I think we'll all be there. I only spent a short time with her, but she struck me as a lovely lady.'

'What about the safe deposit box?' asked Anne.

Bert pushed his flat cap back. 'Blimey, I forgot all about that. Come on, George. What was in it?'

'Fortunately the manager was available to open the bank up.' He allowed James to tell the story.

'Inside were the proceeds of several auctions,' replied James. 'Our government paid Delphine materialistically over the years — paintings, first edition books, that sort of thing. About ten years ago, she sold everything through a number of auctions and transferred the money into gold.'

'How ingenious,' said Anne. 'So what will happen to that?'

GJ continued the story. 'The bank is transferring that into funds, which will be split between me and my Aunt Juliet.'

'A-and what are your plans, G-GJ?' asked Stephen.

GJ smiled. 'Well, I'm actually planning on staying here. Once I get the money sorted, I'm going to give some to the Mission in the East End. I'm also giving a lump sum to the Crabtrees and, hopefully, I can make my peace with them. I know she didn't like me much, but Hyacinth did her best and I believe Peter deserves it. And I'm basing myself at the Coach House.'

'Oh, that's wonderful,' gushed Anne. 'I'm so pleased you're staying.'

'And?' said James.

GJ gave him an inquisitive look. 'Oh yes. And, when those stables are converted, I'm going to launch an artist's studio, so people can learn how to draw and paint while they're here.'

George closed his eyes as he savoured his last piece of spring lamb. 'So, all's well that ends well.'

'I say, George, are you going to try and find Reg Jacobs?' asked James.

'Attempts are underway as we speak. He's probably joined up with another fair at the other end of the country. The likelihood of us finding him is remote.

The likelihood of us talking to him is remote, and the likelihood of him telling us the truth is also fairly remote but we'll keep trying. He's a potential witness and hopefully we'll nab him sooner or later.'

Bert ran his tongue across his teeth. 'I don't fink he wanted anything to do with 'is family.'

'I think you're right, my friend.' James poured more wine for Beth. 'One person who is beginning to talk, though, is our young man here.'

'Yes,' replied GJ. 'Thanks to all of you and the efforts you went to, things are beginning to slot into place. I'm beginning to remember a lot more. Dr Jackson thinks it'll all come back in time.'

'I hope so, GJ,' said Beth. 'And it'll be good for you to get reacquainted with Peter. I believe he thought a lot of you so he can fill in the gaps, I'm sure.'

'Yes, I must admit, it'll be good to reacquaint myself with him,' he said, smiling. 'He did tell the police I'd gone missing but no one found me. I think they were focussing solely on the Wimbledon area and, of course, I'd found myself in the East End by that time and then at the Mission. The search was probably called off by the time I got there.'

GJ then cleared his throat and asked for some quiet as he addressed James, Beth and Bert.

'I've already spent a little of my inheritance by way of a thank you to you three. Lord and Lady Harrington, you could so easily have thrown me out of that barn when you found me, but you didn't. You two, and Bert here, went out of your way to find out who I was and where I came from. Because of that, I've found my identity and my family. And, as I said, things are slotting into place.'

He felt in his pocket and brought out a sealed envelope, which he handed to Bert. 'A little something for you by way of a thank you.'

Bert peered inside at a wad of five pound notes. 'Strewth!' He grabbed GJ's hand. 'Thanks, mate. You're a diamond.'

'Lord and Lady Harrington,' he continued, 'your circumstances are slightly different, so I've taken the liberty of getting something for you. I hope I've done the right thing. I got the idea when I was watching the fair from my bedroom window.'

He got up and waved at Adam, who was standing in the shade at the end of the terrace. The waiter dashed out of sight around the side of the house while James and Beth appeared bemused by such odd behaviour.

GJ continued, 'I know that you were planning to have horse-riding here but that you've set up an agreement with the farm to do that. But, I got to thinking about the small children who are sometimes here and that they may want to have a go on something.'

James held Beth's hand as they both tilted their heads, wondering what on earth he'd planned.

'Well, not to beat around the bush any further, I got these.'

Adam appeared from the side of the house with two of the cutest donkeys in tow. Both Beth and Anne jumped up from the table to greet them.

'Oh, James, these are so beautiful!'

'Aren't they adorable, Stephen?' said Anne with a beaming smile.

James pushed himself up from his chair and thanked GJ warmly. Then, picking up an apple from a nearby fruit bowl, he joined Beth and Anne.

'They are rather splendid, aren't they?' he said. 'And you're right. The children will love them — and they'll keep the grass down. Best speak with our gardener about where to put them.'

'We must bring Luke and Mark over to meet them,' said Anne.

'Yes, you must,' agreed Beth. 'Bring them over later.'

'Do they have names?' James asked, feeding one the apple.

'No, they don't. Any suggestions?'

James announced that he would leave it up to the ladies and returned to the table. After a few minutes, Beth and Anne led the donkeys forward.

'This brown one has soft, twinkly eyes and a gentle nature,' said Anne. 'So we thought we'd call him Sebastian.'

GJ's broad smile lit up his face.

'And this one, sweetie,' said Beth, 'is a gentle lady, so I'm going to call her Delphine.'

James distributed glasses to them. 'Well, ladies, I think they are wonderful names and a reminder of two very dear people.'

'And a mystery solved, Jimmy boy,' added Bert.

'To Sebastian and Delphine.'

'Sebastian and Delphine.'

'Now,' James said as he plonked himself down in his chair. 'Didier let me loose in his kitchen earlier and I was permitted to make my grandmother's lemon pudding. So, is everyone ready for dessert?'

THE END

(See over for Grandma Alice Harrington's Lemon Pudding and Welsh Rarebit recipes)

Grandma Harrington's Lemon Pudding and Welsh Rarebit

Lemon Pudding (Serves 3-4 people)
3 oz/85g sugar
1 oz/28g butter
1 egg (separated)
1 oz/28g flour
1 lemon
Quarter pint/150ml of milk

Cream the butter and sugar; add grated rind and half or all the lemon juice. Sieve in the flour and mix lightly.
Add slightly-beaten yolk of egg and beat well.
Add milk and stir well until blended.
Beat egg white stiff and fold in.
Pour into a well-greased Pyrex dish and stand in a deep pan of hot water
Bake in gas mark 5/375F oven for 30-40 minutes (This results in a sponge top and lemon curd base)

Welsh Rarebit (Serves 4 people)

6 oz/175g Cheddar cheese
2 oz/50g Gruyère cheese
1 tbsp butter
1 tbsp English mustard
2 tspns Worcester sauce
2 tspns flour
4 tbsp milk or stout
Pinch of pepper
Four thick slices of home-made bread
— toasted

Put the cheese, flour, mustard, Worcester Sauce, butter and pepper into a saucepan. Stir well and add the milk/stout in small doses to keep it moist.
Stir until everything melts and becomes a thickish paste.
Put to one side and lightly toast your bread. Spread the sauce over the toast, sprinkle with dash of Tabasco and brown under the grill.

(If feeling adventurous, top with a poached egg or small pieces of crispy fried bacon.)

We do hope that you have enjoyed
reading this large print book.

Did you know that all of our titles
are available for purchase?

We publish a wide range of high
quality large print books including:
Romances, Mysteries, Classics
General Fiction
Non Fiction and Westerns

Special interest titles available in
large print are:
The Little Oxford Dictionary
Music Book, Song Book
Hymn Book, Service Book

Also available from us courtesy of
Oxford University Press:
Young Readers' Dictionary
(large print edition)
Young Readers' Thesaurus
(large print edition)

For further information or a free
brochure, please contact us at:
Ulverscroft Large Print Books Ltd.,
The Green, Bradgate Road, Anstey,
Leicester, LE7 7FU, England.
Tel: (00 44) **0116 236 4325**
Fax: (00 44) **0116 234 0205**

Other titles in the
Linford Mystery Library:

THE MISTRESS OF EVIL

V. J. Banis

John Hamilton travels to the Carpathian Mountains in Romania, along with his wife Victoria and her sister Carolyn, to research the risk of earthquakes in the area. The government provides lodgings for them in the ancient Castle Drakul. Upon investigating a disused basement room, the trio discover a skeleton in a coffin with a wooden stake through its rib cage — and Carolyn feels a strange compulsion to goad John into removing it. Soon afterward, a sinister visitor arrives at the castle — claiming to be a descendant of the original Count Drakul . . .

THE GREEN MANDARIN MYSTERY

Denis Hughes

When a number of eminent scientists — all experts in their field, and of inestimable value to the British Government — mysteriously vanish, the police are at their wits' end. The only clue in each instance is a note left by the scientist saying they have joined 'the Green Mandarin'. Desperate to locate his daughter, Fleurette, a Home Office official enlists the services of scientific detective Ray Ellis. But as his investigations get closer to the truth, will Ray be the next person to go missing?

KNIGHT-ERRANT

Norman Firth

Lance Knight notices a beautiful woman with a notorious criminal in a London restaurant, who is clearly threatening her, and refers to her disparagingly as 'your majesty'. Knight decides to follow her when she leaves — and finds himself saving her after she deliberately throws herself in front of a bus! So begins his most dangerous adventure . . . And in *Passion's Victim*, June Mallory is determined to prove her father innocent of the burglary for which he was imprisoned — and is caught in a tangled web of betrayal and murder.

THE ROOT OF ALL EVIL

Valerie Holmes

When Bartholomew Denton, the owner of Leaham Hall in North Yorkshire, is discovered dead in his bed, Detection Officer Sergeant Hector Blagdon is called in. Young and fit as Denton was, the death seems suspicious. Blagdon is also intrigued by the quick turnover of maid-servants at the Hall, and wonders if there is something else going on. With his old adversary Kendel the butler seemingly trying to frustrate the investigation, Blagdon must delve deep to find answers . . .